NIGHTMARE IN SAVANNAH

Mary Charles

**The Casey Series by
Mary Charles**

**Casey's Revenge
The Reluctant Corpse
Nightmare in Savannah**

NIGHTMARE IN SAVANNAH

BY

MARY CHARLES

Acknowledgements

Where do you start with thanks to all the wonderful people who have helped in the creation of this book? Well, first of all thanks are due to all the faculty and staff at Georgia Southern University for their continued help and support. And then there are the students. It is true that teaching is a first class way of learning, as everyone can bring new and fresh insights to bear, so thanks are also due to all the students for their help along the way. Special thanks go to all the wonderful folk at the Waffle House on Northside Drive. And then there are the Statesboro and the Savannah and Georgia Southern police who, together with the counseling office, have provided valuable technical help. Thanks to the real Ben Appleby and Destiny Lynn Durden - your friendship means a great deal to us - and to the real Misty and Tango and their owner author Rowan Wolfe. And of course to our editors Fred and John Piechoczek without whom we would never be in print.

Thanks a million - Mary

Dedication

We dedicate this book to our children in order of appearance: Steve, Carla, Julie, Karen, Katherine and Christopher. And to our grandchildren: Mathew, Maggie, Hannah, Samuel, Nicholas, Isabella and those yet to appear!

List of characters in alphabetical order

Ben Appleby: an antique dealer
Jacques Archambault: works for Francois Michaud
Bob Barton: captain Savannah PD and Adam's boss
Ed Branch: a witness to a crime
Greg Burke: an art restorer in Statesboro
Hilda Carnes: a witness to a crime
Ashley Carmichael: Joey's boss
Adam Carter : a lieutenant in the violent crimes division of Savannah PD
Jerry Curtis: an antiques dealer
Sharon Davidson: a friend of Casey's
Jean Dunne: a friend of Casey's
Destiny Lynn Durden: Greg's partner in the restoration business
Casey Forbes: a professor at Carter University
Sylvia Gordon: works for the medical examiner's office
Hans: the bodyguard of Klaus
Klaus Kruger: a German looking for paintings
Larry: the bartender at the Mirror Image Club
Jack Malloy: a detective in the Savannah PD
Francois Michaud: an antique dealer in Paris
Mildred: Ben Appleby's wife
Billy Moran: a detective and photographer in the Savannah PD:
Joey Morrisey: works for the Savannah First Trust Bank
Julia Morrow: a victim
Megan Muller: a professor at Carter University and Casey's best friend
Patricia Newland: a friend of Casey's
David Rothschild: an Israeli citizen
Kurt Schultz: an art appraiser
Catherine Sherman: a counselor at Carter University and Adam's partner
Sherri: a waitress at the Waffle House
Elizabeth Snow: a victim
Jessica Stillwell: a victim
Marla Waters: a tour guide and Megan's partner

PROLOGUE

Jessica Stillwell was sure of only one thing in her young life, and that was confusion. It stalked her mind and body like a jungle animal, stopping here and there to gnaw away at the fiber of her sanity. She really, really didn't want to be going through this ordeal. Hadn't she spent the last few hours screaming that exact sentiment at whoever was doing this to her?

"Please, just leave me alone, and let me go. I swear I won't tell anyone; I promise."

Her 5'9" body was stretched as taut as a drum, hands tied over her head, legs spread wide, and each foot secured - to what, she had no idea. The evening had started great, just a fun girls' night out on the town with her two best friends, Jill and Carrie. Everything had been going so well, a few drinks, a little dancing, just the thing to loosen herself up after a long week of classes at the Savannah College of Art and Design, also known as SCAD. Around midnight she had begun to feel a little dizzy and slightly nauseated. She definitely hadn't wanted to get sick in front of her friends and a large group of strangers, so she had left the club and headed for her car. As she had got into her car, the strange feeling of disorientation had taken over. Then there was sudden darkness and the loss of consciousness that left her unaware of her existence until she awakened in this horrible condition.

She was one of the golden girls, sweet and innocent, protected from harm. That was her heritage from birth - to be adored and treated with a caring and understanding that befitted her station in life. She stared helplessly out from beneath a pool of frightened tears. The full, sensuous lips, so many had coveted in her nineteen years, were pulled back in a grimace of pain. She felt she might choke with every breath she took, utterly violated from the ordeal this unknown entity was forcing upon her.

"Please, say something. What do you want from me? Why are you doing this? Please, just let me go."

1

Her voice was starting to get raspy from her efforts to let her captor or captors know she needed to be released from this terrifying occurrence. Again she scanned the area, trying desperately to sort out the who, why and where of what had happened to her. Her vision was limited to the few details she'd already seen a dozen times, the bare wooden walls with peeling paint and the spider webs woven against the old stained boards. She felt as though she herself was spread-eagled in the deadly trap of some giant spider, lurking just outside her limited field of vision, waiting to devour her young body.

"Talk to me, God damn you! My parents have a lot of money. I swear I'll get you whatever you want; just please let me go."

She'd had the briefest glance of some tall, hooded figure passing by her feet, but it had been more like a shadow than a living thing. If it hadn't been for the physical sensations inflicted on her powerless body, she might even have believed it was part of some strange nightmare.

She felt the sensations of warm water against her flesh. Her captor was giving her a sponge bath from the bottom of her feet to the top of her head. Now her hair was being washed and rinsed ever so gently, the sensations accompanied by someone breathing regularly and softly humming a tune she didn't recognize. If this whole episode weren't so incredibly bizarre, it would have been almost pleasant.

"Who are you? What do you want from me?"

At last the washing stopped, and she was being dried with a soft towel smelling faintly of lemon. Eventually the drying halted, and she sensed her captor moving away from her.

Once again she was left in a silence so deep and complete that the only sounds she heard were her own breathing.

From far off, someone was playing a piano. The sound sparked a distant memory of something she'd heard briefly in music appreciation class. She thought it was called Ragtime and was the creation of someone called Scott something or other. The sparkling notes superimposed against her abject terror created an odd, other-worldly sensation, as though she were here, but not here at the same time. Maybe if she tried really hard, she could release her mind to some other universe and leave her body trapped here on its own.

She heard the return of the shadowy figure. Her mind flashed back to the pictures of a coweled, shrouded form with a scythe she'd seen in countless books from childhood - the bent, stooped form of Death himself. This could not be real. What was happening to her could not possibly be happening.

"Please, don't hurt me. Please, let me go. Please, say something."

Again nothing, just the sound of breathing and then the prick of something that felt like a needle against her armpit. It didn't hurt any more than someone drawing blood, but the effects were much more immediate. As she quietly slipped away, even the sound of her own beating heart stopped, and the last thing she heard was a low, mirthless chuckle.

Chapter 1

Klaus Kruger rested his head against the softness of his first class Lufthansa seat and let himself relax. He'd be in Paris in a couple of hours and well on his way to becoming a rich man. Hans was already asleep beside him, and he was slightly envious of the big man's ability to sleep anywhere, anytime.

Klaus was fast approaching eighty, and it was definitely time to spend what years were left to him in the luxury of total financial security. It all seemed so odd the way his present circumstances had come about.

He'd cared for his doddering elderly father until the old man's death six months ago at the age of 98. It had been a major problem for him having to deal with the senility of what had once been a strong tough man. But he'd done the best he could.

They had, after all, both served the Third Reich, he as a very young soldier and his father as an officer directly under the command of Hermann Goering. The war had bonded them for life, and they had often spoken of the good old days until ten years ago when his father had started to slip mentally, but all that was in the past and no longer mattered.

It had been weeks after his father's death before he could bring himself to go through his private papers. Most of them were junk, the ravings of an individual who no longer had a firm grip on reality. One journal entry, however, had caught his attention immediately. It spoke in great detail of an exploit his father had undertaken while he had been stationed in Paris. The old man had actually found two paintings he thought to be of enormous value, which he had decided to keep for himself. He had hastily painted scenes of peasants over the originals and hidden them in the wall of the room where he had been billeted with every intention of sneaking them home to Germany to insure his own financial future.

The fall of Paris had come so quickly that he'd never had the chance to retrieve them before he was shipped to the Eastern front to fight the advancing Soviets. Because of his rank, the old man had been held in a Russian prison for over thirty years as a war criminal, and by the time he was finally returned to Germany, he was a broken man. He had been

4

incapable at that point of doing much of anything except sitting by his favorite window and scribbling notes on what his life had been.

When Klaus had read more of his father's journals, he had found himself excited beyond belief. Not only had his father described in detail what the paintings looked like, but he had also listed the address where he'd hidden them. Everything was now in place, and Klaus was prepared to reap the rewards of his father's cleverness. Since he didn't like the feeling of carrying large sums of money on his person, he'd already wired sufficient funds to a Paris bank to cover all his expenses and those of his large companion.

Hans was no rocket scientist, but he was big enough to provide protection for the extended trip to Paris and then on to the southern United States. Some moron there had put three Degas pastels up on the Internet for sale, but when Klaus had asked for provenance, he had received no reply. Further messages had gone unanswered.

The Degas might be a wild goose chase, but the two paintings were a certainty, of that he was positive. Being filthy rich was now only a matter of time and miles away, and he was certainly still plenty healthy enough to take care of business.

In the event that the pastels proved to be real, he had called upon a few of his friends from the old days to set up a bank credit line of $1,000,000. Even if he had to spend that much to acquire them, he had little doubt that he could triple his money with ease simply by selling them to German collectors to whom he was already well known. He intended to come back from this trip a multi-millionaire no matter what it took to accomplish that goal.

François Michaud was angry; no, angry didn't cover it. Not even furious could properly define what he felt. Utter rage was the only thing that might describe his current state. He found himself pacing back and forth across the limited length of his antique shop on the rue du Cherche-Midi in Paris, muttering under his breath, "espèce d'imbécile." His cousin Jacques stood rooted to the spot near one corner of the Louis IV desk that François used for his work area.

"Sacrébleu! Can't I even leave this place for one hour for a glass of wine and some bread and cheese without you completely destroying my life? What in the name of all that's holy possessed you to sell those paintings? Didn't you realize that if I wanted to sell them, I would have had them on open display in the shop, not hidden behind my desk? God, I curse the day you were born. I swear to you the money will be coming out of your paycheck."

"Bu...but François," Jacques stuttered. "The American was looking specifically for small oil paintings, and he was willing to pay 600 francs for the pair. How was I to know? They've been in the shop for a long time now; I thought you'd be pleased."

"Jacques, I curse you. And I curse your mother and father for sending you to me. Two days ago I had an offer of 10,000 francs from an old German gentleman, who will be arriving in approximately two hours to pick them up. He said they reminded him of some paintings his mother had owned, and he was going to check with his sister if these were the ones. What in the name of God am I going to tell him? Let me see the stupid receipt. Maybe I can catch up with the American and get them back."

"François, I'm so sorry I didn't write a receipt."

"What the hell do you mean you didn't make a receipt? You moron! Excuse me, Jacques, would you be so kind as to hand me that Third Reich dagger sitting on the table next to you. I think I've found a use for it."

As Jacques worked at becoming a part of a 19th century étagère, François's thoughts turned to finding some sort of excuse with which he could placate the German. The man's French had been excellent, but to a person of expertise, the slight German accent had been obvious. François hadn't spent twenty-two years dealing in antiques for nothing. He'd become very good over that period of time in determining the origins of his customers.

He thought back to how he'd found the paintings. A heavier than usual rainstorm had caused some damage to the roof of his private quarters over the shop and resulted in a loss of plaster on one of his bedroom walls. He'd cursed the rain in general, and the exorbitant rates some local buffoon would charge him for the repairs, so he'd set about doing the job himself, and in the course of removing an old section of the plaster, had spotted the two small paintings nestled up against a stud in the outside wall.

He had removed them with great care, his heart in his mouth, sure that his fortune was at last staring him in the face. Further examination had determined them to be unsigned and of not very good quality. Not only that, but they too had suffered water damage, which meant that in a short time he'd be able to observe the paint chipping away, reducing their value to a point of near worthlessness. With this in mind, he'd resolved to dump them on the very first interested party. Better to wind up with something rather than nothing.

Both paintings had been of peasants working in the fields, but the figures had been rather crude and the colors less than imaginative. François had reflected at the time that he himself probably could have done better, given a week or two. That, however, was beside the point. The German had seemed almost sure that these were the paintings he'd been looking for, and François had already spent several hours contemplating what pleasures he could afford himself with this unexpected windfall. Now it had all been taken away in an instant by his idiotic cousin. Rubbing the ache that was beginning to form in his temples, he turned to find the ashen-faced Jacques edging his way toward the front door.

"Oh, no, you don't. Get your skinny little butt back in here. When that German shows up, you're going to be the star of this little fiasco. I want you front and center, Jacques. I think I just may sell him the dagger and let him have his way with you, you idiot."

Jacques, who was pale skinned under normal circumstances, was turning even whiter and visibly shaking. He was indeed endowed with a skinny butt along with a skinny everything else. His 6' 1" frame supported perhaps 140 pounds. His glasses were continuously perched at the end of his long, hooked Gallic nose, and his watery brown eyes had a way of seeming to be constantly in motion, almost as though focusing on a particular thing or person was more than they could handle. His moustache was as thin as a piece of dental floss and did little more than accentuate his mouth. The thinning black hair, which he combed from the left side of his head over the top part of his head to hide a large and obvious balding area, completed the picture of a man who probably had little success in any phase of his life. He also talked with a constant stutter, which built neither enthusiasm for conversation nor a desire to be a friend or lover in others.

François stopped himself in mid-curse as the reality of the situation set in; there was little else he could say to Jacques that would make him feel any worse or himself any better. It was, of course, at this tender point in time when the elderly German entered the shop. His eyes were nearly hidden under his bushy white eyebrows as he stared from one man to the other.

"Ah, Monsieur Michaud, I have come for my little paintings. I have brought you cash since I thought you might prefer that method of payment."

"Mr. Kruger, I have some rather bad news for you, I'm afraid. I am sorry to tell you that my assistant Jacques sold them without my knowledge not two hours ago to an American gentleman. I do hope you will accept my most sincere apology for this unfortunate occurrence."

Silence hung in the little room like the blade of a guillotine suspended in the air, ready to drop with a terrible sickening speed upon the neck of the first person foolish enough to utter a sound. Mr. Kruger's eyes narrowed. He maintained his frozen stance until he at last regained his composure. The man looked to be in his seventies, with a full head of white hair and an equally white beard and moustache. Despite his age, he was obviously in good condition, with a massive barrel chest, and powerful looking arms. Though he stood no more than 5'9" or 5'10", he cut an imposing figure.

"Ah, how unfortunate, Monsieur Michaud. You wouldn't, by any chance, have the name of this American, would you?"

"No, I am terribly sorry, Monsieur Kruger, but I'm afraid Jacques did not make out a receipt; however, I'm sure he could give you a very good description of the gentleman, couldn't you Jacques?"

"Y-y-y-ess s-s-sir. He was about sixty-five, approximately 5'10", and he wore glasses. He had g-g-graying hair, thinning on the top, and a very jolly look to him. H-h-h-he spoke with that accent of an American living in the Southern part of the United S-s-states. T-t-that's about all I can remember, sir."

"I don't suppose the American happened to mention where he was staying, did he?"

"W-w-why yes, sir, as a matter of fact, he did. It was the Crillon, but I seem to remember him saying something about leaving tomorrow."

"Thank you. Perhaps I can catch him before he leaves for home. Gentlemen, adieu."

As the German exited the shop, François saw not a person leaving, but rather the embodiment of 10,000 francs, which he'd already spent several times over. He couldn't believe he hadn't asked Jacques where the American was staying before. He should have asked him that earlier. He really was getting forgetful in his old age. He resumed his mutterings, most of which pertained to the early and painful demise of Jacques Archambault.

Chapter 2

Benjamin Appleby (Ben, to his many friends) sat at the bar of the Hotel Crillon and quietly contemplated the glass of sherry that he was turning slowly with his right hand. The color was excellent, and he loved to watch the glass sparkle as the lights behind the bar turned it into a gleaming kaleidoscope of gold, amber and reds. Ben was not a man who often imbibed, but this was a special occasion. He'd had a very good day. He was a passionate man, but not a man of excesses, unless you included his great love for the buying and selling of antiques or his extraordinary ability to tell a good yarn. Ben had often been described by his multitude of friends and customers as the man whose picture you'd find next to "Southern gentleman" in the dictionary if you were to look up the definition of that phrase.

He'd picked up a lovely little 18th century French sterling silver tea service at a very reasonable price, along with several very fine pieces of Louis IV furniture. He'd also found a pair of small oils with which he'd become intrigued. Although they would never be confused with great art, he found them to be quite acceptable in a folksy sort of way. There was some serious flaking going on with both the pieces, but he had a restorer just outside Savannah who should be able to correct that situation without undue difficulty. All in all, he was pleased with the day's purchases.

Ben pushed his glasses a little further up on his nose, a nose he liked to think of as rather noble and classically Roman in structure. What other people might think, or not think, of his nose was not an issue he dwelt on. The pale blue eyes, widely set below his inquisitive eyebrows, were his best feature anyway.

He let his gaze wander across the richly glowing mahogany of the bar. It almost required one to touch it. The wood was all 19th century, imported from the Philippines. How many thousands of times had elbows rested on this very spot? How many bar rags had wiped away moisture from it? The patina was so rich that it almost drew him into it like a mirror. The place was expensive, but it was worth it to hear the squeak of real leather when he shifted position on his stool. Ben even liked the way the staff spoke English, well enough to be easily understood, but with that lovely hint of Gallic flavoring that let him know he was in a place that was far removed from Savannah, Georgia.

"*Garçon*, may I have just one more glass of this excellent Tio Pepé, please?"

"But of course, Monsieur. I'm glad you're pleased with it."

"Yes, it's lovely, *merci*."

Ben was not a speaker of French. He, like most American tourists, had a smattering of words that allowed him to order the basic food groups and ask where the bathroom was located. Beyond the most simplistic phrases, he was quickly lost in the flurry of foreign words that the French used when communicating with each other. He'd be back in London by tomorrow - the Brits also spoke a language often incomprehensible to the American ear, but at least with them he could ask them to repeat what they'd said and could usually pick up the meaning on the second run-through.

A flicker of a smile crossed his face as he thought back to his first visit to England, when he'd asked a waitress if they had a restroom. He'd been rewarded with "'Ay, Maude, we got any place where this gentleman can rest?" It hadn't taken very long for words like loo, w.c., petrol, boot and bonnet to become a normal part of his vocabulary. He found the British to be rather aloof as a general rule of thumb, but this characteristic was counterbalanced by the magnificence of their architecture and the numerous flea markets where a real treasure might be lurking only a booth or two away.

Ben liked what he did for a living. Sometimes he made money, sometimes he didn't, but at least he was his own man. The only one who could fire him was himself. He also liked the way the antiques connected him to the past. The artisans and artists of the past lived on in their works and would for as long as those works existed. He felt himself to be a valuable link in the process of maintaining the physical proof of days long past, in some way insuring his own link to the future.

He looked up at the mirror just in time to catch sight of a man heading his way with a rather purposeful stride. The man was close to his own age, very distinguished looking, emanating an aura of power and purpose.

"Excuse me, sir. I don't wish to impose on your evening, but may I ask if you are the American who bought two paintings this morning from François Michaud who owns the antique shop at 34 rue du Cherche-Midi?"

The man spoke English with the slightest tinge of an accent, not French though, possibly German. Ben was intrigued as much by the man who had been following behind his visitor as the visitor himself. The second man was much younger and much larger. He had to be at least 6'4" or 6'5" with closely cropped brown hair. This second individual could have been no more than thirty at the most and was built like a center linebacker for a professional football team. Even the brief gaze he gave Ben was enough to make him uncomfortable. The eyes were dark lasers that didn't just look at him but cut right through him. Ben was pleased that the man did not accompany his companion to the bar, but instead chose a booth near the door and worked his considerable bulk into it. Even though the area the man sat in was darkened in a mood-enhancing fashion, there was still enough light to pick up the ugly white scar that ran from cheek to ear. This was definitely not a person Ben would have chosen to meet in a dark alley at midnight.

"Why, yes, I did happen to buy a couple of small paintings from François today. How in the world did you find me?"

"His assistant gave me a rather good description of you and, most fortunately, remembered where you were staying. I would like to ask you if you would consider selling the paintings to me. I would give you a very good price for them. They originally belonged to my family but got lost somewhere during the Second World War. I've been looking for them ever since. It would mean a great deal to me if I could bring them back into the fold."

"I'm awfully sorry. I wish I'd known this earlier. I took everything down to the United Air Service this afternoon and had it all crated and shipped to my shop in Savannah, Georgia. I'm afraid they're already over the Atlantic at this point. If you could give me a number where I can reach you, I'll call you from the States and perhaps ship them to you if we can agree on a price."

"What a shame. I'm on the move at this point touring Europe, and I don't have an address or a number where I can be reached. Please, give me your card, and I can visit you in the States. Perhaps you would you be so kind as to hold them for me. My name is Klaus Kruger."

The man extended a hand with fingers the size of sausages. Ben shook it and was not surprised by the strength of the grip. This was a hand that could yank the heads off small animals.

"Glad to make your acquaintance, Mr. Kruger. I'm Ben Appleby, and I should be back in Savannah by next Tuesday the 21st. Here's my card."

11

"Thank you, Mr. Appleby. Shall we say next Thursday or Friday for my little visit to you then? I appreciate this very much. As to the price, does $5,000 American give you a reasonable profit margin?"

"Why yes, that's more than reasonable, but I'm not sure that I want to sell them at this point."

"Let me give you a traveler's check for half up front and the remainder when I see you next week. Is that agreeable with you Mr. Appleby?"

"Thanks for the offer, but as I said, I'm not sure I'm ready to let them go yet, and please call me Ben."

"Please reconsider. I'll see you next week in the States, and hopefully you'll be ready to sell by then."

Kruger pursed his mouth in what passed for a smile on his thin-lipped, heavily lined face and left the bar area without another word. His large companion laid some money on his table, rose and silently followed. Ben was left staring after the pair, wondering about the true nature of what had just occurred. It made no sense for him to be offered this amount of money for two paintings that weren't worth a tenth of that, even if they were family heirlooms.

"Bartender, please can I have another sherry?" As he sipped the pale yellow drink, Ben thought, better take a closer look at those two little darlings when I get back.

Chapter 3

Newly promoted Lieutenant Adam Carter of the violent crimes division in Savannah's police department rolled over and hit the alarm button in one fluid movement. He squinted at the clock. 5:55. Good, yet again he'd managed to wake just five minutes before its harsh jangling woke him. This waking five minutes earlier than the alarm was becoming a habit, but quite a useful one. He lay back, enjoying the way the early morning sun filled the bedroom. It intensified the yellow of the walls and picked out the colors of the still life he had hung opposite his king-sized bed. The heavy nighttime rains had finished, and he could hear the cries of the marsh birds and see the brilliant blue sky outside the open windows.

Life hadn't always seemed so pleasant at this time of day. There had been a time when waking up after a night of boozing was a major league effort; a time when the only thing that would jerk him into reality was a shot of whiskey and a half a dozen cigarettes; a time when brilliant blue skies only intensified his hangover and made him wish the sun could find someplace else to rise. Another thing that made being awake much more pleasurable nowadays was his relationship with Catherine Sherman. It never failed to amaze him how having someone special in his life could alter his outlook.

The first visit of the day would be to the bathroom, no argument from his protesting bladder there. As he peered into the mirror, he noted that he looked about the same as he had the night before. He was still 6'1" with just the tiniest paunch that would have to go on his forty-three-year-old body. He found exercising a lot easier since he'd given up smoking and drinking heavily. Today the lively brown eyes were clear without a trace of red. His brown hair also looked healthy, and the slightest streaks of gray at the temples just accentuated his craggy good looks. Even his straight aquiline nose looked better these days, even if it was just a tad too long.

Having showered and dressed, he took his cup of strong black coffee onto the deck and leaned over looking at the activity of the marsh, which

13

surrounded his townhouse on Thunderbolt. He'd only moved to his three bedroom older townhouse three months ago but continued to be filled with delight whenever he contemplated his peaceful view. One of these days he would persuade Catherine to move in full-time with him, and maybe he'd even get a dog.

The buzzing of his beeper broke his reverie. "Jack, yeah, oh great, where? Yeah, I know it. I'll pick you up. " He felt in his jacket pocket; the Nicorette gum was there. Although he'd weaned himself off cigarettes by using a patch, he still felt the overwhelming need to smoke on numerous occasions. The gum really helped, and he knew with certainty that he'd be needing it before the day was over. That was the nature of his career.

An hour later, he was standing with his partner, Jack Malloy, in an old, disused barn on Skidaway Island, watching one of the members of the forensic team examine what had probably once been a very attractive young woman who lay spread-eagled and naked in front of him. The minute he ducked under the yellow tape cordoning off the scene, he felt his stomach start to heave. The stench was horrific with hundreds of flies dancing furiously around the body. He quickly unwrapped a piece of Nicorette gum and popped it into his mouth; maybe the taste of peppermint would help. Billy Moran, who was acting as the photographer today was still taking photos while the Scene of the Crime technicians were gathering evidence from the surrounding area.

"What you got?"

"She's dead. No doubt about it. I don't need to hear that from the EMT although he did agree with me!"

Billy had been a member of the forensics team of the violent crimes unit for several years and was known for his caustic wit and often misplaced sense of humor. He was, however, a good cop and excellent at using both the still and the video cameras.

"Thanks a lot. I was thinking more along the line of how long and by what means. From the state of de-composition, it looks to me like a week or more. What did the medic say?"

"It's hard to say; several days, but that's only a guess. I expect the autopsy will tell us what killed her and possibly if she's been raped. I don't see any immediate cause of death, but she's pretty decomposed. Of course the rats have had a meal or two."

Billy's grin seemed particularly macabre to Adam. "Jack, would you go over with the uniforms to make sure we've got all we're going to get from the two guys that found her?"

Thirty-year-old, Jack Malloy turned his head in the direction of the small group a few feet away silhouetted in the small doorway leading into the barn. The two fishermen who had wandered into the abandoned barn to avoid an earlier rainstorm were still fish-belly white, their eyes wide open in stark horror. Jack loved being a cop, especially a homicide cop. He was tall and athletic-looking with closely cropped light brown hair and light blue eyes that never ceased to sparkle with excitement, even in the most mundane situation. He'd been a street cop for three years before joining violent crimes and had good instincts for the job he was now required to do. He lived for moments like this when his enthusiasm could be given full rein to find the solution to a major crime.

Billy moved closer to Adam. "That's it for me for now. I think I'll go grab a stack of pancakes and some bacon. All this naked dead body stuff makes a man hungry."

Adam stared briefly into Billy's broad creased face, taking in the unruly gray hair framing the wide-set dark eyes and watched the shaggy moustache bounce up and down in happy anticipation of breakfast. Maybe when he got to be as old as Billy, he'd be able to develop an equally cavalier attitude toward the horrendous things human beings were capable of doing to each other. On the other hand, a beach somewhere in the Keys or the Caribbean seemed a more appealing place to be when he got to that age.

"Thanks, Billy, I'm glad to see that none of this shit is getting you down."

"Sure, Adam, be talking to you soon. Don't take any wooden bodies."

Adam watched Billy get into his truck and with one last look at the remains of what was once a probably bright and attractive young woman, Adam headed over to Jack and the fishermen to listen to their story. He thought briefly, Shit, this was going to be another one of those days in paradise, but he'd have to get through it.

Chapter 4

Casey Forbes, walking to Clary's from her carriage house apartment, noticed that the restaurant was bustling as usual. Clary's had always been popular because of its good food and the sidewalk tables, which offered the plus of tourist watching - a favorite activity of Casey's. However, ever since it had been immortalized in the book and the movie *Midnight in the Garden of Good and Evil*, it was always crowded with tourists hoping to catch a glimpse of the owner Mike Faber, who had appeared briefly in the movie.

Casey watched as Megan walked towards her. Dressed in designer jeans and a cerulean blue tee shirt that exactly matched the color of her eyes, Megan caught the attention of an older man who held the door to the restaurant open for her. She smiled gently at him and nodded in the direction of Casey, sitting at one of the sidewalk tables. The man smiled ruefully and said something which made Megan laugh and shake her head. Casey reflected that Megan looked younger than her thirty-three years. She might be a few pounds overweight, but she had a great figure and never failed to attract men no matter where she went.

As Megan sat down, Casey joked, "Breaking another heart there, I see."

"Yeah, he asked me if I was alone and could he could buy me breakfast. My new hair cut is working well for me." Megan ran her fingers through her cap of fair hair. Maybe my latest diet is also working."

"You look great. I don't know why you worry so much about your weight; you're tall enough to get away with it."

"That's all right for you to say. How much do you weigh, 115 pounds?"

"I wish, closer to 120 and remember I'm only 5' 6," three whole inches shorter than you."

"Yeah, but you can eat anything and you're always exercising. Whereas me, I just have to look at a cake and the pounds go on."

Casey and Megan had been friends for over two years now. Both composition teachers at Carter University, they once shared an apartment at a very difficult time for Casey. It was during this time that Megan's older brother Paul died in a car accident caused by the evil McLean father and son. Casey was anxious about her friend since it was coming up on the anniversary of Paul's death. She'd noticed that Megan had been very quiet recently and had suggested this breakfast meeting since she knew that Megan hated to be alone at this time. Marla, Megan's partner, was in Europe again with one of the tour groups she guided around the major capitals as part of her job.

Casey deliberately tried to lighten their mood. One of the many horse-drawn carriages carrying tourists was meandering slowly down Abercorn Street with its load of curious and slightly embarrassed looking passengers.

"Megan, take a look at the hat on the older lady with the bright red blouse. Want to take a shot at where she comes from?"

"Got to be a New Yorker. No one who lives here has that kind of nerve."

"Okay, I'll buy that, and the guy next to her with the nose and the loud shirt has got to be hubby. The way his eyes squint tells me he plays the stock market. New York and money, what do you think?"

"Sounds good to me. Catch the group headed here. It's almost the end of September and unusually chilly today, and they're still wearing shorts and tank tops. Got to be Wisconsin, Canada someplace like that. My guess is Mom and Dad taking the two kids on a little vacation. What are your thoughts on that?"

"Sure. And they're taking a walking tour; see the little guide maps in Daddy's back pocket? They might have money, but they're none too anxious to spend it on a bus or horse tour."

"Daddy could be a used car dealer; he kind of looks like one."

Casey smiled. She put her own gloomy thoughts to one side and reflected that it was good to see Megan appearing happier this morning. She wasn't sure how to ask her how she was doing except by coming right out with it.

"Paul's anniversary's coming up next week. How are you feeling?"

"God, I don't know. It's been two years, and I should be over it. Today's a pretty good day, but some days, like last week for instance, are too grim for words. I just keep thinking it was all such a waste. What did he do to those two McLean creeps? Nothing. Thank God Earl is dead and Jimbo is in prison. At least there's some justice in the world. The only good thing that 's come out of the whole tragedy is that Fred and I are much closer."

Casey remembered Fred, Megan's other brother. "Does he e-mail you a lot?"

"Yeah, at least twice a week, and we talk on the phone as well. It was good to see him this summer, and he's talking about coming here for Christmas."

"Oh, it'll be fun to see him again. If you want to do something special on Friday, just let me know. You know how fond I was getting of Paul. I still feel so guilty that it was because you were driving my car, that Paul was killed. Perhaps we could do something just the two of us."

"You don't need to feel guilty. I've never blamed you for the accident. I've told you that often enough. Whatever would I do without you? Anyway, what are our plans for this afternoon? How about some antiquing? We haven't been to Alex Raskin's shop in ages, and he always has some neat things. We can't go to Ben's because he's out of town till next week. Perhaps that's what we could do on Paul's anniversary. We could buy a little painting or something. Ben always makes me feel good."

"You're on. Let's shop today and next week. That'll be bound to make us feel better." Casey laughed and was happy to see Megan smile back.

Chapter 5

Jerry Curtis was looking for his glasses for the twentieth or thirtieth time that day. He'd get himself involved in something, and the damn things would be lost again. *I should have gotten the friggin' bifocals. At least I wouldn't have to take the damn things off every time I need to see something up close,* he thought.

Jerry was a vain man, fighting his age every step of the way. He plastered Rogaine into his head every evening and spent hours in front of various mirrors in the desperate hope of finding new growth. Unfortunately, he remained in that percentage of men who achieve no success whatsoever. *What the hell is that, a pimple? For Christ's sake, I'm fifty-seven years old. Do I really need a pimple? Shit.*

He tore himself away from the bathroom mirror, his shoulders sagging. "What the hell's the use?" he muttered. He was chubby, almost fat, especially in one place, his gut. His belt buckle was being driven lower with every passing year, and only his hips held on for dear life to hold up his pants. His chest looked almost sunken in comparison to his stomach, and the Pillsbury Doughboy legs and bulbous knees made the beach a trial instead of a joy, and shorts were definitely out. A sallow complexion combined with his washed-out blue eyes gave him the overall appearance of a man who probably couldn't even claim that the advancing years had robbed him of his good looks. *That's okay. I've got something nobody else has, and it's going to make me rich. Then let's see who has the last laugh.*

Forgetting about his glasses for the moment, he headed back to the desk in his private office, where he did his accounts and kept his most confidential papers. This was really what it was all about - the real reason for his jittery nerves and burgeoning anxiety - the pastels. He'd known the artist the second he'd laid eyes on the little jewels now in his possession. Three Edgar Degas pastels, the biggest 7"x 8". He remembered every word of his conversation with the seller, a disreputable thief and narcotics user known only as Chuck. He'd stopped by Jerry's place two days earlier with the pastels discretely packaged in a brown envelope.

"Hi Jerry, got something you might be interested in, but it's gonna cost you."

"What you got, Chuck, another fake Inness?"

"Not this time, buddy, these are for real. Rumor is they got swiped out of the Berlin Museum during World War Two. You interested now?"

"Yeah, sure, let's take a look."

Jerry was in an indulgent mood, and nothing much else was going on anyway. He went from indulgence to excited wonderment in thirty seconds flat. He made his best effort to appear cool although he was having difficulty keeping his hands steady.

"I don't know. If they're real, and I emphasize the word if, I might be able to do something with them. What are you looking to get for them?"

"I gotta get $50,000, Jerry, and no trying to knock me down. It's $50,000, or I'm on my way." I tried puttin' 'em on the Internet for big bucks but everyone that replied kept askin' for provenance. I ain't got no time for that kinda shit. That's why I'm lettin' you have 'em for so cheap.

Jerry settled back into his chair and pretended to be musing over the idea. He put on his best perplexed look for Chuck, managing to wrinkle his brow and purse his lips, even though he felt like he was going to burst through his skin at any moment.

"Well, I guess that would be okay. I just hope I'm not hanging myself out to dry. This is a pile of money you're looking for. A check okay with you?"

"Sure, we've known each other a long time. Just the same, it'd better be good."

"It's good, Chuck. Want me to walk you over to the bank?"

"No, that's okay. I'll trust you."

Chuck took his check, left through the back door, checking both ways as he always did, and got into his 1972 green Oldsmobile with a satisfied grin. Jerry was more than satisfied; he was ecstatic. Neither man noticed the little blue car parked at the end of the alley.

That's when Jerry's troubles actually began. He hadn't gotten a good night's sleep since he acquired the pastels and his days were an endless series of Tums, which did little to relieve the constant annoyance of his upset stomach. What to do with them became his mantra. When he was at the shop, he worried about how he was going to market the pastels.

When he was at his home near the Savannah Mall, he worried about someone breaking in and stealing them. He absent-mindedly ran his hand through what was left of his hair and discovered his glasses. They'd been there all the time, probably laughing at him. "Son of a bitch!"

He stood and stretched his cramped muscles; it had been another long, worrisome day. Time to head home for a little supper and a couple of drinks. Maybe he'd just hop on the Internet tonight and see what he could come up with. He'd recently had a couple of interesting conversations with a gentleman in Munich, Germany, who seemed quite interested in art. Maybe there's something there. I've got to get rid of these things before they drive me nuts.

Greg Burke allowed his gaze to wander with a jaundiced eye over the mural, six feet high and twenty long, he and his assistant were in the process of restoring. He turned to his partner, Destiny Lynn Durden, with a grin suspended somewhere between paternalistic and incredulous. Her willingness to tackle any project, no matter how difficult, always secretly pleased him. Her usually positive attitude linked to her uncanny ability to match color was what caused him to hire her in the first place. He had patiently taught her all the restoration skills he had acquired over the thirty-five-year period he had been involved with the conservation of paintings, watercolors, pastels and prints. She was an apt pupil and a quick learner, with just the occasional difficulty cropping up, such as the time she was a little overzealous cleaning an oil painting and erased most of one hand in a portrait.

"First thing we've got to do is make ourselves a stretcher for this little baby, Des. Feel like a trip to Lowe's?"

"Sure, let's go. Might as well get started as soon as possible. You know that after we've had lunch, I 'll need a nap."

"No nap for you today, Des, nice try though."

Greg worked his sixty-one-year-old body out of the comfortable fabric chair he spent as much time as possible in and made a valiant effort to ignore the stiffness in his back and legs. He took a moment to clean his glasses and rub one hand over his chin. Had he shaved this morning? Yes, he had, good deal. His angular frame was doing the best it could, considering he'd been a smoker for forty years and ate too many things that weren't good for him or the diabetes he'd acquired. In some ways it was a minor miracle that he felt as good as he did. On occasion, he envied Destiny her twenty-nine-year-old body. She was a young woman of spirit and intelligence with lively dark brown eyes that flashed like lightning when she was angry. The three children she'd borne had inserted some extra padding on her 5' 4" frame, which was a constant source of aggravation for Des. Southern born and raised, she was not a woman to be trifled with, considering she had once knocked her husband Bobby out for an hour with a solid right cross to the jaw.

The two piled into Greg's van and headed for Lowe's, intent on acquiring the lumber they'd need for framing the mural.

"How're you coming along with the pair of portraits with the smoke damage? I haven't even had a chance to see what you've been up to."

Des turned towards Greg. "They're coming along okay. I've got the dirt and smoke off; all that's left is a little minor in-painting, and we're ready to re-varnish."

"Great, let's get them done and back home to their owner. I'm sure they're being missed."

The two portraits, husband and wife, dated back to the late 1700s and were attributed to the English artist Sir Joshua Reynolds. Fortunately for the owners, the small fire they had in their home did not seriously damage the pair, and a good cleaning carefully applied would restore them to their previous brilliance. Greg loved the two pieces but wouldn't be terribly unhappy to see them go. Despite the fact that he was insured against such losses, he hated the very thought that something might be damaged or lost while in his care.

"When does Ben get back? Didn't he say Tuesday?"

"Yeah, I think so. I wonder what he'll have for us this time."

"Something fun, I'll bet. Ben knows his stuff."

"I bet we'll be getting a call by Wednesday morning, what do you think?"

"Yup, I'll buy that. It'll be good to see the little rascal. I miss him when he's not around."

"Yeah, me too; he is absolutely the nicest man, our Mister Ben."

Destiny always referred to Ben Appleby as Mister Ben out of the respect and admiration she felt for him. She had also referred to Greg as Mister Greg for a long period of time, until Greg diplomatically suggested she shorten it to just plain Greg, in light of the fact that they were equals in the area of restoration, even though he was technically her boss.

They pulled into Lowe's parking lot with an air of happy anticipation. There was nothing quite like the starting of a new project, and who knew what Ben might be bringing for them.

Chapter 6

Ben Appleby sat in his favorite Sheridan armchair with a quizzical expression on his face. Once again he examined the two little French paintings but still couldn't come up with a clear idea of where their attraction lay, or even why he'd bought them in the first place. An even greater puzzlement was why the German was willing to pay so much money to purchase them. They were an enigma, and so far they seemed unwilling to give him any insight into their true nature. "Come on, talk to me. Where did you come from? Where have you been? The least you could do is give me a little help with this."

Despite the careful manner in which they'd been packaged for their long trip from France to Savannah, the flaking of the surface paint was continuing unabated. Ben felt that the process was taking place almost before his eyes, that if he looked away for even a second, he'd find more little paint chips in his lap. But if they were going to the German on Friday, what difference did it make? The restoration would be his problem at that point. The only real and continuing doubt for Ben was whether or not he actually wanted to give up the two little paintings. All the way home from France, he had bandied that query back and forth in his mind like a tennis ball in the last game of the last set in a major tournament and still hadn't come to a decision.

Ben glanced around the apartment he kept over his antique shop. There was little, if any, wall space left for paintings. That had always been a problem; he had a strong tendency to get attached to things, especially paintings. These two were no different; they were already singing their siren song to him. "Keep me. Keep me." After all, they were quite small. Ben was sure that if he put some effort into it, he'd find just the right spot for them. What would he tell the German? Simply that he didn't want to sell them - they were his, after all.

"I'll give Greg Burke a call first thing in the morning. Maybe he can get down here tomorrow and take a look, maybe give me an opinion on whether or not they're worth fixing up and keeping." He muttered to himself.

It bothered Ben more than a little to ignore the German's impassioned plea to regain family treasures, but this was an exception. The meeting had troubled him from the start. Selling things in a Paris bar at 8 o'clock at night was not his style, especially after a couple of glasses of sherry. More than that, he didn't like the man who seemed determined to have the paintings.

It was nothing he could put a finger on, something in his eyes. They'd been hooded, almost like those of a cobra, and somewhere in those fathomless depths had been the hint of dishonesty and cruelty.

Ben was used to selling his wares to people he knew and liked. Okay, so he didn't like them all, but at least he always felt secure that the parties buying his "children," for that is what his antiques were to him, would not do them any serious harm. He wasn't sure if this was the case with the German and the two little paintings. He'd get the guy's name and address and give himself some more time to dwell on whether to let them go or not.

Greg Burke and Destiny Lynn Durden were headed down Highway 80 from Statesboro to Savannah, a route they'd taken hundreds of times before. Des had had a difficult night with her youngest, a three and a half-year-old girl by the name of Brianna, so she was already threatening to grab a nap, something she was normally able to put off until the return trip. The call from Ben Appleby had been enough to get the two restorers into their van on a typically blue-skied Georgia morning. It was Friday, and neither had particularly felt like working that hard anyway. It was a good day to visit Savannah.

"Are we gonna stop in Brooklet for gas? I need cigarettes and something to drink; I can't go on without my caffeine."

"Don't worry, you'll get your caffeine and some Fig Newtons. Maybe that'll be enough to keep you awake until we get to Ben's. Where do you feel like eating today?"

"I don't know; how about you?" A large part of any trip to Savannah for Greg and Des was picking out a place to eat, the one chance to escape the rather mundane nature of dining in their hometown, an opportunity for a more exotic and interesting cuisine.

"How about Snapper Jack's? I could do with some shrimp."

"Sounds good to me. Wake me up when we get there."

"Des, you're hopeless."

With both the van and Des refueled, Greg pointed the vehicle once again on 80 east and continued in the direction of Savannah. The little hamlets of Ivanhoe Junction and Blichton sped by as they made the turn onto I-16, which would carry them the rest of the way into town. The scenery flashing by the windows was so familiar to the two that they scarcely noticed it, flat and unchanging, punctuated only by the occasional double-wide trailer, house or farm. Traffic was light, as it usually was, and it was a constant fight for Greg to keep the van within the confines of the speed limit. The tendency was always to get there as fast as they could, get business taken care of and get to the high point of the day, lunch.

"What's Mister Ben got for us?"

"He said he had two paintings he picked up in France that were into some serious flaking."

"He say if they were good?"

"No, he didn't mention that. I suppose we'll find out when we get there."

They were passing the exit signs for the Southwest Bypass and Lyons Parkway, signifying that they were now close to their destination. The 37th Street exit flew by, and they were at the Collier Street Exit, home of Ben Appleby's antique shop. Des continued on with her litany of complaints about the difficulties of raising two young boys, twelve and ten, with little assistance from her husband, who seemed more in tune with spending time with his buddies than with her. Greg nodded at appropriate intervals; it was a topic of conversation he was quite familiar with, but one he could do little or nothing to correct. His thoughts were centered on what he'd find at Ben's, and he found his mind drifting away from Des and her problems.

". . .and then do you know what the son-of-a-bitch did?"

"What? Oh yes, what did he do?"

"He actually expected me to let him make love to me after spending half the night getting drunk with his pals. Can you believe that?"

"Hard to believe, Des, hard to believe."

Greg had spent most of his life living in the North. After five years of living in the Deep South, he was still in the process of getting acclimated to it. He and his wife, Emma, were both convinced that they'd found Erskine Caldwell's *Tobacco Road*. At the very least, it was *Peyton Place* revisited. Both, however, loved the down-to-earth feel of southeast Georgia and enjoyed their involvement with the people there. Even though Des and most of her family and friends spent more time fighting their way upstream than salmon trying to spawn, they were extraordinarily proud and delightful people, full of love and warmth.

Forsythe Park loomed ahead, and it was only a couple of jigs and jogs to Ben's. As they rounded the last turn onto Collier, they could see his gray van parked in its accustomed spot on the right, enjoying the shade provided by a large oak. Greg pulled his van into a spot behind Ben's, and he and Des got out of the vehicle and walked in the direction of the steps leading up to Ben's shop. They were only about half way up the short stone staircase when they were greeted by an extremely unusual event. An older gentleman was leaving Ben's house in what seemed to be an extraordinary state of rage.

"You'd better find those paintings for me, Mr. Appleby, and quickly. I want them, and I don't intend to allow you to put me off. Do we understand one another, sir?"

"I'm terribly sorry, Mr. Kruger. I still don't know if I want to sell them."

"I want the paintings, and I want them in a hurry. You'd better make up your mind to sell them to me."

"I'm doing the best I can, sir, in considering your offer. There really isn't anything else I can do for the moment."

"Appleby, I'll be back next Tuesday, and you'll have them for me. That's all I have to say."

Greg and Des stood rooted to the spot at this inconceivable turn of events. How could anyone be this angry and threatening with a man as nice as Ben Appleby? Without a backward glance, the burly white-haired man shoved his way past them and headed in the direction of a waiting taxi. He entered the cab and slammed the door with enough enthusiasm to let the bewildered couple on Ben's steps know that his fury was full-blown.

"Jeez, I know this is none of my business, but what in the hell was that all about?"

"Come on in, Greg. You too, Des; it's a long story. I'll fill you in."

Chapter 7

Jerry Curtis was lost in the magnificence of her. She didn't just move; she flowed like a sultry sea against a welcoming shore. Like the lyrics of an Elton John song, slow and warm and uniquely sensual. There was a single word he could extricate from his lust-enraptured brain to describe her: exquisite. Yes, that was it; she was exquisite. Exquisitely supple and soft, long sinuous legs and small but perfectly rounded breasts that rose and fell in rhythm with his own wildly beating heart.

Their encounter had a simple enough beginning. She came into his antique shop at about 3:00 p.m. He was captivated by her from the first - a slender six feet or so of pure female beauty, strikingly blond hair cut shoulder-length with the ends turned in to frame the perfect oval of her face. The dark brown eyes beneath her long lashes had promised universes of fulfillment, as did her beautifully sculptured mouth that would drive Hugh Hefner crazy beneath a perfect slender classical nose. She was the personification of someone whom every man would love and every woman would hate.

She browsed casually through the shop, touching nearly every item with her long, beautifully tapered fingers, lingering here and there with one item or another, more a caress than just an application of flesh to an inanimate object. They talked, nothing specific, just in generalities about the various pieces of furniture, objets d'art, and paintings he had on sale. Inside of an hour she took his heart as surely as Sherman had taken Atlanta. Whether he was in love or in lust was beside the point; he wanted her, and after a point, that's all that really mattered.

After a lengthy period of time, he finally stuttered out a dinner proposal, which she had, much to his astonishment, accepted. The evening went more smoothly than even in his wildest dreams he could have hoped for. He knew he wasn't that much to look at - aging, balding, myopic, and more than a few pounds overweight. She didn't seem to notice, much less care. He simply could not believe his good fortune to have found this living goddess who seemed to be as entranced with him as he was with her.

Having eaten an exquisite meal at Elizabeth's on 37th Street, they returned to the apartment that he maintained over the shop; everything progressed with the precision of a movie scripted in the romantic style of the best of Hollywood's golden era. He was Bogie; he was Gable; he was Grant, nothing was off, and nothing existed except the perfection of the two of them coming together as a single unit. He was involved to the point of soaring through previously untouched climes. With some depth of pride, he showed her his latest acquisitions, with the hope that in seeing them, she would hold him in even higher esteem than she seemingly already did.

The Degas pastels appeared to do exactly that. Her warm, liquid brown eyes seemed to widen even further, absorbing the little sketches into their bottomless depths. She seemed excited by them, by their beauty as well as by their immense value. He translated her excitement as a need to be with him and summoned the courage to touch her, to caress her silken softness. She had yielded to him with a force of passion he had never known.

Now it was time for the final conquest, the removal of her black bra and panties. Lying on the bed, as he gloried in her unique sensuality, he'd felt the first sensation of something odd, out of place. His vision began to blur and he felt disoriented. There was a sudden pain in his arm and then a total blackness.

Casey, in preparation for the greatly anticipated trip to Ben's antique store, was busy wrapping up her morning. There were the usual last-minute questions from her students and phone calls to return. She waited for the arrival of Megan and Marla, fluffed her short dark curly hair and adjusted her lipstick.

"Hey, Case, how was your morning?"

"Great, Megs, how about yours, any budding Hemingways yet?"

"Sure, a George Hemingway, maybe, but no Ernests though. You?"

"I've got a couple of kids that are doing really well; they've got a shot at being writers if they knuckle down and keep at it. Where's Marla?"

"She's right behind me; she just stopped in the ladies to perk herself up. God, she can look better in ten minutes than I can in three hours; it's enough to drive a girl nuts."

The brown-haired, brown-eyed Marla appeared in the hallway, headed in the direction of her two friends, drawing admiring glances from two of the cleaning staff as she walked by. She was stunning enough to elicit looks from both males and females. At 5'10" she was a little taller than Megan and her slender body type made her look taller still. Her complexion was flawless, and she always seemed to maintain a perfect tan no matter the time of year.

"Ah, there they are, my two favorite academics. What's up, troupe?"

"Same shit, different day. How about you?"

"Good as gold. We ready to hit the road?"

Casey turned to Megan. "You and Marla looking for anything in particular today?"

"I'm not, but Marla's been into art since her last trip to the Tate Museum in London. Maybe Ben will have something to catch her eye. Let's see which galleries you've visited so far: the Hermitage, the Louvre, the Prado. Life is such a bore for you, isn't it?"

"Now don't be jealous. You know I always bring you back nice presents and phone you when I can."

"God, I wish I had your job as a travel consultant, getting all those free trips to Europe! What a horrible way to have to make your living. Too bad you're no longer in education with Megan and me; then you could look forward to getting stuck here in good old Savannah month in and month out."

"My heart bleeds for you. You academics who only work for eight months in the year."

"Oh yeah, have we heard that one before? No one mentions that during our supposed time off, we have to write articles, apply for grants since we're so badly paid, and of course if we want any sort of promotion, we should find the time to bang out a book or two. So much for having four months vacation each year."

"God, I'm so thankful for good friends. Can we just get on with this, ladies?"

The three women piled into Marla's green Ford Taurus and headed out for Ben Appleby's with happy anticipation. When they arrived at Collier Street, they found the blue van belonging to Greg Burke, parked behind Ben's. Casey and Megan were well acquainted with Greg and his young partner Des Durden, having had several of their paintings restored by the pair.

"Hey, great, looks like a real party. Greg and Des are here too," said Casey. "Have you ever met them, Marla?"

"No, but I love that pastoral scene they restored for Megan."

"You'll like them. You can buy a painting which looks crummy for a low price, let them fix it for you, and bingo, instant great art."

The three ascended the steps to Ben's door and rang the bell. All three noticed that he was not his normal happy self as soon as he answered the door. The Ben that greeted them looked flustered and pressured. "Hi Casey, Megan, Marla. Come on in. Des and Greg are here and we're having a little tête-a-tête in the living room."

After Marla had been introduced to Greg and Des, Ben brought their attention to the reason for his current out-of-sorts condition. The two little paintings lay in the middle of the dining room table, looking rather pitiful in their tattered, dull state. Des picked one of them up, being careful not to disturb their already fragile condition.

"Mister Ben, have you noticed that there seems to be an initial of some sort on whatever's painted underneath this?"

"No, I didn't see it, Des. Where did you find it?"

"See, down here in the lower left, where the paint's flaked away from this woman's skirt."

Greg Burke took the painting from Des and shifted it at an angle in an attempt to get better light.

"I think she's right, Ben. Looks like an O, maybe even an R-O. Can't be sure, but there definitely seems to be something there.

Everyone took their turn examining the little genre piece, and each voiced the opinion that there was definitely some sort of lettering under the surface paint.

"I don't know. What do you think we should do with it?" Ben looked enquiringly at Greg.

"I think we should take a little more paint away in that area to see if we actually can find a signature. A little more paint lost on this item isn't going to make a lot of difference. It's already in such tough shape that we're going to have to do a fair amount of in-painting anyway. A couple more little spots aren't going to hurt anything. We could try an X-ray on it; that might give us an idea as to what's really under there."

"No, I don't want to get carried away with this; I didn't pay that much for these two anyway. Just take 'em with you and see what you can find out."

Marla and Megan had been listening to the conversation with some interest. Both were taken with the paintings, undeterred by their condition or the obvious lack of talent displayed by the artist.

"Have you yet decided what you're going to be asking for these? I think they're adorable."

"God, I don't know, Marla. I suppose it depends on what Greg here charges me for fixing them up. I'm still not even sure if I want to sell them at all. I think I'll wait to see what they look like when they're cleaned up."

"Okay, but please do keep me in mind if you do decide to sell them. I'd be interested."

"I will, if I don't get beaten to death first by that German that wants them."

Ben went on to explain the rather odd confrontation with the angry man they had met exiting the shop and his puzzlement at the man's insistence. All of the friends came up with their own fanciful versions of why the man might be so desperate to get his hands on the paintings - the wildest version coming from Casey, who proposed that he was an ex-Nazi dealing in great works of art stolen during the Second World War. This elicited a round of snorts and chuckles from all present. Everyone there knew that what they were looking at was not great art, even under the wildest stretch of the imagination.

Chapter 8

Sylvia Gordon adjusted her glasses and went back to the ordeal of filing the paperwork for the latest arrival at the Medical Examiner's office in Savannah. When she was busy assisting with the autopsies, she reveled in her job, but when she had to fill in the numerous forms every time a new arrival showed up, she was bored to tears.

She ran a hand through her short fair hair and got up to check some information in the filing cabinet, cracking her knee on the edge of the desk. Usually she loved being close to 6' tall, but her desk at work was obviously built for someone far shorter and caused her numerous bruises.

"Did you do the toxicology report yet?" Dr. Frazer's voice startled Sylvia, causing her to knock her elbow on the file cabinet.

"Ouch, sorry, yes I meant to give it to you. She had some Rohypnol and 2000 units of insulin in her system."

"Interesting, first the date rape drug and then a lethal dose of insulin. Doubt that she accidentally injected that herself. So, that pinprick might have been the site where it was administered. Very interesting. I think I'll just have another look at Jessica Stillwell before we release the body. Take a few more photographs. Don't want to have missed anything."

Sylvia looked at Dr. Frazer's departing back, wishing he'd asked for her help again. She didn't want him to think of her as only a glorified clerk. After all this was an internship and he should be using her skills.

She looked back at the pile of filing and deliberately thought of the evening ahead. She enjoyed life in Savannah, especially the night-life with all the clubs, bars and good restaurants to go to. Maybe she'd go to the Mirror Image again soon. It would be nice to wear her new dress and go dancing. That would take her mind off the boring aspects of her work.

Lieutenant Adam Carter was hard at work. He sat quietly at his desk in the squad room, absent-mindedly drumming the fingers of his right hand on the scarred metal surface. The desk had been there as long as he had. It was definitely of the no-frills variety, with enough dents and scratches to prove it.

Adam wasn't appreciably happier than he'd been two weeks ago when they'd found the body of the young girl spread-eagled on the old barn floor. Catherine was away for a week at a conference in Tucson. Although he spoke to her on the phone every evening, he was missing her calm presence and easy laughter. The last few days he'd worked sixteen-hour days and the desire to smoke was driving him crazy. Not only was this latest killing on his mind, but he was also handling the Jerry Curtis death, another enigma with absolutely no leads going anywhere. He hoped that Curtis was something simple like a heart attack. He could easily deal with that at the moment. Jerry's neighbor had found him naked in bed but without any apparent wounds. Perhaps there weren't any complications there.

The girl, on the other hand, had been found in a deserted barn in the middle of a field with no occupied buildings within half a mile. He'd sent Jack to check out the closest neighbors anyway, just in case. The FBI's VICAP system hadn't helped with the data he had from the young girl. There were no crimes of a similar nature.

The 5' 9", slender, blond young woman had been dead approximately five days and she died from a massive dose of insulin administered by needle in her armpit. According to the toxicology exam, she also had Rohypnol in her system. She had rope burns on her wrists and ankles, which unfortunately meant she was probably still alive when she was injected. There was no sign of semen anywhere on her, and she had more liquor in her than food. The medical examiner said that she had been bathed before death and a couple of fibers from a towel were found in her long hair. Scavenging animals, probably rats, had done a fair amount of damage but not enough to make identification impossible.

"I wonder what the hell happened to her clothes or the rope for that matter," mused Adam. His team had notified her family, and now was trying to run down any friends or associates who might have seen her or been with her prior to the time she wound up in that barn. It wasn't going to be easy; he just had that kind of feeling. They were lucky to have even identified her this quickly. Thank God Georgia put fingerprints on file for drivers' licenses, and that she had a Georgia license.

Adam picked up the photo ID of Jessica Stillwell they'd received from SCAD and tried to think of anything this pretty, vivacious-looking nineteen-year-old could have done that would have caused her to wind up tied down on the floor of a musty old abandoned barn with some psycho injecting her.

Her driver's license gave her address as a SCAD dormitory, which was surprising considering no one had even reported her missing. This was a comment on the fast-paced, 'who cares?' nature of current society in itself.

Her parents had been completely devastated by the news. They were used to getting irregular phone calls from Jessica, so were totally unprepared for what had occurred. They were New Englanders, who saw their daughter on breaks and during the summer, and didn't even have a clue as to who her friends might be. That was the part of the job that Adam hated the worst, notifying people of the death of someone close to them. It still pulled his guts out every time he had to do it, even after all these years.

Adam unwrapped a fresh piece of gum and got ready to start another day of trying to track down someone who might have seen or been with this unfortunate young woman prior to her demise. Maybe just one more cup of coffee might do the trick and give him an insight into something he hadn't thought of yet. He needed to find some friends of hers as quickly as possible, so he could at least begin to start eliminating some of the questions nagging him.

Klaus Kruger was angry. The stupid American antique dealer was still proving obstinate. He unconsciously clenched and opened his hands as though some part of his mind visualized the American's throat in their iron grip. His eyes drifted back and forth across the confines of his self-imposed one-room cell at the Holiday Inn. There were two double beds with a night table situated between them, generic prints staring back at him vacantly from the opposite wall and a large television housed in an ornate armoire. His partner was busy, as usual, watching some vacuous drivel. Hans seemed to be intrigued with American television and particularly loved the Jerry Springer Show. Klaus hated all television since it was largely garbage in his estimation.

"Hans, will you please turn that goddamned crap off for a few minutes. We've got to come up with a plan to get those paintings, and soon."

Hans turned his broad hard face in Klaus's direction. His large hands fumbled with the remote and finally succeeded in getting the power off. His 6'5", rock-hard frame extended the full length of the bed and looked massive and intimidating, even in a prone position.

"Yah, okay, so what do we do, break in?"

"I don't know what kind of alarm system he's got in that place. We need to get a good look at it to see if it can be disarmed."

"Sure, when do you want to give it a look, tonight?"

"Yah, there is no time to be wasted. We've got to get those paintings before he does something stupid like sell them to someone else."

"Why don't we just go in and take them?"

"Maybe it'll come to that. We'll see."

"Okay Klaus, you're the boss. Just let me know what you want me to do and when."

Hans turned the TV back on just in time to catch one participant on the Springer show lunging in the direction of another with fists flying. As Hans began laughing out loud, Klaus turned his head toward the window overlooking the parking lot, and began dreaming of what the weather might be like back home in Munich. He wearily pulled out his laptop and logged on. It was time to check the Internet to see what new information might be out there on the Degas pastels. It seemed they were moving around more than he was.

Chapter 9

The death of Jerry Curtis upset several people in Savannah and its surrounding area, mainly because some wished that they had been the one who killed him, and some knew that now that he was dead, they would never get the money he owed them. Since he was largely thought of as a second-rate dealer of dubious moral character, Jerry was not well liked by a large percentage of his contemporaries. He had been involved in several lawsuits over the years brought by customers who had purchased items from him that proved to be something other than what he guaranteed them to be. His death made the news in all the local papers with provocative banners like 'Local Antique Dealer Found Dead in Home', although the articles went on to say that the cause of death was unknown. Many of the more moral of Savannah's society questioned Jerry's sexual affiliations. There were those that swore he was straight, those that swore he was gay, and those that swore he was a little of both. But his unfortunate end led to conversations all over the city regarding his life-style and the possible cause of his death. If the police had any leads, they were keeping them to themselves and answered all questions with the standard 'no comment'.

Marla Waters stopped her perusal of the newspaper long enough to cast a sidelong glance at Megan. "What do you think about this guy Curtis dying, Megs? Did you know him?"

"Not well. I've been in his place a couple of times; he always seemed like an okay guy. He had a little trouble keeping his eyes in his head, but other than that, he never gave me a problem."

Megan could never get over the fact that she was with someone as incredibly attractive as Marla. Marla didn't just sit in a chair; she coiled in it. She was sensuous enough to make a cobra jealous. Her robe was open a little to reveal one long tanned leg, which gave Megan one more opportunity to marvel at its perfection. Megan pursed her full lips and ran her hands through her cap of blonde hair and considered whether or not she wanted to change from her tee shirt and shorts to something sexier. It was amazing that even at her height she could feel small when beside Marla. Yet she couldn't help but feel they made an attractive looking couple.

"How about Casey? Do you know if she knew Curtis?"

"Yeah, I think she bought a couple of small things from him. Why do you ask?"

"Just curiosity. I've got to spend more time hanging out with you guys. You know really interesting people - like sleazy antique dealers who wind up dead. I'm really missing out."

"Marla, I love you, but you do have the strangest sense of humor at times."

"Of course I do. Look who I'm living with."

Marla went back to her reading, and Megan picked up the crossword puzzle she'd been working on. She decided she really didn't know the eight-letter word for an Indonesian herbivore, and did she have the slightest clue what the word was for the ancient Etruscan god of fertility.

She threw the paper disgustedly into the basket next to her recliner and got up to check the view from their front window overlooking Vine Street. She liked this little two-bedroom apartment. They'd decorated it together with some help from Casey and only the occasional clash of wills, and now it felt like home. She especially liked living with Marla; they rarely fought, and when they did, the making up was almost worth it.

"What's happening out there? Anybody beating a path to our door?"

"Nope, not a soul in sight. Looks like it might rain any second; a very good day to get some R & R."

"Sounds good to me. Get your rest now, and we can do some relaxing later."

Megan smiled at her reflection in the window. She looked like a happy woman. If she moved her head just a couple of inches, she could pick up the reflected image of Marla sprawled contentedly in her armchair, long legs flung at divergent angles; one over the arm of the chair, and the other stretched full-length in front of her. Life really could be good when you had someone special.

She reflected back on her life and the difficulties she'd endured in the past - the estrangement from her parents when she'd finally gotten up enough nerve to tell them she was a lesbian, the sidelong glances of colleagues whose silent disapproval cut her like knives. She always maintained as low a profile as possible, but it always bothered her that she felt it necessary to do so. What right did anyone have to make judgments about who she was and how she lived her life? Thank God for a friend like Casey, who accepted her exactly as she was. That, and the fact that she'd found Marla, made life not just tolerable but fun.

She wondered briefly if the dead antique dealer - What was his name again? - Curtis, had someone who cared about him. How horrible it must be to have someone taken from you unexpectedly. She turned from the window with a tiny shudder at that thought and went over to Marla to get in a little quality snuggling time. She fervently hoped she'd never have to find out.

Halfway across town, another set of eyes was reading the news of Jerry Curtis's death. These were older eyes, deeply set under shaggy eyebrows; eyes the color of an angry sea, eyes that refused to believe the words printed in front of them. "*Mein Gott.* This can't be happening. First that swine Appleby and now this. It just can't be possible."

Klaus threw the paper across the room, where it hit the wall and fluttered back to the floor in sections. Hans cast a mildly curious glance in his direction, then turned his attention back to a rerun of the *Andy Griffith Show.*

"I was supposed to meet with that klutz today to look at the Degas he put on the Internet and now this. What in hell is going on here? Hans, we're going out to get some answers, and I do mean now. I've taken all the crap I intend to from these idiots. It's time to get what belongs to us and get out of this miserable, annoying country."

Greg watched over Des's left shoulder as she completed the final step of removing flakes of paint from the signature they'd uncovered beneath the surface paint on one of the small paintings. It was a time-consuming, back-breaking job requiring the use of a tiny ivory stylus to scrape away the over-paint one millimeter at a time. It had taken Des nearly four hours working under the illuminated magnifying lens they used for such jobs, but after some gentle cleaning the signature was abundantly clear - Camille Pissarro, 1882.

Greg stood behind Des and slightly to her left, holding a copy of one of the signature books they so often used in the identification of paintings. "Holy shit! It looks like the real thing, Des."

"You're kiddin'. How much is he worth?"

"According to Davenports, the last sale went through Christie's of London for $2,500.000. I think it's time to put in a call to Mr. Appleby."

Simultaneously their eyes centered on the second little piece sitting innocently on a shelf waiting for its turn for cleaning.

"Oh my God! If this is a Pissaro, who do you suppose painted that one?"

Chapter 10

"Did you do the valuation on the Wright estate yet?"

Joey looked up from the computer into the perfectly made-up face of Ashley Carmichael.

"I started it, ma'am, but I'm not quite finished."

"If you could get it done by lunchtime, I'm meeting with the executors this afternoon. What do you think of the paintings so far?"

"Two American impressionists in excellent condition. The Mary Cassatt is especially saleable, as, for that matter, is the Singer-Sargent. The other paintings are fair, nothing above $5,000."

"And the Cassatt and Sargent what would they fetch?"

"I'll check the latest auction figures, but at least a million and a half each."

"As much as that? The family will be pleased. Good job, Joey. Put the figures on my desk as soon as you can."

"Certainly, Miss Ashley."

Joey stared at the back of his boss as she walked swiftly down the hallway. Today she was wearing a very simply cut black sheath with a matching short-sleeved boxy black jacket piped in white. Understated elegance that was always the trademark of Miss Ashley, vice president of Savannah First Trust Bank, Joey's mentor and idol. She was perfect in Joey's eyes, from her shining auburn hair, which she always wore in a chin-length bob, and her long-lashed brown eyes to her slender legs always shod in high-heeled Italian shoes. Joey ran his fingers through his own short wheat-colored hair. "One of these days I'll be just like Ashley," he muttered and turned once again to the computer and the valuation.

The old house was silent for the most part, with the exception of the creaks and groans that are a natural part of old age. She'd been standing there anchored to the same spot since 1882, watching newer and much less attractive dwellings go up around her. She bore her years with a dignity and a resigned resolve befitting her station in life. Yes, there were times when she missed the old days when she'd stood alone, a tribute to the beauty of Victorian architecture. Now she felt more like a rose among thorns, which she attributed to the unfailing ability of man to destroy what is beautiful and to erect something wretched and ugly in its place.

The quiet footsteps padding softly down her hallway did little to disquiet her. She'd known the tread of thousands of feet in her time, and a couple more would do little to draw her attention. Now and again one of the two figures, currently occupying her second floor, ran into one stationary object or another and let out a muffled oath. This, too, didn't trouble her at all. She was the fine old lady that occupied the corner of Collier and Abercorn Streets. She had her own alarm system, one that would have daunted your average thief.

Hans, however, was not your average thief. Trained in the German army, he was an expert in electronic systems, and had been able to disable the one protecting the old house with relative ease. Now he and his older companion were able to search the house containing Ben Appleby's antique shop at their leisure, pausing only to avoid being seen by the lights of passing cars. Even that was not a significant problem at 3:30 in the morning.

The search was thorough and methodical. The two investigated every possible hiding place in which the two little paintings might have been hidden and came up with absolutely nothing. Klaus's fury increased with every passing minute, and he was perilously close to picking up something breakable and hurling it across the room. "Let's get the hell out of here. Wherever he has them hidden, they are definitely not here."

As Klaus and his large companion left the old house, his mind returned to a former, and in his way of thinking, a better time, a time when he had been an eighteen-year-old youth, full of the furious sound and excitement of the Third Reich. Entering houses then was no problem - he simply broke down doors and took what he wanted and laughed openly at the terror-stricken cries and moans of the less than human Jews. Now he was seventy-eight years old, though he knew he looked little more than sixty-five, and he had never forgotten the pride and power of the black uniform he'd worn in those early days. How he longed for that period in his life; if only it could be that way again. In these modern times, he could no longer use a Luger to convince people of his determination and resolve. God, he hated that! Now he was going to have to lower himself once again and go through the motions of talking to that fool Appleby.

The sole occupant of the little blue car watched the departure of the two shadowy figures from the old house on Collier Street with more than above average concern. It was apparent even in the dim light that they carried nothing with them - an interesting development. As the two men departed the scene, the little car began its own trip home. Nothing to do but wait for the next move the Germans would make. The solitary figure absent-mindedly fingered an antique silver Star of David hanging on an equally old gold chain as the small vehicle made the right hand turn onto Drayton Street and headed south with another day of clandestine observation completed.

The tall blond sat on the bed of the simply-appointed motel room and unlocked the black leather briefcase for just one more look at the recently acquired treasures. The room itself was generic, no different than any other of thousands of rooms for rent in Savannah: a king-sized bed, a comfortable armchair, a round table with an upright office chair, and two night tables. The art on the walls was typical tasteless prints and commanded no attention from the observer. The art in the briefcase, the Degas pastels recently acquired, however, was an entirely different matter.

The new owner gave a brief thought to their manner of acquisition. It was unfortunate that the man had died, but sometimes bad things happened. The blond wouldn't worry about it.

"God, you are so beautiful, my little friends. It's sort of a shame we have to part, but money is money."

With a final wistful glance, the blond re-locked the briefcase and put it back under the bed. It was time to find a buyer for the little cache of pastels. They would be able to provide something never acquired through a miserable childhood or in the years lived as an adult, security.

Chapter 11

The illusion had to be perfect, the carefully applied makeup without a single solitary flaw. "This is the real me. This is who I really am, the perfect beautiful woman." This was the real Joey Morrisey in the mirror, not the shy, introspective young man who daydreamed about his boss and worked so industriously at his desk at the Savannah First Trust Bank every working day of his life.

He'd known for years about the trap he'd been born into, the falsehood he'd been forced to live since his earliest memories as a young boy. No one had understood then; no one would understand now, how it felt to be a woman locked in a man's body. Only he could understand completely the injustice of the situation. But in his heart he and the mirror knew how truly lovely and feminine the real Joey was. He always promised himself that someday he'd find the courage and the money to do what should be, must be done - the final transformation from Joey Morrisey, into the real Joyce. He shifted his slender frame left and right to catch the full impact of the blond haired, perfect face in the mirror.

The mirror stared back with its usual indifference, and Joey once again began to feel the stirring of anger at the bizarre inequity of his situation. He could think of ways to put those feelings to rest. It was rather simple really, all he needed to do was let a few of those beautiful blond young things, who took their gender for granted and flaunted it in his face, know how it felt to be in the sort of misery he had to live with every day of his life. Joey stood to get one more good look in the mirror, adjusted the padding in his bra, smoothed the silky blue sheath against his slim shape, and headed for the door for a night of possibilities at his favorite club.

Catherine Sherman walked slowly from her red Toyota Corolla toward the Counseling Center at Carter University. It was one of those perfect fall mornings with a clear blue sky and no humidity. She was dressed in her usual work clothes of a straight knee length skirt (today's was navy), crisp white blouse and brightly colored silk scarf knotted around her neck. She looked professional yet approachable. Her scarf choice this day was emerald green with a border of navy and white stripes. Her scarves were like her signature tune: some were fairly plain, but others had exotic fish, insects or animals on them, or were boldly striped and in lurid colors. Her colleagues and clients often commented that they transformed Catherine, who was by nature rather serious, to someone with a quirky humor. Today's choice was deliberately subdued owing to the first client she was seeing at nine o'clock.

Mary Beth Reid had been recommended to Catherine at the request of the Health Center. This in itself was fairly unusual, since usually the students themselves would come to the counselors asking for help with a problem. However, on some more serious occasions, faculty or health personnel would call the center and say that they had recommended a student to seek help. Sometimes the students never then showed up, but usually they did.

As she walked very slowly and in obvious pain into Catherine's office, Mary Beth glanced around her. The office walls were painted a soothing pale green, and healthy-looking plants filled every corner. There was a beautiful large photo of a sunset dominating one wall and several other photos matted and framed of exotic looking locations on the other walls. She looked at the woman in front of her and summed her up rapidly: elegant, cool, calm, but at least she was smiling.

"Hello, Mary Beth, I'm glad you could make it. I'm Catherine Sherman; please take a seat." Catherine gestured to an upholstered sofa with several cushions and took a matching armchair herself.

"Thanks, Dr. Sherman, it was good of you to see me at such short notice." Mary Beth's voice was low and quiet, not much above a whisper. She lowered herself cautiously into the chair, leaning forward slightly as though to put as little weight as possible on her bottom. Her thick, long fair hair fell forward hiding most of her face. I'm not quite sure what I'm supposed to tell you, but the doctor in the health center seemed to say that it would help me if I came and told you what happened to me. But I must say right away," Mary Beth's voice grew stronger, "I don't want to go to the police."

"That's fine, Mary Beth; you don't have to go to the police," replied Catherine. "Why don't you just tell me what happened, and we can take it from there."

"It all happened three days ago on Friday night. I'd met this guy, Will, at the Mirror Image in the historic district last week, and we'd arranged to meet up again last Friday. My cousin, Teri, was supposed to come with us, but at the last moment, she called me and said she had to take her mother to the hospital; she's diabetic and she hasn't been well. Anyway, I decided to go alone since my roommate was out of town, but I know a lot of the crowd who go to the club, so I felt sure there'd be lots of people there that I knew.

"Will was there already when I arrived about nine o'clock, and he was cool. He looked really nice, dressed in black; he's blond-haired and tan, so he looked great. We made a nice couple I thought, and a couple of people made some remark that we looked good together. I'm so tall, close to six foot, that it's great to find someone who's taller than me and doesn't mind a tall woman."

Catherine smiled encouragingly at Mary Beth. "You're doing fine; keep on telling me about your evening."

"We danced. Will's a terrific dancer, lots of rhythm. At one point we sat at the side of the dance floor and he got me a drink, rum and coke. I'm only twenty, but Will's twenty-two, and they rarely card people, so he got the drinks. I was thirsty and hot, and I guess I drank my drink pretty fast. And then... then..." Mary Beth's voice faltered, "I just don't remember anything else."

"When did you wake up?" asked Catherine.

"The next morning. I was on the bed in my bedroom and there was blood, so much blood. Oh God!" Mary Beth started to cry, great heaving sobs, her shoulders shaking.

Catherine got up from her chair, sat next to the crying girl and put her arms around her. Mary Beth turned and buried her head on Catherine's shoulder. "I feel so guilty, so dirty. What did I do wrong?"

"Oh, Mary Beth, you didn't do anything wrong. That's the whole point. From what you're telling me, I think he probably slipped Rohypnol or GHB into your drink. They're really popular at clubs and here on campus. They're what people call the date rape drugs. They're odorless, tasteless, and in rum and coke you might not have been aware of the floating particles that Rohypnol often leaves. I'm thinking it was probably that one since it has an amnesiac effect, and you say you can't remember anything. The health center said something about your injuries; do you want to tell me anything about them?"

"That's really why I'm here. He hurt me so bad. I can't stop bleeding. I wasn't going to go to the health center, but I couldn't stop the bleeding. And now they're saying I have to go to the hospital because the X rays they took show that I'm damaged internally and maybe... maybe..." Mary Beth stopped speaking.

"You're afraid you might not be able to have kids?"

"Yeah. And no one's really talking about if he might have had a disease. They've given me a whole lot of antibiotics, but I just don't know what's going to happen, and I'm so scared."

"Mary Beth, where are your parents? Have you called them?"

"They're away on vacation. They're somewhere in the Caribbean, and it's really hard to get a hold of them. They'll be back in a week."

"Do you have any other family who could help? You mentioned your cousin; do you have an aunt who could come here?"

"Yes, my aunt Jean. I really like her. Perhaps I should call her and maybe I can go to her local hospital. She lives outside Augusta. But her next door neighbor's a cop, and I don't know."

"You don't want to talk to the cops. Is that what I'm hearing?"

"No, oh I know I should have called them right away, but I just couldn't face it. I just couldn't bear all the questions, and what good would it have done? He'd still have done it. He'd still have treated me like an animal. But you know what's really scaring me now?" Mary Beth turned her head violently from side to side so her fair hair swung. "I don't even know if it was only Will who did this to me. I heard the doctor say something about the severity of the penetration, and I'm afraid there was more than one person. Also I vaguely remember telling Will where I lived, but how did he get me out of the club, with no one suspecting anything?"

"Well, that's easy. The initial effect of Rohypnol is drunkenness, so Will could have just told people you were feeling a little drunk, and he was taking you home."

"I feel so guilty. Why did he do this to me? What did I do wrong?"

"Oh Mary Beth, you have to remember that for men like Will, you're just a target like in a game. It wasn't anything personal against you. You were just a convenient victim. Remember, rape isn't about sex. It' s about power. The frightening thing is that he'll most likely do it again."

"Oh, I know I should tell the cops, but I just can't; I can't." Mary Beth began crying again.

"Okay, let's leave the cops at this time; we can always contact them at a later date when you feel strong enough to cope. I think what we should do now is phone your aunt and get her to come and fetch you."

"But what about all my classes? What about my tests and things?"

"You don't need to worry about those. I'll call all your professors and ask them to give you a week off. Then, when you find out more from the doctor in Augusta, we can plan if you need more time off. Is that okay with you?"

"Yeah, thanks, Dr. Sherman."

"Now, I'm going to give you a couple of pamphlets to read. Maybe you can look at them with your aunt. I want to tell you again, Mary Beth, you were the victim here. You're not to blame yourself. You're a fine young woman; try and remember that. Here's my card; please give me a call when you come back from Augusta, or if you want to talk while you 're there, you can also just phone me here during the day."

As she ushered Mary Beth out of her office, Catherine pondered as to whether or not this Will would rape someone else soon or worse. Was Will even his real name? She knew she couldn't tell Adam about Mary Beth, but maybe he should be made aware of the Mirror Image and predators like Will.

Chapter 12

It was a typical early October evening in Savannah. The rain that had been falling during some part of the day or night for the past week was not ready to give way to dryer cooler weather yet. However, neither the light rain nor the sticky heat seemed to be a concern to the tall, shadowy figure moving slowly down River Street at an hour when most people had hours before tucked themselves into bed.

River Street runs along the waterfront of Savannah. Home to a myriad gift shops, restaurants and river boat cruises, it is an area largely devoted to tourism, and is the focus of the annual Saint Patrick's Day celebration, which often brings thousands of visitors, mainly young people, to the city.

There is usually something going on in River Street late into the night, especially on Friday and Saturday nights when several live bands and street musicians ply their trade, hopeful of picking up enough money to make it through to the following weekend. It is an old street of cobblestones dating back to the earliest days of Savannah, difficult to drive on, difficult even to walk on if you've had too many drinks. It is a place well-known to the police, an area prone to too much drinking, fist-fights, and even the occasional totally drunk individual who falls into the river.

It was the perfect setting for the predator.

The predator didn't drink liquor, at least not when he was hunting since he needed the advantage to bring down his targets. To complete a successful hunt, one had to be quicker, more alert and focused, for that was what made the difference between the victor and the loser.

The selection of the target had already been made earlier that evening. Now all that was required was careful stalking and selecting the precise moment when an attack could be swiftly and successfully completed.

The intended victim didn't have the slightest notion of the fate that was intended for her. She had started the evening with three of her friends, hitting several spots that catered to the young crowd with loud music and heavy drinking. Two of the group had packed it in about 1 a.m. and headed off in separate directions. That left the brown shoulder-length-haired girl with glasses and her taller blond companion, whose hair was nearly waist length and seemed to swing back and forth in rhythm to her melodious laughter. They were both obviously young, no older than their early twenties. The tall blond wore jeans, which looked sprayed on, and a tee shirt which emphasized her perky up-thrusting breasts. There was just enough of a gap between the shirt and the jeans to allow the predator a glimpse of a twinkling diamond in the place of honor in her navel. The stalker paid little notice to the shorter brunette; she was not the prey and mattered little in the drama. Her only role was to get the hell out of the way as soon as possible.

The girls continued on down River Street past the entrance to the Hyatt, swaying as they walked and occasionally bumping hips, which invariably induced new gales of laughter from both. They turned left after passing the Hyatt and began the trek up the steep steps that led them to the Bay Street level. At no time did they seem to be aware of the two cold, calculating eyes that intensely followed their every step.

The mind of the predator shifted into overdrive with full focus on the endgame. The oppressive heat was of no concern; even the tiny rivulets of sweat, caused by the wearing of a light hooded jacket on this unusually warm night, were ignored. What mattered was what lay ahead, and the reassuring weight of the ten inch needle filled with Rohypnol that pressed against the predator's ribs. A gentle touch assured its owner that it was still in place and ready for action.

The girls reached Bay Street and were continuing their happy stroll in the direction of Martin Luther King Boulevard. Were they walking home, or did they have cars? If they had cars, had they each brought one, or were they riding together? Together would provide a problem, but only time would tell.

Bay Street seemed even darker than usual at this hour. All the bars were closed or closing, and all that remained were the streetlights that seemed dimmed by the haze left by the rain and the stifling humidity. The huge oaks on the river side of the street loomed menacingly, their limbs weighed down by the Spanish moss hanging like grey sodden shrouds; it was a perfect night for a nightmare.

The girls stopped by a small black Ford Escort. This was the moment of truth. What happened now would determine whether or not the chase would continue to its logical finale. The predator took in a breath and held it for what seemed like minutes as if afraid that its breathing could be heard in the fifty or so feet that separated it from the two laughing young women. The old oak sheltered the tall, slender figure with its massive trunk, providing a perfect haven for watching without being seen. Only snatches of conversation could be heard: "Had a great time," "next week," "call me." Finally, the brown haired member of the duo unlocked the driver's side door to the little vehicle and got in, bumping her head on the doorframe as she did so. This elicited more laughter and some final shouted goodbyes. With a cough and a spurt of smoke, the little car worked its way out of its parking space into the street and was quickly gone.

Now the tall blond was alone and continuing her walk down Bay Street, a solitary figure that seemed to be realizing how truly alone she was. The laughter was gone, replaced by a more apprehensive look on a face that turned left and right as she walked. Her pace was much quicker now that she was alone. By the time she'd reached her own car, a small green two door Honda Civic, she was nearly running as if all the possible dangers of the night had come rushing into her mind along with the departure of her companion. Had she known what followed so closely behind her, she would have broken into a full-fledged sprint, but of course she had no way of knowing. The remaining bravado brought on by the liquor still had just enough effect to give her a false sense of her own invulnerability.

The right hand of the stalker found the comforting feel of the needle's plunger and tensed for the final act. The timing of the next move was critical. It had to be the exact moment when the victim had unlocked her door, gotten into the driver's seat and was fumbling to put her keys into the ignition. Those few seconds before she adjusted herself in her seat and remembered to lock her door were the time to pounce. A quick chop to the back of the neck and a hard shove, pushing her into the passenger's seat, then plunging the lethal weapon into the side of her neck which would render her helpless until a much safer, quieter spot could be reached where the game could begin in earnest.

The predator had begun to take a step from behind the oak tree where it had taken refuge in the shadows about twenty feet from the young woman, when it became aware of headlights approaching from the opposite direction. There was nothing to do but wait for the lights to pass and hope that the opportunity hadn't vanished. The car stopped and the upper part of a uniformed figure appeared in the open driver's side window.

"You all right, Miss?"

"Yes, thanks officer, just getting ready to head home."

"You haven't had too much to drink by any chance, have you, miss?"

"Oh no, I had a couple of drinks earlier, but I'm just fine now, and I just live over in the Oglethorpe apartment building next to the Civic Center."

"Okay, but be careful. It's too late at night to be out by yourself. How about if we just follow behind you till you get home?"

"Thanks, officer, I've got to admit it did get a bit scary under all those oaks. I didn't realize how late it was."

"Okay, have a good night miss; we'll just follow behind until we know you're safe."

"Thanks again, I appreciate it."

The predator dug itself as deeply into the shadows of the old tree as it could. It wouldn't do to be spotted at this point. Even though the disappointment of getting so close without achieving the final goal was agonizing, there would be another night. That night would have to come soon, though; the predator was hungry, very hungry.

Lieutenant Adam Carter watched Jack Malloy as he handled a phone call that was probably from some old lady, who was convinced she'd just witnessed some horrible event taking place, which more likely would turn out to be nothing more than an everyday occurrence blown out of proportion by bad eyesight and an over-active imagination.

Jack talked in a perfectly modulated tone, never once raising his voice. The guy was good, no doubt about it. There were times when Adam envied Jack his free and easy existence, but then he thought about Catherine and what a good life he had now they were together and quickly remembered how lousy life had been for him before they'd met. As Jack put down the phone, Adam asked him, "You got a sec?"

"Sure, buddy, what's up?"

"We got that cause of death on Jerry Curtis. It was a heart attack. The only kicker is that his system also had Rohypnol in it, just like Jessica Stillwell's had. What do you make of that?"

"I don't know," Jack fiddled with the telephone cord, "weird coincidence?"

"No, surely not. I might have expected Viagra in a fifty-seven-year-old, but not Rohypnol. That's a date rape drug. He might have been putting it in some female's drink, but that he had his coffee laced with it? That's too odd."

"You think it caused his heart attack?" asked Jack.

"Not according to the ME, although he did say his heart was in such bad shape he was a disaster waiting to happen. It was just a matter of time."

"Well, that's good, so we don't have another murder to worry about."

"No, just Jessica's." Adam looked at his notes. "Did you get anything else out of those two women who were with Jessica at the Mirror Image Club? What were their names again? Jill and something?"

"Jill Mason and Carrie Swartz. Nothing more than we got in the first interview. They drank; they danced till about midnight, but then Jessica said she wasn't feeling well and split. They couldn't seem to remember very much about who was there. Carrie mentioned that Jessica danced with a tall blond woman. It's a gay bar, so I'd imagine you'd get a fairly diverse group of people in there."

"Was Jessica gay?"

"No, the girls said she was straight like they are. Lots of SCAD students go there because the music's good. How do you suppose the perp got his hands on the Rohypnol?" Jack looked enquiringly at Adam.

"No, problem, pal. You can get it almost anywhere nowadays. Could have been downtown or even the Internet. Want to know how to build a pipe bomb? Want to buy some magic mushrooms? No problem, just go online. A couple of clicks and you can get all the information or buy pretty much anything. It's a weird world we're living in."

"You got that right. I think I'll get myself an M16 for those bigger jobs we need to handle." Jack laughed.

"Listen, I'll try tracking down the Rohypnol if you're willing to take a trip to the Mirror Image. I'd do it, but I'm booked solid this weekend. I swore to Catherine we'd go out on Friday unless there was an emergency, and Saturday I'm at the Kiwanis."

"Okay by me. Besides you're taken. I might just find somebody there I'd like." Jack laughed.

"Just make sure that somebody passes a sex test before you get too carried away. I don't wanna have to come here and bail you out." Adam smiled.

"That's why I need the M16. There wouldn't be enough of the victim to identify."

Chapter 13

Ben Appleby began his day, as he almost always did, with a shower and a small bowl of corn flakes topped with a banana. Mildred bustled contentedly around the kitchen as she had done for nearly all of the forty years they'd been married. The bright blue eyes were a little faded with time, and the hair was no longer waist-length but a shoulder-length bob with numerous streaks of gray woven into the dark brown. There were an additional thirty pounds on the compact 5' 2" frame, but none of the physical changes had dimmed the cheerful nature of a basically happy woman. Ben's glasses were suspended halfway down his nose as they usually were, and he took a moment to look over the top of his morning paper to watch his wife flitter around the little kitchen. He could not suppress the small smile of amusement and affection that was so often brought to his lips by just watching her.

They had had a life with far more ups than downs, something he was eternally grateful for. Mildred had been there through the thin times as well as the fat, never failing to keep him as trim as possible, neat and well taken care of. He was just the tiniest bit ashamed that he hadn't related the information that Greg had uncovered about one of the little paintings, but he thought it wiser not to get her hopes up unnecessarily. Time enough for that when he could prove them to be what they seemed to be; and if it were true, they would both soon be enjoying the fruits of many long years of hard work. Ben had stopped believing in fairy tales years ago, but now it seemed that the ultimate in fairy tales, the discovery of two very valuable paintings, just might be unfolding. He knew he'd be on pins and needles until he heard from Greg and Des about the second painting.

"Ben, honey, are you okay? You seem preoccupied this morning."

"Oh, sure, hon, I'm fine. I'm just thinking about what I've got to get done today."

"Well, finish your breakfast, or you'll be late opening the shop."

"I'm not really that hungry this morning. Maybe I'll take an early lunch. But you're right; it's time for me to shove off."

With a kiss to Mildred's rosy cheek, Ben headed out the door and started his van. He began the trip up Victory Drive as he did every day, his mind totally focused on what information he might receive during the day from Greg. A horn blasting on his right let him know that he was drifting into someone else's lane, and he was rudely jolted back to the realities of Savannah morning traffic.

What if it really is a Pissaro? What if they both are? What am I going to do with them - auction, private sale, what? Where did they really come from; who was the original owner; what if their family wants them back? Think, Ben, think. What the hell are you going to do with them if they're for real? Did the German know about this? Is that why he wanted them so badly?

Confusion whirled through Ben's mind like a firestorm. All he was coming up with were questions that had no answers. By the time he made his turn onto Abercorn Street headed toward his shop, he had resolved absolutely nothing, except for the knowledge that if they were the real thing, he certainly wasn't going to keep them in the shop, or even in his home for that matter.

"Oh, shit!"

"Now what, Des?"

"You'd better take a look at this. I've got a "P. Ceza" to this point. Can this possibly be who I think it might be?"

"The signature looks good."

"All I'm sure of is that if it's a Cézanne, you'd better get ready to give Ben mouth-to-mouth when we tell him."

Casey woke up in what could be best described as a pensive mood. She'd enjoyed the previous evening with Megan and Marla watching *The Taming of the Shrew* by the university drama department. While the performance was a tad or two short of something from the Royal Shakespeare Company, it was still fun watching the young students give it their all. She had finished the evening with a bottle of wine at Megan and Marla's apartment, with the usual complement of bad jokes and ribald laughter. Megan's favorite label of the moment was the three Musketeers, D'Artagnan, Aramis, and Shorty, which Casey failed to find humorous. Even though the early evening had some of the pleasantness which Casey had begun to take for granted when they got together, later there was an undercurrent of something darker hiding just below the level of conversation.

Megan had made a comment again about Marla's job, which had caused her to respond quite sharply. "I do wish you'd shut up about my work. I'm bringing in lots of money, which you seem more than happy to spend, and while we're on the subject, what about all the times you say we can't go out because you have a pile of grading to do. You don't hear me bitching and moaning about those times, do you?"

Megan had gone quiet, but Casey could see she was upset. What was happening between her two friends? She thought. They certainly did seem to be going through a rough spot in their relationship. She decided to try and change the subject, and they had gone on to talk about the article in the *Savannah Morning News* about the body of a young girl that was found in Richmond Hill.

"I wonder if she was one of our students. Did the paper say anything?"

"No, it didn't. Just that she was nude and found in an old barn by some fishermen. God, it's so scary when you read this stuff. I like to pretend that nothing bad happens in Savannah."

"Gee, Megs, that's a bit unrealistic," said Casey. "After all this is a big city with several colleges. Obviously not as big as New York or Boston, but still, murders are bound to happen."

"Yeah, I guess you're right. I just don't like to read about it all the time. Now my beloved here just loves the gory details, don't you?" Megan turned to look at Marla.

"That's not totally true."

"Yes, it is. Just the other day you were asking me about Jerry Curtis and you were positively licking your lips." The anger in Megan's tone surprised Casey, who immediately changed the subject. There were obviously problems between her two friends, which might just be normal between two people who were involved. Just because she and Megan had never argued when they lived together didn't mean a thing. Theirs had been a very different relationship. But the whole evening had left her with a strange disquiet. She needed to talk to Megan about what was bothering her. After all she was still her best buddy.

Klaus was becoming more and more frustrated with life in general. Not only had he been unable to make any headway with acquiring the two little paintings, but he was stuck in a claustrophobic little motel room with Hans, who had become hooked on American television. Nothing he could have done in his youth or since could have been bad enough to doom him to the fate he currently found himself captured by. He was beginning to think that he had died and been sent to a purgatory that included reruns of every bad American sitcom ever produced.

"Hans, can you turn that God damn thing off for a while? I can't even think."

"But Klaus, it's just getting to the good part. Gilligan may have just thought of a way to get off the island."

Calmly reaching into the night-stand just to the right of his bed, Klaus slowly withdrew the vintage Luger given personally to him by Herman Goering, and very carefully, very deliberately, took aim at the television.

"You have to the count of three Hans - *eins, zwei...*"

"All right, all right, I'm turning it off - see - now are you happy?"

"Yes, Hans, I couldn't be happier. Now, get off your lazy butt. It's time for another visit to Mr. Appleby, and this time we don't leave until we know the whereabouts of those paintings, understood?"

"Okay! I get it; let's go."

The two men left the motel and headed off in the direction of Ben Appleby's antique shop in the small rental car they'd had since their arrival in Savannah. Klaus was seriously considering going back to Avis to acquire the next size up. He was getting tired of being cramped and uncomfortable and having to look at Hans, who looked like a ten-pound banana stuffed into a five-pound can next to him. It was getting close to two weeks since they'd arrived, and they were no closer to having either the two paintings owned by Appleby or the Degas pastels he knew to be in the area. If killing was what it took to get what he wanted, Klaus was now more than ready to pursue that course. He knew full well he was reaching the now-or-never phase of the operation, and it would have to be resolved quickly. There was simply no more time to waste. If someone was going to be eliminated because of this fiasco, the one thing that he was certain of was that it wouldn't be him.

Ben, Greg and Des sat around the 1920's enamel-topped kitchen table in what acted as the kitchen/dining area of the second floor apartment over Ben's shop. Even this room had not escaped Ben's avid desire for the collecting of paintings. Every wall, no matter how small the surface, housed at least three or four pieces of artwork of various sizes. In addition to the art, there were dozens of tins dating back to the 1900s, advertising products long absent from the American scene. Several even evidenced the smiling faces of the royal family of Britain at various stages of their reign. Greg was currently captivated by the picture of the smiling face of a very young Elizabeth II, which graced a biscuit tin whose cookies had been long since consumed, while Des pondered the fate of some long forgotten model who had lent her visage to the sale of a medicine container which guaranteed a cure for everything from warts to colic.

"Okay. We're pretty sure we know who painted the little darlings. Do you want us to continue removing the rest of the outer layer of paint?" Greg asked.

"You know, I don't have the slightest idea of what to do at this point. If they're for real, which they seem to be, where do I go from here? I've been thinking about it since you let me know about the signatures, and I still haven't got a clue as to what to do next."

"How about auction? Sotheby's or Christie's would die to get their hands on this pair."

"I know, Des, but what if they're stolen? That might explain the break-in I had."

"Break-in?" Greg said worriedly. "What break-in?"

Ben explained that when he'd come to work, he'd noticed that his alarm wasn't working and some things had been disturbed, although with the huge inventory he carried, it was almost impossible to see if anything had been taken. He continued, "I don't want to get myself into some kind of hot water over these paintings. I think what I'd like to do at this point is let the two of you finish cleaning them and send some photographs to a friend of mine at the Metropolitan in New York, maybe let him do a little probing around and see what he can come up with. I'll need provenance to sell them. What do you think, Greg?"

"You could maybe check the Internet if anything is known about their provenance. Let's continue the job, get some pictures of the finished products and go from there." Greg stood up.

"Okay, just one thing. Please don't mention what we've got going on here to anyone. There may be people already after these, possibly even that German who was in such a bad mood the day you met him here. I'm not sure to what extent someone might be willing to go to get these, so if we keep it to ourselves, maybe we can get through this without any real difficulties."

"No problem, Des and I aren't about to let anyone know about these little gems; your secrets are safe with us."

As the other two rose from the table and headed toward the staircase leading down into the shop section of the old house, the sound of a buzzer from below indicated new arrivals to the shop.

"Wait here a sec. Let me see who this is before you leave."

Even though the two little paintings were now wrapped back into their protective layer of Styrofoam and cardboard, both Greg and Des took a couple of steps backwards, more out of reflex than thought. Ben peered through the curtains masking the windows of the door and opened it in what Greg thought to be a distinctly tentative fashion. Two figures, one of them quite large, entered the hallway.

"Mr. Appleby, I have come for my paintings, and you need to know I do not intend to leave without them."

Quickly handing the paintings to Des, Greg motioned her further back into the shadows and began his own descent down the staircase.

"Ben, that was the cops on the phone; they're coming over to check out that break-in. They'll be here in a couple of minutes. Oh, I'm sorry, I didn't realize you have customers. Please excuse me, gentlemen."

The older man was turning burgundy, his eyebrows knitting together to the point they almost seemed like one solid connected bushy line. His eyes flashed like flint struck against a stone with an anger that seemed almost lethal in its intensity. The very large person standing next to him seemed equally upset.

"I'm sorry about the paintings, Mr. Kruger, but I've already sold them to someone else, a long-time customer who just couldn't live without them. Maybe there's something else I can offer you in their place."

"No, Appleby, there is nothing you can offer me in their place. Will you tell me who you sold them to?"

"Sorry, I'm afraid I couldn't do that. I never reveal the names of customers to anyone."

"I see. Then we shall bid you good day. And you, sir, who might you be?"

"Oh, I'm just a friend of Ben's; name's Bill - Bill Green."

"I see, Mr. Green. You wouldn't happen to be the person who bought those paintings would you?"

"I'm sorry; I'm at a loss. What paintings is he talking about, Ben?"

"Oh, just two little not very well done pieces I brought back from France, nothing you would have been interested in. Well, as I said, I am sorry, Mr. Kruger. I wish I could be more helpful."

As the angry pair left the shop and headed back to their car, Ben and Greg shared a long and quizzical look over what had just taken place.

Chapter 14

Megan Muller rested her head on her hands as she looked over the twenty seemingly dedicated young people currently involved in the pop quiz she'd given them. Her other hand played with her hair, a habit she'd acquired whenever anything was troubling her. And something *was* troubling her; she only wished she had a clear idea of what it was.

School was fine; her life was good, if somewhat routine, and her romance with Marla was going, or seemed to be going most of the time, quite well. But something was troubling her. She thought back to last night's lovemaking; it had been superb as usual. She knew on some level what was wrong but simply refused to face it, positive that the problem lay within herself and not Marla.

For one thing, she could not ask Marla to talk about her early life, since she was loathe to reveal much about her own traumatic upbringing. The second thing was that after they made love, no matter how fulfilling it was sexually, she invariably lay awake afterwards with a feeling of emptiness. There was some thing, some place in Marla she could not reach, and even though Marla was a masterful lover, Megan felt she never really gave from her soul. Indeed, she felt at times she was no closer to the hidden Marla than she was when they first started dating. She had tried everything she could to be the trustworthy lover and confidante she was sure Marla needed, but she had no real idea of how to proceed to achieve that goal of sharing her life with Marla, instead of just being a part of it. "Maybe I'll talk to Casey about it; could be she'll have some insight into what I'm doing wrong."

Casey Forbes had discussed with Tarka over breakfast her feelings of unease that something wasn't quite right. Tarka had been manfully working at trying to extract a fur ball from his throat at the time and hadn't proved particularly helpful. Last night as she'd brushed Tarka's long grey fur, she'd mused that she'd talk to Megan at lunch and try to discover the problems. Megan had, after all, always been there for her when things were bad. It was only right that she should be helpful when Megan was clearly having troubles.

Tarka was getting fidgety, "I really don't need your help, human. I can take care of my own fur balls, thank you very much." Showing his disdain, Tarka stomped off in the direction of his favorite paper bag, determined to ignore this unappreciative being, at least until it was time for supper.

As Casey sat down across from Megan in a booth at the Olive Garden, she could not shed the feeling that for the first time in their friendship, there was a tiny wall between them. Megan had barely touched her spaghetti, a definitely un-Megan-like occurrence. Even though she constantly complained about being overweight, Megan seldom sent her plate back in any condition other than clean.

"Megs, are you okay, honey? You're not eating, and it looks to me like you've even lost a few pounds."

"I'm okay; maybe I'm just coming down with something. I haven't felt really terrific for a couple of days now."

"Are you sure that's all it is? You haven't seemed like the old you for a while. You know if there's something bothering you, I want to know about it. I want to help if I can. How's everything with Marla; you two okay? You seemed a bit angry with her the other night. Is it her job that's the problem?"

"Yeah, sometimes. She's away such a lot and I do get fed up in the apartment all alone. But in some ways I've never been happier. She just seems to be on remote control sometimes, and that bothers me a little. Other than that, we get along pretty well."

"What do you mean by 'remote control'?"

"I don't know; maybe it's just me being silly, but there are times she drifts into a world of her own, and I can't reach her, no matter how hard I try."

"Have you tried talking to her about it?"

"All she says is that she's concentrating on something and not to worry about it. I can't get her to go into it any more than I can pry out any information about her life prior to our getting together. It's very frustrating at times."

"Do you really want to know about her past? After all you're quite a private person. Perhaps she is, too. I'm sure she'll tell you everything when she's ready; just give it a little time. You'll get there."

"Yeah, I know you're right. I do love her, and I guess I'm silly enough to want everything to be perfect all the time."

Megan idly twirled a piece of spaghetti on her fork and then pushed the nearly untouched meat balls away from her with a shrug of resigned defeat.

"If I tell you something, will you promise not to think I'm nuts?"

"Don't be silly. Of course I won't think you're nuts. I love you, you know that, and I want to help if I can."

"Well, the other night, Marla and I were watching the old version of *Psycho* on television - you know the one with the horrendous shower scene where Norman Bates stabs Janet Leigh?"

"Yes, I know the one."

"Well, right in the middle of that scene, I happened to glance at Marla, and guess what? She was smiling! Am I crazy to let a little thing like that bother me?"

"Well, I don't think I'd build it up into a major big deal. She's probably just seen it too many times, and it's sort of lost the impact for her. Maybe she was just smiling about how scared she was the first time she saw it. And you said something about her liking gory things. Does she like horror movies?"

"Yeah, she loves them."

"Well then, that's it. She's probably seen *Psycho* lots of times, and she finds horror more funny than scary. Lots of people are like that."

"You're probably right, Case. There was just something in her eyes at that moment that I'd never seen before, and it scared me for just a second, but you're probably right. I'm getting myself worked up over absolutely nothing. Thanks for talking to me about it. I feel much better, just getting it out in the open."

"God, you know I'm always here for you and Marla, no matter what."

"Thanks, best buddy, I appreciate that."

"Unfortunately, it's time for us to jam some writing skills into the stressed out brains of our charges. And don't forget to eat a good dinner tonight. You hardly touched your lunch and you're getting too damn skinny. You know how I hate competition in skinny. I'm already way out of it on tall."

"As long as I don't start getting shorter, so you're still in a class all by yourself, Case. I'll talk to you later."

Sylvia Gordon organized her desk into two neat little piles, one representing completed projects and the other those waiting to be done. Those awaiting completion were in order of priority for her return to work on Monday. She took a long last look around her office before she was ready to leave for the weekend to make sure she hadn't forgotten anything important.

There were times when she seriously thought about moving to a larger city where she could better utilize her schooling and her talents, but her roots were in Savannah and just the thought of moving all her possessions and looking for a new job somewhere else gave her a headache.

"Hey, Syl, you ready for the weekend?"

"You bet, how about you? Any big plans?"

Harley Jamison, one of the pathologists, gave her his best man about town look and a wink. Sylvia knew he was dying to ask her out, but thankfully he'd never been able to work up the nerve, which was a good thing since she definitely would have had to turn him down. He was at least four or five inches shorter than she was and both balding and quite overweight. He dressed like he was still lost in the '60s, and while Sylvia liked the little man's personality, there was no way she'd ever be seen in public on a date with him.

"Well, not really, I thought I just might hit a couple of the local hot spots and see what's happening. How about you? You going any place special tonight?"

"I don't think so. It's been a tough week; I think I'll probably watch a little TV and hit the sack early."

"You really should try to get out more. You know what they say: All work and no play makes Sylvia a dull girl."

"That's me, just a little country mouse. Well, have a good weekend. I'll see you again bright and early Monday morning."

"Night."

Country mouse, that was a good one. She wouldn't have to worry about Harley showing up at any of the places she liked to hang out in, at least she certainly hoped not. There were the usual rumors floating around the place about a pretty young woman who wasn't married and didn't seem to have a regular boyfriend. Nothing was ever said to her face, of course - that wasn't the way it was done in polite Southern society, but she knew there were those that probably whispered about her being a lesbian when they were doing their thing in the men's room and needed something to gossip about.

"You still here, Syl?" Dr. Andrew Frazer's voice caught her by surprise. "I thought you'd be halfway home by now. By the way, did I mention that you did a nice job on Jessica Stillwell?"

"Thanks, I appreciate that. Wanna walk me to my car?"

"Sure will. It's not often I get to be seen in the company of a gorgeous young woman. Let's get outta here."

"Ready when you are."

It was only six o'clock. That would give her plenty of time to get home and fix herself something to eat. She wasn't really hungry, but she knew she'd be drinking later on, and she needed something in her stomach or she'd face the possibility of looking stupid after the first couple of drinks.

Losing control was something Sylvia never did in public. There were times, of course, when it was perfectly all right to let herself go, especially when making love. That was her favorite time for giving herself completely to the lovely feel of two bodies grinding together with nothing held back. The touch of hands and lips caressing every part of her drove her wild and allowed her to express a passion she withheld from nearly every other part of her life save one. That other hidden passion was buried deep within her most secret places and known to no one except herself, and that would be the way it would stay. She enjoyed giving her body with wild enthusiasm and hedonistic abandon when the time was right, but she would take her other special secret to her grave.

As Adam Carter pulled into the crowded lot of the Abercorn Street Waffle House, he was quick to note that Jack's car was already there as was the blue van that belonged to Greg Burke. Good, that meant that Greg and Des were in Savannah to pick up or deposit some paintings. He enjoyed talking to both of them, especially Des, whose Southern accent and sense of humor never failed to pick up his day. When he took a moment or two to think about it, he was a little surprised to find out how many people he'd met through visiting the Waffle House on a regular basis.

He'd soon learned that Waffle Houses are different from most restaurants in that the customers are for the most part regulars, and the whole atmosphere is more like a family gathering than strangers in a diner. The cooks and waitresses know nearly everyone, and it's fairly common for them to call out, "Give me a Charlie breakfast," with the knowledge that the cook knows who it's for and prepares it accordingly. Adam had noticed how people who go into Waffle Houses tend to talk to one another whether they've met before or not.

At the Abercorn Waffle House there was a regular, an older man who had spent much of his life in the Navy. He would stroll from table to table talking with the customers even if they might not be interested in conversation. Most of them took his behavior with a smile and a laugh, except for the occasional customers who would try their best to avoid eye contact and eat as fast as they could.

As Adam pulled open the inner door, he immediately spotted Joe, the ex-navy man, standing beside a table occupied by a man and a woman and a couple of kids. Joe looked at the children expectantly, a wide grin on his craggy face, dark brown eyes twinkling behind his glasses. "What did one eye say to the other eye?"

The children both shyly shook their heads, obviously lost for an answer while Mom and Dad just nodded their heads in a benevolent manner.

"Something between us smells." To the accompaniment of gales of laughter from the kids, Joe headed back to his regular spot on a stool at the high bar next to Greg to wait for the arrival of a new group that he could amuse. Des, who was sitting next to Greg, covered her eyes with her hands in mock surrender.

"Hi, Greg, Joe, Des, what's new?"

"Nothing much, how about you? I was just about to tell Des here the one about what you tell a man goes in one ear and out the other, but what you tell a woman goes in her ear and out her mouth. Isn't that right, Joe?"

"Greg, Joe's elderly, and I wouldn't really want to hurt him. You, on the other hand, are fair game. What would you like broken, an arm or a leg?"

Greg smiled at Des, "Oh, you are indeed the perfect example of shy demure southern womanhood. Don't you agree, Adam?"

"Don't try to pull me into that one, you guys. I have no opinion at all regarding anything Des wants to say. It looks like Jack has already finished eating, so at least I don't have to watch him mixing his food; my day's looking up already. Who's working the booths?"

"Sheri is; if you listen close enough, you can hear her dulcet tones in the back room."

Sheri was one of Adam's favorite people. An attractive thirty-five-year-old, she had an almost unceasing sense of good humor, bright intelligent eyes and a laugh loud enough to be heard in the parking lot. She also seemed to know half the people in Savannah and what they were currently involved in. If Sheri didn't know what was going on in town, it probably wasn't worth knowing.

"Hi, Adam, you sittin' with Jack?"

"Yeah, since he's finished eating, my stomach should be okay."

"I could bring you some grits, how 'bout that?"

"Right, when pigs fly. I'd rather have road-kill."

"Greg, what are you and Des doing down here? Life got too boring in Statesboro?"

"Not really, we're headed over to Ben Appleby's; he's got some paintings we're working with him on."

"Yeah, I know Ben; he's a good man."

One of the things that Adam liked about the Waffle House was that nobody ever asked him about his work; not even he and Jack discussed the job when they were in there. It was like a little island of tranquility set apart from the pressures they would face again as soon as they stepped out the door. The only problem with being here was that most of the people he liked sat in the smoking area, but Jack liked to sit in the no-smoking area and since he'd given cigarettes up, it made sense he should, too. But it didn't make life any easier to watch the other customers so happily enjoying their after breakfast smokes.

"Well, it's good to see you guys again. Give me a call if Des breaks any of your body parts. I'll try to get her bail set high enough to give you time to mend. Let me go talk to my partner."

"Good to see you, too. Have a great day."

As Adam plopped himself down across from Jack, he knew that they'd spend the next few minutes discussing sports, Jack's love life and other trivial subjects, but he also knew that in the back of both their minds would be the much more ominous topic of murder.

Chapter 15

The tall blond was pleased. She'd found a possible buyer for the Degas pastels over the Internet. A German seemed quite interested. The details of the upcoming meeting had been very carefully worked out. Someone would deliver a bank draft for a million dollars to her in the parking lot of Publix grocery store at Twelve Oaks at noon. Such a place and time would allow some measure of protection.

Life was beginning to pull itself together and there would soon be enough money to support a very comfortable lifestyle. It was time to end the rat-race and exit the maze one last time, this time for good. Just a few more little details to clean up before being free to slip into darkness.

Silence is not necessarily golden; at least that was Ben Appleby's current outlook on the matter. The quietude he found himself locked in had an ominous quality to it that was more than restrictive; it was closer to terrifying. He was bound hands and feet, lying face-down on one of his own oriental carpets, and worse still, in the living room of his own home, a place that should have constituted sanctuary. The buzzing in his head continued unabated.

He'd never seen who had hit him from behind or with what. All he could see from under the blindfold was a very small area of the oriental pattern of blues, greens and reds, and even that not very clearly. Of all the emotions currently racing around in his mind, the one that took predominance was confusion. The others - fear, anger, and an overall helplessness - bobbed up and down like the ducks in a carnival shooting gallery. He had absolutely no idea of the what, who, or why of this thing. Who could possibly want anything he owned badly enough to resort to this kind of behavior? The two little paintings jumped into his mind with a frightening clarity just as he heard the soft hiss of words coming from an unknown source next to his right ear.

"Mr. Appleby, I need to know where those paintings I want are, and I think you need to tell me rather quickly. My friend has your wife tied to

66

that lovely easy chair just next to your Sheraton sofa, and I sense he just might become impatient if you do not tell me what I want to know."

Ben heard a muffled cry of pain from Mildred to his left.

"See there, Mr. Appleby, he's already started hurting her. He's so hard to control. Don't worry; he hasn't done anything that will show, at least not yet. Do you want to tell me where the paintings are?"

The series of low, muted groans coming from Mildred drove Ben crazy as he struggled hopelessly against the ropes binding him. He had never felt such a helpless rage in his life.

"Our friend Mr. Appleby seems to have become a mute. How unfortunate for his wife. Let's take out something. I think this time a molar, don't you? Or should we start with her fingernails? What do you think, Mr. Appleby? Do you have a preference in your wife's disfigurement?"

"Please, just stop, for Christ's sake. I told you I already sold them, and there's nothing more I can do about it!"

Ben realized as soon as the words were out of his mouth that he had given away the fact that he was positive his assailants were the two Germans. Had he just signed his and Mildred's death warrants?

"Assuming you're not lying to me, Mr. Appleby, give me the name and address of the purchaser and my associate and I will be off, allowing you to comfort your poor wife in peace."

"I don't know their address, God damn you, but their names are Bert and Alicia Farmington."

"I see. May we have the nail on her index finger please?"

This time the scream of pain from Mildred was loud enough to overcome whatever they had over her mouth, and echoed along every fiber of Ben's being as it ended in a long series of choking sobs.

"All right, all right! Just stop! I'll tell you anything you want to know. Just leave my wife alone."

"Much better, Mr. Appleby. Now where are they, before my friend decides to do another nail just for the pure pleasure of it?"

Ben took a deep breath to calm himself. "They're with a friend of mine, Greg Burke, who lives in Statesboro. He's doing some restoration work on them."

"Ah, good. Now we're getting somewhere. Has he taken any paint off, Mr. Appleby? Is that why you're forcing us to go through all this? Is it because you now know who did them? Does this man Burke also know?"

"Yes, he does, and if anything happens to me or my wife, he'll also have a damn good idea who did it. He's seen you, and he'll be able to point you out to the police."

"Oh, I don't think it will come to that, sir. We really have no desire to hurt anyone seriously. We just want what should have been ours from the beginning, then we'll be on our way. I think what we'll do for now, Mr. Appleby, is leave you here just the way you are. However, I think Mildred needs to stay with us, until the situation is resolved. Then we'll get her back to you almost as good as new. How does that sound? Good, I knew you'd agree. Goodbye, Mr. Appleby."

Ben heard the sounds of footsteps headed toward his front door accompanied by more pitiful moans from his beloved Mildred. The door made a quiet sliding sound as it closed behind the departing group, one of whom had been the focal point of everything he had done or been for fifty years. He had virtually nothing left to do for the next few hours except to try to release himself from his bonds. Sometime during that effort, he'd also have to decide what he needed to do about letting Greg know he was in imminent danger of being severely hurt or possibly even murdered. Ben's heart had gone stone cold; he no longer cared about the money the two little paintings represented; all he cared about now was getting his wife and his good friend Greg out of the desperate situation they were both in.

Klaus had felt every hour of every day of his seventy-eight years as the rental car made the fifty-mile trip from Savannah to Statesboro. This was going far beyond the original plan of simply buying two little paintings and returning them to Germany. It should have been an easy task: buy the paintings from that foolishly stubborn Appleby and get on a plane.

He should have been playing with his grandchildren right at this very moment, bouncing them happily on his knee in his warm, comfortable home in Munich. He should be sitting in front of the fireplace in his very own living room, admiring his father's paintings on the wall with Hilda bustling around in her eternal quest for perfect order, dusting and straightening with that perpetual smile on her round, pleasant face, asking him if he wanted a second drink. But, oh no, here they were, the two of them, the tired old man and the hulking enforcer who had become hooked on American television, headed out to attempt their second break-in within a week. Not only that, but they had managed to add assault and kidnapping to their list of crimes with still no successful result in sight.

Nightmare in Savannah

Klaus shifted his body to try to relieve some of the tension in his aching bones with little success. At least he'd traded up to a Lexus through Avis, which provided more comfort than the small car they'd had. He stroked his beard and watched the scenery flow by with little interest, although it was late at night, and he could see very little. He had the thought in his mind that even if it were daylight, it wouldn't make the view any more interesting. The countryside seemed to consist mostly of fields interspersed with the dark forms of small houses or trailers at rare intervals. Even the 7-11s seemed to have packed it in for the evening, causing him to grab a quick glance at the gas gauge, which fortunately was over the three quarters mark.

All he needed now was for the car to run out of gas; that would be the perfect end to the evening. Thank God Hans had at least had enough brains to keep the tank full. The effort caused him to focus once again for the briefest of moments on his burly driving companion.

Klaus had hoped that leaving the motel room might give him some hours of blessed silence, free from sitcom reruns. Unfortunately, this was not the case. It seemed that Hans had not only been hooked by the television, but also by Country and Western music, and was now droning along in a flat, off-key monotone with some unknown singer on the radio bemoaning the loss of his life and love to whiskey and honky-tonk women. He considered shooting the damned thing out, but the explanation that would be required by the rental agency was more than he could deal with in his tired state. Turning it off would leave him confined in a very small space with a sullen, pouting Hans, something else he didn't need to deal with at the moment. Let the damned thing play. This should all be over soon, and he could be in Savannah Airport checking flight information.

Klaus mentally ticked off the sequence of events that needed to take place before he was finally free of the operation. Appleby's wife was well-sedated, securely tied up in their motel room, so even if the sedative wore off before they returned, she should not be a problem. Appleby would do nothing until he was sure his wife was all right. He would meet the party holding the Degas tomorrow in the Savannah Publix parking lot, and with the art securely in hand, head for the airport. In less than twenty-four hours, he should be well out over the Atlantic, headed for home. He breathed a sigh, born of both hope and frustration in equal measures, and tried to prepare himself for the next step in this horrendous venture.

Joey Morrison waited patiently for the little machine to read his sugar level from the small sample of blood he'd inserted into it. It was an activity he performed at least once a day, every day of his life. He detested the pain that pricking his finger generated, even though it wasn't severe. He hated having to inject himself with insulin even more, but unfortunately it was the only way he could live an even close to normal life. Being a diabetic seemed like one more way that the fates had found to make every day of his existence a living hell. Wasn't it bad enough that he was a woman born in a man's body?

He knew that if anyone ever found out that he liked to dress in women's clothes, he'd immediately be labeled a transvestite and treated like he was the dregs of society. No one really understood him, someone tortured by his present body just waiting like a chrysalis to turn into a beautiful butterfly. At least the hormones he'd been taking were doing wonders for his boobs.

The fact that he was kept from achieving his true destiny by something as mundane as money made things even worse. All that stood between his current life and a perfect one were more medications and an operation. The problem was that he didn't make enough at the bank to achieve his goal, and if he finished his treatment, the looks he'd get from his co-workers would mean the end of his job.

He just hated all those pretty blondes who surrounded him. They didn't appreciate how lucky they were, and the way they were always looking at him in a mocking fashion drove him wild. Every single one deserved to be taught a lesson, and he was learning ways to teach them.

He turned his attention back to the book he'd borrowed from the library and which was keeping him engrossed. *Lost Treasures of the Third Reich* was utterly fascinating and similar to another tome he'd finished, *Stolen Art and How to Identify It.* As he read the lengthy descriptions of the masterpieces that had disappeared during the Second World War, he thought about the time when he'd be free to travel the world as a woman. He'd proclaim his femininity in every magnificent museum and art gallery and make love with whomever he chose to. At long last life would be everything it always should have been, and God help anyone who stood in his way before he took that final step to freedom.

Sylvia watched the crowd shuffle in and out of the Mirror Image, some of them just beginning their evenings and some already in an advanced state of intoxication. She hadn't seen anyone of great interest to her at this point, and as the night wore on, the chances of finding anybody would decrease to where there wasn't much left to do but pick up her purse and go home.

That was the way it went in the singles world. Straight, gay or something in between, it made little difference when you played the mating game. There was always a pending excitement in the air whether anything concrete actually took place or not. If nothing happened tonight, there was always tomorrow night.

She had at least had the chance to dance with a few people, and while there hadn't been anyone that had set off any bells, it was always kind of fun to share the intimacy of being close to someone while swaying to a sultry romantic rhythm.

The only problem, if it could be considered that, was her height. It occasionally got a little strange when you were dancing with a man who was shorter than you. While she didn't give a damn, sometimes they did.

The most interesting person she'd been with was another blond who was as tall as she was. She had short fair hair and wore a beautiful red dress, which showed off her spectacular cleavage. She'd caught several people looking at them when they were on the floor and she knew they made a striking-looking couple.

The conversation had been somewhat stilted, but it most often was in situations like this. It was seldom easy to find the right words to say to someone who was a virtual stranger.

"So what brings you here? Are you looking for anyone special?"

"Not really, I just like to get out after a long week on the job and enjoy myself."

"I guess this is the right place then, there's one of everything in here."

"You're right about that. I kinda like it here. I haven't seen you in here before. Is this your first time?"

"No, I've been here a few times before. I guess we just never ran into one another. What do you do for a living?"

"I work at one of the local banks. How about you?"

"I work at the Medical Examiner's office here in Savannah."

"Your job sounds a whole lot more interesting than mine. Do you actually cut up corpses and stuff like that?"

"No, I'm more into the forensics part of it, you know, testing for what's in the system of the deceased and the like."

"I still think it sounds more exciting than banking. My real love is art though, and I do get to have some fun with that every once in awhile."

"Art in a bank, how do you manage that?"

"Part of my job is dealing with the valuation of estates. On occasion we get one to deal with that has some serious art involved. When that happens, it sort of perks up my whole week."

"That's understandable; I love art myself. I'm always looking around in antique shops and checking stuff out on the Internet. Maybe we could get together some weekend and do a little poking around. By the way, my name's Sylvia, what's yours?"

"Glad to meet you, Sylvia, I'm Joyce. At the risk of sounding immodest, I do think we make a striking couple. I bet most people would take us for sisters."

"Probably, and I suppose we are in a way."

"How do you mean?"

"Well, it's not just that we look alike, but if I had to guess, I'd bet we probably think alike. I sense something in you that reminds me of myself. Maybe it's just my imagination, but I think we might be kindred spirits."

"You know I didn't want to say anything, but I think you might be right. Do you have a significant other at the moment?"

"Nope, how about you?"

"Not for a while. Is there anything special that you require in, how shall I put it, an intimate friend?"

"Only that they've got a brain and a sense of humor. Other than that, anything goes."

"I knew I was going to like you as soon as I met you. Would you like to get together later?"

"Let me think about it. If not tonight, I'm positive we'll meet again at some point. It's really been a pleasure to meet you."

"Same here. Let me know if you change your mind."

Sylvia watched the slender attractive figure of the tall young blond named Joyce sway off in the direction of the dance floor and thought briefly on whether tonight would be a good night to enjoy a special moment or not. She was a bit tired at this point, and she wasn't sure if her energy level was up to the amount of mental and physical effort that an intimate assignation would require.

She had absolutely no qualms about having what society liked to term one-night stands, nor had she any fear of being intimate with someone she'd only known for a short time. Everything came down to whether she felt like it or not. Aside from that, making love wasn't the only kind of excitement out there. There were other activities of an equally exciting and much more dangerous nature she enjoyed as well.

Her eyes caught those of a tall good-looking man at the bar. He was another possibility. She decided to take her drink up to the bar and grab the stool next to his. He was definitely a hunk. Who knew what this evening might hold in store?

Jack Malloy had chosen a table as far away from the small dance floor as he could. This was the first time he'd ever ventured into a gay bar, and he found himself slightly anxious. The club was dark, but he was doing his very best to try to remain invisible, trying to wrap the gloomy smoke-filled atmosphere around him like a cloak. He had a thought flash through his mind about having a date here with him, but that would be pleasure, and this was definitely business, no time to be thinking about the enjoyable things in his life. He nervously turned the half-filled glass of Dewar's around and around in little circles on the glass table top in front of him. Being unseen wasn't quite as easy as he'd hoped it would be; he'd already been hit on twice and secretly wished he'd done something to make himself uglier before he'd shown up in this place. Jack had never thought of himself as a homophobe, but little traces of doubt were beginning to creep into his mind. He'd always expressed his belief that there was absolutely nothing wrong with guys with guys and women with women, but now he was beginning to wonder if he really believed it.

Jack spent a few minutes with the bartender, a clean-cut curly-haired young man named Larry with a broad Southern accent. Larry, however, couldn't help, citing the size and diversity of the crowd on the night in question. He had been on duty that night, but said he paid very little attention to who was there, with the exception of a few regulars he'd pointed out. Jack spent a few minutes with each of the regulars, but again, received very little helpful information.

The conversations assumed a monotonous sameness after a while. He would produce his picture of Jessica and say, "Do you remember seeing this woman in here on the night of September 18th?" The answers, with the exception of one, had been the same: "Nope, sorry, didn't notice her, what's she done?" The one person who did seem to have a recollection of seeing Jessica was a twenty-five-year-old by the name of Collie Brachen. She had been sitting with a group of her friends and vaguely remembered Jessica dancing a couple of times with a rather tall woman with short blond hair. She'd been attracted more by the tall blond, whom she described as extremely good-looking, rather than Jessica, but had not noticed if they left together.

Jack had been drifting into a state of semi-reverie, concentrating more on the little circles he was making with his nearly empty glass of Dewar's than he was the noisy crowd around him, when he heard a voice no more than a few inches from his left ear, "Can I refill that for you?" The disembodied voice yanked him back from the edge of the dreamlike trance he'd been falling into, and Jack spun his head around to the left to find himself staring into the liquid brown eyes of a Rock Hudson clone.

"Oh, sorry, I'm afraid I was drifting away there for a second. No thanks, I'm okay for now."

"Mind if I join you for a bit? Not much happening in here tonight."

"No, of course not. Have a seat. Do you come here often?"

"Not really; my partner's out of town and I was getting tired of sitting around and watching TV. How 'bout you?"

"I'm afraid I'm strictly here on business. I'm a detective with the Savannah Police Department, and I'm trying to pick up some information about the young woman in this photograph. I don't suppose you've seen her before, have you?"

"Nope, sorry. Oh, by the way, my name's George Crane, should have introduced myself before."

"Glad to meet you, George. I'm Jack."

"So what's the story with this girl? Is she a victim or a perpetrator?"

"Unfortunately, she's a victim. I'm just trying to locate someone who might have seen her."

"Can I ask if she's dead or alive?"

"Dead, I'm afraid. That's why I'm looking for someone who may have seen her."

"Pity, nice looking young woman. It's a very hard world out there. Have you made any headway at all?"

"Only that she was seen dancing with a tall blond woman while she was here."

"Be careful with that one. I don't know how familiar you are with the gay/lesbian scene down here, but quite a few of the women you see in these places aren't really women - they're guys in drag. You might not be looking for a woman at all; you might be looking for a guy in a blond wig and makeup."

Jack sat back abruptly. It hadn't occurred to him until that moment that a male drag queen might be the party he was looking for. "Thanks. I hadn't even thought of that."

"I know some of these guys look so good when they're dressed up, it's nearly impossible to tell the difference. Well, good luck with your case; it's time for me to be on the go."

"Nice to meet you, George, thanks again for the tip."

"Any time."

Jack watched the tall figure head for the door, then reached into his pocket for a bill to pay his tab. He knew as surely as he knew that sunrise would follow the night that he wouldn't be learning anything new or helpful on this night.

Chapter 16

Klaus awoke with a start. The car had stopped moving, and Hans was gently pushing against his shoulder with one of his ham-like hands. "Klaus, wake up, wake up, we're here."

Klaus had been having a lovely dream of the early days, dressed in his immaculate black uniform and glistening black boots, the death heads pinned to his collars. How he'd loved the intimidation factor of wearing that uniform, watching the terrified faces of the scum he encountered, especially the hated "Juden." His only regret for those days was that he and his father had been primarily involved in the procuring of art for the Nazi higher-ups, instead of in the process of eliminating enemies of the state.

Klaus tried to shake the cobwebs that had formed in his head during his nap. For a moment he'd forgotten where they were going or why. It all came rushing back with a cold reality. They were in Statesboro, Georgia, at the restoration shop of Greg Burke, and they were once again in search of art that should rightfully be his property. It seemed like every bone in his body ached. He'd fallen asleep with his head against the side window and his shoulders in an unnatural position. He'd be paying for that for the next twenty-four hours - God damn old age and the tortures that accompanied it. He shook himself into as positive a mental state as current conditions would allow.

"Is that the building over there, Hans?"

"Yah, it's ADT wired, but that shouldn't be a problem. Probably no harder to take out than the one in Appleby's shop."

"Any sign of any dogs? Any lights on? Are we ready to take a shot at it?"

"I am if you are, Herr Kruger. Let's get it done; I've already missed most of my favorite shows, and God only knows what will be on by the time we get back to the room."

"Ah yes, what a tragedy to miss a single re-run of *The Brady Bunch*. Let's go."

The two men left their rental car, lost in the shade of two immense old oaks, and worked their way towards the shop through the murky shadows thrown across the landscape by a couple of low density street lamps. Klaus checked his watch in the dim light - 3:30 a.m. - perfect. No one in his right mind would be up at this time of the morning. This should be a piece of cake.

They approached the shop, which was unlit, from the rear. The area was residential, but there were no lights shining anywhere in the surrounding houses, the nearest of which was at least a hundred feet away. As Klaus continued to scan the area for any signs of life, Hans quickly disabled the alarm system and set his attention to picking the locks on the back door of the restoration building. Once inside, the illumination of Hans's small penlight was all they would need to find the two elusive small paintings. The darkened room was dominated by a large studio easel, several tables, and shelves lined with oils, acrylics, watercolors, pastels, charcoals and various cleaning solutions. Various larger pieces of artwork and frames lined the room in differing stages of restoration, but there was no immediate sign of what they were looking for. It wasn't until Hans pointed it out that the floor-to-ceiling wall cabinet caught Klaus's attention. It was grey, made of heavy metal, with a very serious looking combination lock right in the center of it.

"Shit, can you open it, Hans?"

"If I had the right tools, I could, but even at that it would take me a couple of hours or more."

"Damn, now what do we do? They've got to be locked in there, no question about it."

"I don't know; there's nothing I can do without proper equipment or explosives of some sort."

"Then we wait until morning; I'm not going back to Savannah without those paintings. Back to the car; it should be light in a couple of hours, and then we can make our move. Agreed?"

"Whatever you say, Herr Kruger, but I don't like it."

"Neither do I, but it's now or never."

Both men headed back to the rented black Lexus in a sullen mood - one because the project had taken another unexpected and frustrating twist, the other because valuable TV viewing time was being lost.

As the night wore on, Ben Appleby finally worked his way free of the confining ropes that bound him and was now positioned in his easy chair, staring off into space. His right hand was twitching, and there was nothing he could do to stop it. His mind was filled with one terrifying thought after another. Was Mildred all right? Was she being hurt? Was she even still alive? He had no idea in the world what to do. If he called the police, he would almost assuredly be signing Mildred's death warrant. If he called Greg, that would probably amount to doing the same. His only real hope was that Greg would give the Germans the stupid paintings, and they would then release Mildred unharmed. They could go back to wherever the hell they came from, and he, his wife, and his friends, would be free to live in peace again. It seemed logical that if they were going to actually kill anyone, they would have started with him. The fact that he was still alive gave him hope that this sequence of events still might result in an ending that wouldn't require anyone's death. At present it was the best he could hope for, so he continued to grip the arms of his favorite chair and stare off into the nothingness of his darkened living room, with nothing but his frantic thoughts of his companions.

The one recurring thought in Ben's mind was the number of times he had asked the Lord for various and sundry small favors during the course of his life. He fervently wished he could take them all back at this point and cash them in for this one really big one.

It was early Saturday morning and Adam Carter was trying hard to stem the downpour currently running down the neck of his raincoat. The gray Spanish moss which hung in drifts from the branches of the ancient oaks in Bonaventure Cemetery really did resemble old men's beards in the murky half-light that deepened his depression. Why did the worst things always happen at night and usually in the rain? If only he'd thought to wear a hat. If only he'd remembered his umbrella. If only he'd been an accountant like his mother had wanted him to be instead of a detective, if only. But 'if only' counted for absolutely nothing. Adam took another ineffective swipe at his forehead with his already sodden handkerchief in a vain attempt to wipe some of the moisture off his face. He could feel the dampness forming under his arms and in the small of his back; he'd count himself extremely lucky if he didn't catch pneumonia. "Shit."

Adam had visited Bonaventure Cemetery on numerous occasions, but never before at midnight in the pouring rain. In the spring, it was a place of beauty with the multi-colored azalea bushes, flowering dogwoods and sweetly scented wisteria. He was familiar enough with the layout to know that the final resting places of Johnny Mercer and Jim Williams lay somewhere off to his right and a hundred or more yards ahead. Tonight the darkness and gloom of the cemetery was intense, with only the police lights illuminating the tomb directly in front of him and more specifically the nude body of the young woman who lay spread-eagled across the top of it. The inscription on the end of the cement enclosure, Edwina Johanson 1833-1894, meant little or nothing to Adam, captured as he was by the ivory white figure of the naked girl.

She looked no more than nineteen or twenty, with long blond hair that was now a wet tangled mass hanging limply off one end of the tomb. She was probably of medium to above average height, and her body was tan, a pale honey color, except for the clear bikini shaped white parts. She looked more like a perfectly formed life-sized porcelain doll than an entity that had once been an animated living person. Heavy eyebrows framed her closed eyes, and Adam briefly wondered what color they were. The serenity of the face and figure before him was in stark contrast to what might have been a painful death. There was no real way to tell for sure. She didn't have a mark on her that was visible to the naked eye, and thoughts of Jessica Stillwell ran through his head. If this one was also an insulin related death, he'd have a real problem on his hands.

There was something or someone stirring off to the left, probably just another one of the uniforms blundering around in the crime scene. He turned and tried to open his eyes wider than they already were in the vain hope that increasing the surface area of his vision would make anything clearer in the soggy world surrounding him. It could have been a cop, a dog, or a God damned elephant for all he knew. If it wasn't a cup of coffee, or a dry set of clothing, it wasn't going to be of that much value to him in any case. Eventually through the gloom he was able to make out the familiar face of Jack Malloy.

"What's up? Can Billy give us anything?" Jack looked just as wet and miserable as Adam, but at least he had an umbrella.

"Don't know. He's still working on her, and I haven't talked to him yet. You guys picking up anything of interest? Footprints, anything?"

"Not yet. This rain is probably killing any hope of our finding something worthwhile anyway, but we've got the area cordoned off, and we'll keep doing what we can. I've got the kids who found her talking to the uniforms, although I don't think they're gonna be much help.

"Okay, keep at it. I'll let you know what Billy finds."

Adam let his eyes shift back to the broad back of Billy Moran as he worked over the young, still form lying on the cold, wet slab. He already knew in his soul what he was going to find - nothing. A second corpse slain in a manner almost identical to the one found four weeks ago, only in much better condition. Only an autopsy was going to tell him what he really needed to know.

Megan Muller rolled over in bed and checked the small digital clock on her night-stand. It was uncompromising in its faithfulness at keeping time to the second, no matter how painful that might be to its viewer at 6:15 a.m. She briefly thought that catching a few more moments of sleep wouldn't hurt. She'd had a tough night, filled with a great deal of tossing and turning. She'd been awake at 2:00 a.m. and again at 4:00. Megan didn't sleep well when Marla was not in the house, and Marla had been called away for an overnight in Atlanta to deal with the latest group of happy little tourists she would be accompanying on a tour though Europe. As she patted the empty space next to her, she became aware of the tinges of jealousy she frequently felt towards Marla's chosen profession. Being an overseas tour guide was a fabulous job and it paid well, but the downside was the amount of time it kept the two of them apart. The apartment they shared wasn't really that big, a kitchen with attached dining area, a living room, two bedrooms and a bath; it just seemed so much larger when she was all by herself.

Megan rubbed her eyes in an effort to get them to focus well enough to allow her to make the very needed trip to the bathroom across the hall. Duty to her job ought not to be enough to make her abandon the warmth of her bed, but the persistent yammering of her bladder would. Time to get your ass in gear, girl; there are things to be done.

Megan threw her long legs over the side of the bed and headed for the bathroom. After that, it was shower time, one of the times when she was glad to have short hair. She could wash it, dry it, give it a couple of quick fluffs this way and that, and it was good to go. She never used much makeup, so that was not a time-consuming task either. The thing that always took the longest was checking her body for signs of encroaching fat. Fat molecules had an insidious way of creeping onto her thighs and hips overnight and laughing at her when she found them staring back at her in the mirror in the morning. She needed to start walking again with Casey during their lunch break. Damn that little shit anyway: she never puts on an ounce.

Entering her walk-in closet to choose her clothes for the day, Megan couldn't help but think back to the dreadful closet of her childhood. The memories of the times when her father had tied her up and locked her in the dark space for even the smallest infraction of his rules would probably never completely go away. She would always be afraid of the dark and of enclosed spaces. And her hatred and fear of her father had continued until the day he and her mother died in a car accident when she was in college.

She was never sure how much her mother knew about what was going on, but she had never really forgiven her for acquiescing to her father's every whim and reminding Megan several times a day that "Daddy knows best. You just have to do what he says and not annoy him."

Looking at all her clothes, Megan quickly decided on a purple, pink and white workout outfit. If the students didn't appreciate it, screw them; she needed to be comfortable more than she needed their approval of her choice of clothes on this particular morning.

The next task, of course, was to feed the damn cat, which was probably ensconced next to her bowl in the kitchen, waiting patiently for her high point of the day. Megan hadn't wanted a pet, because she liked her freedom. She had argued when Marla had wanted a dog, but when Marla had come home with the small, pretty calico stray, she felt she couldn't really complain any more. However, now the cat was proving quite a nuisance since Marla was always away, and it was she who was forced to always be there to feed it. To make matters worse, Marla had chosen to name it, of all things, Pussy, after a favorite cat she'd read about years ago in a British children's book. Although Megan had accepted the name in good humor, the cat's constant chewing on cords of any nature nearly drove her crazy and left her in constant fear of watching the stupid animal go up in a flash of electrical combustion. The truly humiliating moments were those rare occasions when the cat managed to sneak outside. She was then forced to stand in the front yard and shout, "Pussy, here Pussy, where are you Pussy?" to what she was sure was the amusement of the entire apartment complex.

Pussy also didn't have the personality that Casey's cat, Tarka, did. Tarka seemed more like a human than an animal and never failed to amuse her with his countenance that gave him the look of a Tibetan monk contemplating the vagaries of life. Megan had even suggested to Casey that she buy Tarka a saffron robe and his own altar, but Tarka had made it quite clear that he would not put up with such ridicule. He was not a lap dog after all.

Megan completed her morning rituals, unlocked the door of her 1998 blue Cavalier, and prepared herself for the onslaught of another day of teaching Composition to a group of college students who sometimes appreciated her, but most of the time, only tolerated her because they were forced to be there if they ever hoped to achieve a degree.

Adam did not look forward even a little bit to the day ahead of him. The second bizarre death of the young woman in Bonaventure Cemetery had kept him up until 3:00 a.m. last night and would be the first thing on his desk this morning. Unless his team could come up with something concrete in the line of evidence, which was unlikely, he'd now be faced with two murders for which he had no leads.

At least this one was fresh, thanks to the kids that had found the body while playing some kind of weird game of let's-scare-each-other in the cemetery last night. They'd gotten a lot more than they counted on, and all three had been pasty-faced and on the verge of throwing up when he'd interrogated them. He'd made a silent bet with himself that it would probably be the last time that particular group would be playing their little games in Bonaventure anytime soon after dark.

The young woman had been dead for an hour or so when the teenagers had stumbled across her body tied to the tomb. Unfortunately, they had neither heard anything nor seen anyone. He had the distinct feeling that finding the body so quickly wasn't going to be helpful to him, and all he really had to look forward to was another long and fruitless round of interrogation. He'd be happy, at least, for a quick identification. Even though it was probably too early for someone to report her as a missing person, maybe he could get a quick ID through her fingerprints.

He almost wished for the good old days when the perp in a domestic dispute could be found standing at the scene with the still smoking gun, saying something like "I really didn't mean to shoot her, officer, but she just wouldn't shut up." Or, better yet, the victim of a drug deal gone bad whom you could almost dismiss with a "he probably got exactly what he deserved anyway." What he was faced with now was truly bad shit, two innocent young female victims dead with little insight into motive or who the killer might be. He didn't even know if the murderer was male or female. "God, it's gonna be another crap-ass day. Even that might not cover it, maybe abysmal might do it."

The squad room had been alive with conversation among the half dozen detectives seated there until he'd opened the door and stepped inside. A sudden silence had descended on the room as his compatriots viewed him with expressions caught somewhere between pity and compassion.

"Hey, Adam. What's up, man? Any leads yet on the latest dead girl?"

"If I can do anything to help, let me know, buddy."

"Nothing yet, guys. Anybody seen Jack? He was supposed to be riding in with Murphy today."

"Yeah, he's in; he headed down to the bakery to pick you up a cheese Danish. I guess he figured you'd need it."

"He's got that right. Throw in a bottle of Advil, and I'll be good to go."

"By the way, the captain wants to see you. The press got hold of the story, and they're on him like a basset hound on a coon. He needs you to help him set up a press conference."

"Shit, that's what I needed to hear. How did they find out so quick?"

"Good news travels fast, buddy. Haven't you ever heard that one?"

"Jesus, this is going to be one superior day. It's almost enough to get me back to smoking."

"No chance, buddy, nobody in here's gonna help you get your habit back."

Adam thought they were a pretty good bunch of guys he worked with, albeit a little weird and more than a little jaded by the work they did. "Hell, let me go see the captain and get that over with so I can at least try to get a little real work done."

Adam shrugged his way back into his jacket and gave it a cursory check in the mirror he kept in the top drawer of his desk for just such occasions. Thank God for the new pants he'd bought; at least they looked good. The captain would be aware of his pulling the late night job and hopefully overlook his rumpled appearance. He did the best he could with his hair and ran his index finger over his teeth, which he'd forgotten to brush this morning. As he closed the squad room door behind him and headed down the drab hallway to Captain Barton's office, he could hear the voices of his fellow detectives once again rise in a din of conversation, no doubt discussing poor Adam and the lousy cases he'd gotten stuck with.

Captain Bob Barton was a straight-up guy - ex-military, he had stuck with the closely cropped hair look and the ramrod straight back. He was known as a fair man by the detectives but with a temper no one tried more than once. The hair was gray now, but the face remained cut in granite and the body as lean as it must have been in his days in Vietnam. The topper was the eye patch over his right eye, supposedly a reminder of his days in combat. The remaining eye was jet black, and he could cut through a man with that one good eye like a laser through butter. Captain Barton always made a commanding and intimidating figure at any press conference he ran, which made good points with the upper echelon. He also seemed to be a favorite with the press with his no-nonsense approach to the criminal element of Savannah.

"You wanted to see me, captain?"

"Yes, Carter, have a seat. Bring me up to the minute on what you've got on this latest death. Do we have a second murder on our hands or not?"

"Sure looks probable, unless it was just an OD or accident. The M.O. is similar, but we won't know until we get the autopsy results.

"Shit, I don't like the feel of this. Anything on the identity of the latest victim yet?" The one black eye stared hard at Adam.

"Not yet. I'm searching AFIS for a fingerprint match."

"Okay. I've set up a press conference for eleven downtown, and I'd like you to be there."

"Yes, sir. Anything else?"

"Oh, yeah - one thing, Carter."

"Sir?"

"Shave, and try and get your eyes open enough so I can see the pupils and don't be chewing that gum on camera. It makes you look like a cow chewing the cud."

"Yes, sir."

Fifty miles to the north of Savannah, two men were shifting uncomfortably in the front seat of a rented black Lexus, getting ready to begin their own activities for the day. "Keep a close watch on the house, Hans. I want to know the second he comes out to go to the work shed."

"Yah, it should be soon; his wife came out about ten minutes ago and got into a little red car and left. He shouldn't be far behind. It's almost nine."

"Look! There he is now, but he's not heading toward the shed, he's getting into his van. Now what? Do we follow him?"

"No, we stay right where we are. It's a work day; he's got to come back soon. We'll wait and go after him as soon as he opens the shed."

Klaus had never in his life felt more conspicuous than he did now, sitting in the bright morning sunshine of a Georgia day in the parking lot of the Statesboro Hospice. The two old oaks no longer provided cover, and they were now obvious to the world at large, two men parked in a rented Lexus who could easily be observed by even the most casual passers-by. Klaus pulled his old fedora as far down over his face as he could and silently cursed the day he'd ever left Germany.

The blue Chevy van appeared about a half hour later, and its occupant, carrying a cup of coffee, headed toward the side door of the restoration shed. Greg Burke was confused as soon as he turned the handle of the shop door. Something was wrong: it was unlocked. This was one of the few things that Greg never forgot to do, even on his worst days. He entered the room with tentative steps. Everything seemed to be in order, no paintings missing, nothing that seemed obviously out of place. He crossed the room to get a better view of the wall safe. The lock was untouched, and the vault remained locked. He ran a hand through his thinning hair and adjusted his glasses, pushing them further up on his nose, a gesture he repeated dozens of times every day, to the point that it was now more habit than necessity. Greg was perplexed; it simply wasn't in his nature to forget to lock the door to the shop. So concentrated was he on looking for something amiss, that he failed to hear the entry of the two men, until they were nearly on top of him. The first thing he became aware of was the feel of cold metal at the base of his skull, and the sound of a voice he'd heard somewhere before.

"Mr. Burke, we are here for the two small paintings you are restoring for Mr. Appleby. If you would be so kind as to get them, we will be out of your way immediately, and let you get on with your day."

"I'm terribly sorry, sir, but I don't know what you're talking about. I don't have anything for Ben here at this time."

"Perhaps you would just open your wall safe for us, Mr. Burke. Then we can make that determination for ourselves. We are not here to play games. Just do as I say and quickly."

"Maybe if I could just talk to Ben. We could clear this up."

"I'm sorry, but Mr. Appleby is tied up at the moment, and we have allowed ourselves the pleasure of taking his lovely wife Mildred into our custody. Your wisest choice, should you wish to prolong the lives of your friends, is to simply follow my orders."

"How the hell do I know if you're telling me the truth about any of this?"

"You don't, Mr. Burke, but if you will make a quarter-turn to your left, you will find yourself looking into a silencer which is attached to the barrel of a German Luger, which is extremely functional, a fact, I assure you, you do not want to find out about on a personal level. It would seem to me that you need your hands to do your work, and my large friend here could easily make that an impossibility for you, at least for an extended period of time. Can we stop this little game now, Mr. Burke?"

"You don't seem to leave me any alternative. You're the two men I've seen at Ben's, aren't you?"

"Yes, and I assure you we do not have to meet again if you will simply open that safe for us."

"Okay, just give me a second. You are making me extremely nervous with this pistol. Could you just move it away from my face, so I can remember the combination, and I'll get you the God damned paintings?"

"Please do so, and we'll be on our way and out of your life and Appleby's life the very minute we have what we came for."

It was of course at this moment that Des, with impeccable timing, chose to enter the shop.

As she said, "What?" the look on her face was that of a woman who had just given birth to a baby without even the remotest knowledge that she was pregnant.

Hans turned, fumbling with the Walther PK in his shoulder holster in an attempt to bring the weapon to bear on the totally shocked Des. All Des got out was "Greg?" before she turned and bolted from the shop with Hans in close pursuit.

Greg watched the two figures race past the rear window as though it were a pursuit scene from a Grade B movie. It might have even been funny if it weren't for the deadly seriousness of the situation. He even heard the dull plunk of the Walther being fired as the two disappeared from his field of vision. He was quickly brought back to his own reality by the painful thrust of the Luger against his neck.

"Goddamnit, man! Get me the paintings now!"

Greg spun the dial of the wall safe at the best speed he could muster. Trying to stay calm, he was acutely aware of the painful thumping of his heart against his chest as he finally got the vault open on the second try. That was the last thing he would remember for a while, other than the flashes of light and pain caused by the Luger connecting against the side of his head. He reeled sideways into the studio easel, which in turn somersaulted him into a stack of bubble-wrap and cardboard cartons used for shipping. He wasn't even vaguely aware of the elderly German leaving the shop with the long sought after little paintings under his arms.

Hans, on the other hand, wasn't doing a great deal better in the handling of the situation with Des. Des was no delicate shrinking Southern Belle. Raising her three children with, but mostly without, a husband with a roving eye had not only made her as hard as nails mentally but also physically.

Des had simply circled the building until she found what she was looking for, a stack of two-by-fours used for the crating and shipping of large art pieces. As Hans rounded the corner in hot pursuit, he was completely unprepared for what awaited him. Wielding a five-foot section of the wood, Des swung it like a baseball bat head high and connected with some considerable force directly into the center of Hans's face. Hans's look of anger changed to a look of astonishment in an instant as what he had considered easy prey turned in a fraction of a second into someone who resembled Mr. T in jeans and a Mickey Mouse T-shirt. He continued to clutch the Walther in his right hand while his left hand dazedly tried to determine what was left of his nose. He staggered forward for a few feet before plunging headfirst into an azalea bush.

While Hans was desperately trying to focus his attention on what in the name of God had befallen him at the hands of the diminutive Des, Klaus came from the other end of the building at as close to a run as his seventy-eight-year-old legs would allow. Klaus fired a shot in Des's general direction, which went high and wide to the left and harmlessly impacted with a pine tree. "Let's get out of here you moron - back to the car quick." Klaus put his free hand under Hans's arm and helped the big man to his feet. The two then headed back to the rental at the best speed they could make under the circumstances. Once again neither of them noticed the little blue car that pulled out discretely behind them, so busy were they in trying to make their next appointment of the day at Savannah International Airport.

Des's first thought was for Greg's condition and getting her hands on a phone to dial 911. She paid no attention to the retreating Germans as she rushed inside the studio to help her friend and partner.

Chapter 17

It wasn't an extraordinary event. Nothing that would reshape mankind or cause even a ripple across the vastness of the universe. It was something that occurred everyday in hundreds if not thousands of places around the globe. If the event was unremarkable in nature, the man involved was even less so. He was a very average looking thirty-year-old male in a neatly pressed brown suit with matching brown wing tips, who stood quietly observing the off loading passengers at gate three in the main concourse of Savannah International Airport. He checked his watch. It was 9:30 a.m., and the Continental jet had arrived precisely on time, bearing its full load of passengers eager to reach their final destinations in Savannah. He adjusted the simple placard bearing the name Schultz to chest level and simply waited. The man's hazel eyes observed the departing passengers with a calm serenity. They were the eyes of a man who had seen perhaps too much of life's little incongruities.

Savannah International lies northeast of the city and caters primarily to Continental and Delta Airlines. It is not a large airport as international airports go, having one main concourse and two electronic portals to scan boarding passengers. The entrance area is graced by paintings done by local SCAD students and a display of weapons taken from those egotistical enough or stupid enough to believe they could board an airplane with a knife or gun concealed in their carry-on baggage. What it lacks in size it makes up for in charm and lack of clutter. Greeting someone in Savannah is an easy task uncomplicated by the great legions scurrying back and forth in an airport like Atlanta, Kennedy or O'Hare.

He spotted the man he was looking for long before the man became aware of the Schultz sign he was holding, another unremarkable person much like himself - closely cut, neatly combed light brown hair in the thirty-year-old range, with eyes he knew would be brown when they got close enough to be seen. The large briefcase he carried would be his only luggage. This particular gentleman didn't intend to spend enough time in Savannah to need a change of clothing. As the brown eyes came up and recognition of the sign came into them, the man headed towards him with a slightly puzzled expression on his face.

"Excuse me, my name is Kurt Schultz, but I was expecting to meet an older gentleman by the name of Kruger. Are you here for me?"

"Yes, I am. Mr. Kruger had an unexpected problem he had to deal with and sent me in his place. May I help you with your bag?"

"No, no that's okay; it's not heavy. I wonder why I wasn't told of this change in plans."

"Sorry, but there was no time. Herr Kruger was involved in the acquisition of the product you'll be authenticating and hit an unexpected snag. He and Hans will be joining us shortly in Savannah for the exchange. I'm just here to take you to their motel."

"All right, I don't like unexpected changes, but I guess it can't be helped. Let's get out of here and get this over with."

"Sure, my car's in short term parking; just follow me."

As the two men walked the three hundred yards separating the terminal building from short term parking, anyone who took the time to bother to look at them would have taken them for brothers; as it was, no one did.

Joey Morrisey stretched his legs under his desk and checked the large clock suspended over the entrance leading from Market Street into the main area of the Savannah First Trust Bank, his employer of the last seven years. He nervously shuffled the stack of loan applications in front of him with very little thought about whether they'd be approved or not. He had other things on his mind for this particular day. He'd even begun talking to himself. "Looking at that stupid clock every three minutes isn't going to make lunchtime get here any quicker, you idiot. You've got to settle down and pay some attention to what you're supposed to be doing. A couple of the tellers are starting to stare at you."

He tried to concentrate on something other than what he needed to get done at lunch. He tried momentarily to concentrate on the new pink silk panties he was wearing. Usually, that did the trick and brought him back to reality. However, not even that was working today. He abruptly thought that a trip to the men's room might help. He'd get himself away from his desk for a few minutes and try to pull himself together.

"Jake, gotta take a trip down the hall; be back shortly."

"Okay, Joey, hope everything comes out alright."

Jake was one of the older bank employees, a lending officer for nearly thirty-five years, and his rather old-fashioned sense of humor reflected both his age and his tenure on the job.

"Right, see ya in a minute."

"Sure, take your time; it's quiet in here today anyway."

As Joey rose and began his walk in the direction of the men's room, he was immediately aware of the sensual feeling the silk panties made when they rubbed against his groin. He wished he were home in his own space, somewhere where he could indulge the wonderful feel of silk to its ultimate conclusion. He also wished he didn't have to wear the uncomfortable binder over his lovely new chest, but he had no choice in that matter either.

He passed one of the newer female employees as he neared the door to the john, Cindy, Mindy, something like that. She was a secretary for one of the big shots upstairs, and he'd hated her on first sight. She was of medium height and blond with a large imposing bust, which she seemed to take great pride in thrusting out in front of people, especially men, at every opportunity.

"Good mawnin', Mr. Morrisey."

"Morning."

She even spoke with that broad snobbish Southern accent he so despised.

"God, you superior bitch. Who are you to act so la di dah? I could teach you a few things."

"Excuse me, Mr. Morrisey, did you say sumthin'?"

"Ah no, nothing, just talking to myself I guess."

"Ya don't wanna do that Mister Morrisey; people will start to stare at ya."

"Yes, you're right; I must watch out for that, mustn't I?"

Joey pushed open the door to the men's room as quickly as he could and entered the only sanctuary in the building where he could be free, if only for a few moments, from prying female eyes and irritating female voices. He chose a stall to relieve himself in. Wearing women's panties in a men's room, he had to take every precaution he could to avoid prying eyes.

All too soon he had to go back to work. It was time to spend a couple more slow, painful hours at his desk getting ready for the excitement that would occur when lunch finally arrived.

Nightmare in Savannah

Adam's Sunday had been a respite of calm after the last days of hard work. Catherine and he had got up late, had breakfast at the Waffle House on Abercorn and then lazed the afternoon away. That evening they'd met up with Casey and a young colleague of his, Jim Davies, and danced till the small hours at Tubby's. As usual they'd all laughed a lot and he'd managed to forget the horrors of the latest murder.

Now, it was Monday morning, and as Adam entered the station and glanced around at the happy little troop gathered there, he once again was brought to the realization that institutional yellow-green was not the perfect color to inspire creative thought. The general feeling in the squad was that the walls looked more like the color of baby diarrhea than anything else, and the gray desks and speckled gray floor were no more attractive. There had been an elderly detective who had retired shortly after Adam arrived in violent crimes who had even sworn the floors had once been white. To a man, the current occupants agreed that white was not even a remote possibility.

After acknowledging the grunts and indecipherable mumbles he received by way of greetings from his colleagues, Adam flopped himself into his well-worn swivel chair and prepared himself for the mountains of information his computer was determined to give him. Jack was somewhere in the field right now doggedly trying to catch them some kind of break but so far no deal. At least they'd been able to identify the latest victim from her fingerprints as Julia Morrow, 5' 8", 135 lbs, age twenty-one, born and raised in Savannah, and been able to notify the next of kin, but they had found out little more than that. From every indication, she too had been a nice straight kid working as a teller in one of the local banks. Her roommate had indicated that the last time she'd seen her was when Julia went down to the ATM machine on the corner to take out a few bucks for food. When Julia didn't come back by midnight to the apartment they shared, she began making calls and wound up calling the police department at 7:00 a.m. the following morning. Julia had been dating a couple of guys off and on, but both of them quickly turned into dead ends, having excellent alibis for the night in question. It was right back to square one. He wished he could hurry up the autopsy results as he just had a gut feeling that the two deaths were similar. He was just about to find himself a piece of Nicorette gum when the phone rang.

"Violent Crimes, Carter."

"Hi, Adam, it's Jack."

"Yeah, what's up?"

"I may have caught us a break. I'm out here doing a door to door at Bonaventure, and I'd worked my way nearly all the way around when I ran into a Mrs. Hilda Carnes, who thinks she remembers two figures going into the cemetery at about the time of the latest killing on the night in question. She didn't get a great look at them, but it's a possibility. Want to join me down here?"

"Sure, what's your twenty?"

"304 Woodlawn, on the south side of Bonaventure."

"Okay, buddy, see you in about fifteen minutes."

As Adam shrugged his way back into his worn sports jacket, he began to feel just the slightest lessening of the tension that had been riding his shoulders for the last few weeks. Maybe they might finally have something other than two female corpses and a dead antique dealer to go on.

Chapter 18

Adam slipped behind the steering wheel of the nondescript tan Crown Victoria that would serve as his ride to Bonaventure cemetery. While it was supposed to be an unmarked police vehicle, Adam knew that any drug dealer worth his salt would spot it as a cop car four blocks away. It always gave him a sort of perverse pleasure to give the dealers he knew the V for victory sign as he drove by. Cracking the window just enough to keep his mind alert, he headed out to join his partner on what he dearly hoped to be their first break.

While Adam worked his way through the heavy mid morning traffic on Victory Drive, he fought the urge to stick the bubble light on the roof of his car and move some of the doddering assholes in front of him out of the way. He decided against his need for speed and thought taking a little extra time on the ride would give him a few more minutes to get his head together on what he wanted to ask Miss or Mrs. Hilda Carnes.

As he pulled around Bonaventure and on to Woodlawn Street, he saw Jack's car parked in the driveway of a small white house about halfway down the block. The well-kept lawn and proliferation of shrubs and flowers suggested someone who took pride in its ownership. He got out of his car and headed for the front door, noticing the variety of red, white and yellow roses, one of the few flowers he actually recognized. His ex-wife had been the gardener in the family and knew dozens of varieties by name. Adam's expertise pretty much stopped at roses, mums, azaleas and wisteria. After that they all became a mystery to him.

Jack greeted him at the door before he even had a chance to ring the bell. "Hi, partner, I'd like you to meet Mrs. Hilda Carnes who may have some information for us concerning the murder that took place in the cemetery. Mrs. Carnes, this is my partner, Lieutenant Adam Carter."

"How do you do, Mrs. Carnes. I can't tell you how happy I am to meet you. We're most anxious to get the person or persons responsible for this terrible crime, as I'm sure you know."

Mrs. Hilda Carnes had the look of someone whose normally mundane life had been suddenly thrust into a starring role. She was short, no more than 5'2", and plump, with a round motherly face that probably spent more time smiling than it did frowning. Her lightly curled white hair was short and served to accentuate her dark brown eyes, which were sparkling with the possibility of this unexpected adventure.

"I'm pleased to meet you, Detective Carter; I only hope I can be of some help. I've already told your partner what I saw, so I don't know if there's anything more I can add."

"Yes, I appreciate that, Mrs. Carnes, but if you would be so kind as to go over it just one more time for me, I'd be very grateful."

"Okay, as I told your partner, it was about 11:30 on last Friday evening that I noticed this couple going into the cemetery. I happened to make a note of the time because I was waiting for my dog, Jet, to finish up his business so I could go to bed. I'm past sixty-five you know, so I try to make sure I'm always in bed by midnight. The late Mr. Carnes owned his own accounting business, and he'd be up until 1:00 or 2:00 sometimes. I'm sure that contributed to his dying at sixty-two. That's one of the reasons I make sure I'm always in bed before midnight."

"Yes, that's very wise, Mrs. Carnes. I wish my partners and I could do the same. Did you notice anything unusual about the couple? Anything in the way they were dressed or the way they walked, and could you show me from your window exactly where it was you spotted them?"

"Well, they were both dressed in dark clothing, slacks and sweaters as I remember. They were headed down my street in the direction of the cemetery, which I found a little odd at that time of night since I rarely see anyone out walking in this neighborhood that long after dark. Here, come to the door for a minute, and I'll show you exactly where I saw them."

Adam hoisted himself out of the over-stuffed chair he was sitting in and crossed the little living room trying his best to avoid the numerous photographs and knick-knacks which obviously represented a lifetime of collecting by Mrs. Carnes. He made a mental note that every single one of the mementoes in the room would be worth at least an hour's worth of conversation and did his level best to avoid looking directly at any single object for fear of being sidetracked by the story of its acquisition. When both he and Hilda Carnes had reached the open door, she pointed enthusiastically at a street lamp about fifty feet down the road.

"See, that's where I first noticed them as they passed underneath that street lamp. They were walking side by side, but they weren't touching.

One of them was quite tall with short blond hair, and the other was shorter with fairly long blond hair. I notice these things because sometimes I like to pretend I'm Mrs. Fletcher, you know, the lady on *Murder She Wrote*, Angela Lansbury. I hope you don't think I'm just a silly old fool for indulging in fantasies like that, but it does help to pass the time."

"Not at all, Mrs. Carnes, sometimes I like to pretend I'm Mike Hammer. Did you hear them say anything? Were they carrying anything?"

"No, I'm afraid I was too far away to hear anything, but I'm pretty sure the taller one was carrying a paper bag. And I got the impression she was female."

"So the taller one was female. What about the shorter one?"

"I don't know, probably;"

"Were they slender or heavy? Do you remember that?"

"Oh, both of them were quite slender. That's another reason I thought they were both women."

"Am I correct in assuming that you only saw them from behind going in the direction of the cemetery so that you didn't actually get a look at a vehicle they might have arrived in?"

"Yes, I'm sorry; as I said, I saw them as they passed underneath that street lamp and watched them until they reached that second streetlight further down. After that, they just sort of faded into the darkness. Then Jet showed up, and we both went back into the house, and I went to bed shortly after that."

"Well thank you, Mrs. Carnes; you've been most helpful, and here's my card in the event you happen to think of anything you haven't already told us."

"Oh, can't you gentlemen stay for just a bit? I was just putting on a pot of coffee, and I made some cookies just fresh this morning."

"That's awfully kind of you, Mrs. Carnes, but this is our first good lead, and I think we should get right on it with all possible speed. Don't you, Jack?"

Jack's slightly raised eyebrows let Adam know that he'd probably done his share of reminiscing while he'd been waiting for Adam's arrival and was more than ready to hit the street.

"Yes, ma'am, I'm afraid it's duty before pleasure. Perhaps we can get a rain check for a later date?"

"Any time, you're both so very polite. I'm so glad I was able to be of some help. Please feel free to call me. I'm usually in every morning."

"We will. Thanks again, Mrs. Carnes."

As they left the small house, Adam turned to Jack. "Would you do me a big favor and stay out here a little longer? Maybe somebody else saw something, possibly even the vehicle they came here in."

"Yeah, okay. I'll see what I can do. What are you gonna be up to?"

"I'm headed back to the station to see if the ME's got anything new and exciting for us; I'll see you when you get back."

"Okay."

Des Durden's first act after attempting to fell Hans was to check on her partner's condition. She found Greg trying to disentangle himself from the heap of bubble wrap and empty cartons he'd wound up in, one hand on the floor, the other gingerly exploring the growing egg on the back of his head. "Greg, are you okay?"

"Yeah, Des, just a little groggy. How about you? I thought I heard gunshots."

"Can you believe they were tryin' to shoot me? It was them two German guys we saw at Ben's shop."

"Yeah, I know. God, I knew they wanted those paintings, but I didn't realize until now just how badly they wanted them. How about you? Are you okay?"

"I'm fine; I hit the one that was chasin' me with a two-by-four; then the other one showed up and took a wild shot at me, and then they both took off in the direction of the hospice. I'm callin' 911. Do you need an ambulance? I can do emergency treatment you know; I am studyin' to be an EMT after all."

"Thanks for the offer, but I hurt bad enough already. I'm okay. Just get the cops over here as soon as they can make it. After you do that, call Ben. We've got to get a handle on what the hell's going on here. God, I hope he and Mildred are all right."

As Greg finally extricated himself from the jumbled pile on the floor, he was seriously wondering if art restoration was getting to be too dangerous a business to be in.

Casey was eager to finish her morning classes and meet Megan for lunch. Megan had arrived at school later than usual and had been acting cheerfully all morning. Casey was determined to find out at lunch what was going, one way or another. She'd even resort to fat jokes if that was what it took to pry information out of her friend. Lunch would be doubly interesting because of the new person joining them. Sharon Davidson had just recently been hired as a counselor, and Megan had immediately liked her. She was a vibrant redhead a full two inches shorter than Casey herself, and she was overjoyed at the thought of having someone join their group of friends who didn't actually make her feel like a height-challenged outcast.

When Casey reached the cafeteria, Megan and Sharon had already secured a table by the window, and they exchanged waves as Casey fell into place in the lunch line. She selected a salad with low cal dressing and worked her way down the counter desperately trying to locate an entrée she could enjoy which was not greasy or had overcooked vegetables with it. From her vantage point in the line she could see Megan already attacking a fried chicken breast with mashed potatoes and gravy on the side and butter beans. Sharon had a salad like her own along with the meat loaf. Casey finally decided on some fish, picked up a rather tired looking apple and headed toward the table. The fat jokes were definitely going to be on the menu today. They were both just begging for it.

"Hi, people, my, my, my, aren't we all just in calorie heaven today?"

"Why don't you try the chicken, Casey? Maybe it'll help you grow a couple of inches."

"What you've got will make you grow too, Megs, only not in an upward direction. And how come you can get away with meatloaf, Sharon? You're smaller than I am."

"Just an unbelievable metabolic rate, Casey. Some of us short people are blessed, you know."

"Well, as usual I couldn't find anything really healthy. I do wish they'd serve something that isn't swimming in butter. So how come you're looking so cheerful today, Megs?"

"Well, Case, Sharon has had a great idea. What if a bunch of us got together for a Saturday or Sunday sleep-over somewhere, ladies only? What do you think? We could bring Marla along, and I know that Jean would love a weekend away from home once in a great while. Of course Jean is 5'11", so we'd need to get at least one more short person for you too."

Casey had always liked Jean Dunne, a vivacious, African-American, leggy forty-year-old biologist with a great sense of humor who always had a ready smile for everyone.

"That sounds like a pretty good idea to me, Megs. How about Patricia Newland? She told me Harold might be away one of these weekends, so she might even have us stay over at her big house, and the best part is she's shorter than both Sharon and I are. I like the idea."

"Great, let's get started on it. I'll talk to Jean and Marla; you talk to Patricia. Let's see if we can't all get together over some Mexican food some night, plan a date and see if Patricia offers her place as a venue. What do you think?" Megan turned towards Sharon?"

"Hey, I'm all for it. It would give me a great chance to get to know some of the folks here better, and I'm all for that."

"It might even prove to be beneficial in several ways, Sharon, since you're a counselor. Maybe you could counsel Casey on how to accept being short."

"I'll have you know, Megs, that for most people 5'6" is not considered short at all. Do you think we should ask Catherine, too? I'm not sure if she sees Adam every weekend.

"Sure, ask her if she's free. That reminds me - I haven't seen Adam in a dog's age. How is he?"

"He's fine, very busy with the murders."

"I've been meaning to contact him and have him and Catherine over to dinner, but I just haven 't gotten around to it."

"Gosh, look at the time! I've gotta run."

"Okay, bye folks. I'll see you later. It's time for my next rumble with my beloveds."

The three women left the cafeteria, all pleased with the course of events that had taken place over lunch and all eagerly anticipating their upcoming venture.

As the morning wore on, things were going from bad to worse for Klaus. He hated driving on American roads, especially on secondary American roads where the maximum speed was usually 55 miles per hour. He wondered exactly how fast he could drive the Lexus on the autobahn where there were no speed limits. They were already very late for their pick-up of the art expert from Germany, who was probably pacing back and forth in Savannah International right at this very moment. As though that wasn't bad enough, Hans's moaning over the condition of his face was driving him crazy as well.

"Che broke my node; che broke my fugging node."

"Shut up, we'll take care of it as soon as we get back to the motel. At least the bleeding's stopped; be happy for that."

"I'b gonna kill her. I'b gonna kill 'em both."

"We have no time for that, you fool. All we need to do is pick up the rest of our art at noon, and we' re finally out of here. Now shut up and let me concentrate on driving."

"Che broke my node. I'b gonna kill her."

As the Lexus sped down highway 80 in the direction of Savannah, Klaus desperately tried to clear his aging mind for the things he needed to get done before their flight departed for Newark at 6:15 p.m.

The tall blond glanced around the little motel room that had been a second home for so long. The pink and green coverlet on the king-sized bed remained as it had from the first day, unruffled and undisturbed. The expanses of the blond hued furniture were uncluttered without even a single ring mark on their surfaces to denote that a human being had spent any time here at all. In fact, the three main occupants of this room had been the Degas, and they had never complained about how good or bad the maid service might have been. Except for the time they'd been in their cozy little nest in the room safe, they too had spent little time in the room itself. If they'd had a voice in the matter, it was likely that the only probable thing they would have commented on was the tasteless nature of the prints, which had supposedly been purchased to pull the room together in shades of pink and green.

Now the three little pastels lay on the bed for the last time, being observed by the eyes of their temporary owner before they began their new adventure in the possession of the purchaser the blond would be meeting in the parking lot of Publix at noon this very day. The blond was experiencing a mixture of emotions on this very special morning, excitement tinged with just a tint of fear, the joy of having possessed, if only for a brief time, these precious pieces of antiquity, and the anticipation of the freedom to be obtained from their sale. A glance at the ghastly pink clock on the pastel wall confirmed that only forty-five minutes now separated her from one million dollars. It had been a trek from the time when the availability of the pieces had been gleaned, through the tracking of them, through the drugging of the idiot antique dealer who'd picked them up, through all the dodging and hiding, through the renting of this plastic room, to this final point of triumph. Had it all been worth it? Yes, you bet your ass it had!

One more check of hair and makeup in the room mirror, and it would be time to go, time to be rich. The eyes looked the same to the owner, wide and brown and full of innocence. If the eyes were indeed the mirrors of the soul, it would have to be up to someone else to find the substance there in those cloudless dark pools.

As the seconds ticked by, Klaus continued his pacing back and forth in front of the Continental Airlines counter in Savannah Airport. He had Kurt Schultz paged twice with no response. The time was nearing 11:30 a.m., only a half-hour away from the rendezvous at Publix. Even though they'd been late reaching the airport, the fool should have had enough intelligence to wait for them.

"Where the hell is he? Some expert, he can't even get to where he's supposed to be. The desk confirmed that he arrived on the flight he was scheduled for, but where the hell did he go? We can't wait here any longer, Hans; he knows the meeting spot and the time. We can only hope he found his own way into Savannah and he'll meet us at Publix. *Mein Gott*! How did everything get so screwed up? Let's get out of here; we'll just have to pray he makes it to Publix on time with the check. If not, we're going to have to play it by ear."

Hans had not been prone to conversation ever since his unfortunate encounter with Des. They'd stopped at a drug store to get a bandage for his nose, and the bleeding had stopped, but his mood had not brightened one iota. A quick check in the men's room mirror at the airport had confirmed that the best he could expect in the morning were two very black eyes. He burned with a murderous rage right to the very depths of his soul, and he silently vowed that some how, some way the little bitch who'd clocked him with that two-by-four would live to regret it.

While Klaus and Hans were pacing the carpeted main concourse of Savannah airport, Kurt Schultz was far beyond caring about the anxiety they were feeling. The ride in from the airport went well. He was a little tired after the long flight, but Klaus's representative was gifted with a good sense of humor, and the trip into Savannah passed quickly. As they pulled into the parking lot of the Holiday Inn, he began to relax and looked forward to the upcoming exchange between buyer and seller.

The room that his new contact Peter Zeller had rented was both clean and attractive. Kurt put his briefcase on the glass table next to the window and removed his jacket. Time for just a few minutes of relaxation.

"Do you mind if I used the bathroom, Peter? I'd like to clean up just a bit after the flight."

"Of course not, be my guest; we have plenty of time."

"Thanks, I'll just be a moment."

The cold water felt good splashing against his face, and Kurt rubbed his eyes in an attempt to relieve some of the strain he felt there. He was just beginning to feel fully human again when the voice that sounded close to his left ear startled him.

"By the way, Kurt, I think you should know that my real name is David Rothschild."

The only other sound he heard, and the last, was the quiet pop of the silencer equipped Beretta being fired against the back of his head. After that there was nothing but silence and the feeling of falling through layers of black clouds towards an unknown destination from which he'd never return.

Chapter 19

Ben Appleby picked up on the first ring of the phone he'd been impatiently sitting by for the last tension-filled hours since freeing himself from the bonds the Germans had placed him in. He was unable to keep his voice from trembling; he'd been both dreading this call, for fear of something terrible happening to Mildred, and longing for it, from the tremulous hope that the Germans had finally released her.

"Ben?"

"Yes. God, is that you Greg? Are you okay?"

"Yeah, I got a little bump on the noggin, and those two nasty people we met at your place took the paintings away from me at gun point, other than that I'm doing pretty well. Ben, what the hell's going on?"

"I'm so sorry I had to put you through this. They came here last night, tied me up, and then took Mildred with them. I was so terrified of something happening to Mildred that I was afraid to do anything or call anyone. God, I'm glad you're all right."

"Yeah, I'm fine. Actually I think at least one of them is in worse shape than I am. Des hit him in the face with a two-by-four, little charmer that she is. I'm sorry that they got the two paintings, but unfortunately I didn't have much choice in the matter. We did call the police though, and they should be here any minute."

"I don't give a damn about the paintings at this point. I'm just grateful that you and Des weren't hurt. Can you keep my name out of it for the time being when the police show up? I want to avoid doing anything at all until I'm sure Mildred's safe. I know it's asking a lot, but I'd appreciate it more than I can say."

"You've got it, my dear old friend. I'll tell them about the assault and the robbery, but for now we'll just keep the fact that the paintings belonged to you out of it. And Ben, call me the very second that you know Mildred's okay."

"You know I will, and please take care of yourself."

"As long as Des doesn't insist on using her EMT training on me, I'm probably going to get out of this alive. I'll talk to you and soon I hope."

"You got it." As Ben put the telephone back into the cradle, he became even more aware of the fact that he probably wasn't going to stop shaking until he got the one call he really wanted, the one telling him that Mildred was safe and free.

The sunshine of high noon on a clear blue, cloudless day in Savannah gave the parking lot of Publix the look of a stage play that had been excessively well lighted. The brilliant rays ricocheted off every windshield and side window of the dozens of vehicles coming and going in the busy parking area. It danced and shimmered on the tops of cars and on every surface of the chrome shopping carts that had been abandoned here and there in helter-skelter fashion by their users. It played in joyful fashion on the little pools of oil and water left behind by departing cars and vans and in general seemed to be having a very good time displaying its versatility.

At first glance, the tall blond standing under the canopy at Semolina's Italian restaurant seemed to be nothing more than a casual observer of the passing panorama. Eyes hidden by sunglasses, she looked like just another patron waiting for someone to join her for lunch. A few people, primarily males, did give her more than just a casual glance, but that was occasioned more by her spectacular face and figure than it was by any real curiosity about why she might be standing there. No one paid any attention at all to the nervous movement of the hands holding the small package in front of her, and even if they had, would probably have placed little importance on it.

The blond's eyes never wavered behind the sunglasses. She was afforded an excellent view of the front of Publix, which was directly across the parking lot from Semolina's. She carefully noted the entrance of every vehicle pulling into the shopping area from Abercorn Street and all of the hundreds of people scurrying busily about completing their errands. She was probably the one person present in the area who was most acutely aware of why she was there and what she intended to do. As the minute hand on her watch reached quarter after twelve, her anxiety increased to the point that she was nearly ready to get back in her car, flee to the relative safety of her motel room, and rethink the whole deal.

It was at that precise moment that she noticed the black Lexus glide slowly by with two men in it, one of them wearing a brown hat with a jaunty red feather in it. He was older than she thought he would be, and his bushy white eyebrows were thrust in an expression that made his face look grim and resolute. The driver was a younger man sporting a bandage in the center of his face. They didn't look like two people who were having a particularly good day.

The Lexus parked in one of the center parking spots about half way between her position in front of Semolina's and the main entrance to Publix. The two men slowly exited their vehicle and began cautiously to scan the surrounding area. The blond began a slow stroll in the general direction of their car, eyes sweeping left and right in an effort to detect anything suspicious in the activity going on around them. She had approached to within a few feet of the men she was positive were her contacts, when she became aware of a third man nearing the Lexus from the opposite direction. This one was about thirty, well dressed and pleasant looking, undoubtedly the art expert sent from Germany she'd been told to expect. Most importantly he was carrying a briefcase which most assuredly must contain the $1,000,000 bank check she was counting on. The two men standing on opposite sides of the Lexus sensed his approach about the same time as she did. Both of them tensed perceptibly and put their hands inside their jackets at the same instant. The young man stopped at the back of the Lexus with an almost boyish grin on his face as though he were completely oblivious to any tension in the air and as though he didn't have a care in the world.

"Mr. Kruger, I presume. I'm Kurt Schultz; it's a pleasure to meet you. And your friend is?"

"This is my associate, Hans; sorry we missed you at the airport, I'm most happy to see you."

"Glad to be here, and the other party we were expecting, has he shown up?"

The blond, after taking in the exchange between the three men, moved into position about six feet away from Klaus and did the bit she'd been instructed to do.

"Uncle John is that you? How's Aunt Martha?"

"Ah yes, Aunt Martha is well, thank you. It's good to see you; did you bring the gift for Aunt Martha I asked you to bring?"

"Right here under my arm. Would you like to take a quick little look before we complete our exchange? "

"Yes, please just hand it to young Mr. Schultz here, and he'll be most happy to give you the gift you've been looking forward to. Then, at long last, I will be able to bid a fond goodbye to your lovely country, no offense meant."

"None taken. Where would you like to view these Mr. Schultz?"

"The back seat of the Lexus seems as good as anywhere. I've always had a great fondness for tinted windows. Privacy is such a lovely thing, don't you agree? Why don't you three just make sure that we're not interrupted while I do my little bit? By the way, forgive me for expecting a male; this is the twenty-first century after all, isn't it?"

"No problem, Mr. Schultz, but I agree with Uncle John here. I think the sooner we can get this done the happier we'll all be."

"This shouldn't take long. I'll be right with you."

The young man got into the back seat of the Lexus, extracting a magnifying glass from a jacket pocket as he did so and closed the door behind him. When he got out ten minutes later, his hazel eyes remained wide with good-natured innocence, and his mouth still curled in what seemed to be a perpetual smile. Both Hans and Klaus had relaxed during the interval, and they were both now in semi-lounging positions against the opposite sides of the Lexus.

"Is everything in order, Mr. Schultz?"

"Ah yes, quite so, gentlemen and lady. These little gems are the real thing. I guess it's time we wrap this up."

As the tall blond waited expectantly, what she saw emerge from the suitcase was not the longed for check but a silencer equipped Beretta. The first round caught Hans just above the left eye, and he slid to the ground without a sound. The second soft pop hit Klaus high in the upper left chest and sent him reeling backwards towards a white Ford Transit van where he collapsed in a heap of muttered curses. As the Beretta swung in a deadly arc in her direction, she dove headfirst behind the small white compact that occupied the space next to the Lexus. She heard the whine of the shell passing through the empty space she'd been standing in and did an amazingly fast half crawl, half duck walk in a direction that would take her as far from the muzzle of the Beretta as she could get. When, after a few seconds, she dared a quick peek at the scene she'd just left, there was no sign of Mr. Schultz, and Klaus had, amazingly enough, managed to get himself behind the wheel of the Lexus and was backing out.

"You goddamned bastards, you screwed me. I'll get you both. I swear I will."

Strangely enough, none of the passersby swarming through the busy parking area seemed to have noticed that something very strange was going on. When the person who owned the Jeep Cherokee against which Hans now lay dead tried to load groceries into a vehicle with a corpse staring back at him, that would probably change.

The tall blond left the area as quickly as she could, doing her best to ignore the pain from the various scrapes and bruises she'd received in her reckless plunge toward safety. She was more determined than ever that this was not going to be the last word on this little fiasco.

Walter Campion pulled his three-hundred-pound bulk out of the oversized leather chair he'd had special ordered from Heilig Myers Furniture and began a stately march across the main floor of Savannah First Trust Bank. He was, in his own estimation, a man of some importance and prestige, an intimidating figure to be reckoned with. As a senior vice president of the bank with over twenty-five years of experience, he dearly disliked anyone who would not or could not display the same type of loyalty and dedication that had been the hallmark of his tenure with the bank. Nothing escaped his notice; no one was immune to his caustic wit, which he used at the first sign of a perceived transgression.

"How's your day, Jake?"

"Fine, Mr. Campion, and yours?"

"Good, good. I don't seem to see Mr. Morrisey in the area. Hasn't he returned from lunch yet?"

"I'm afraid not yet, sir; he must have been held up."

"No call?"

"No sir, but I'm sure he will; he's usually very reliable."

"Yes, I can see that. Have him come see me when he comes in will you?"

"Yes, Mr. Campion, I'll tell him."

"Thanks, Jake, carry on."

Adam Carter went back over his notes for what seemed like the four or five hundredth time. Nothing new was leaping off the pages at him to give him some kind of clue as to where to take either of the murders of the two young women from the current stalemate at which he found himself. He still felt his best bet was somewhere within the walls of one of the gay/lesbian nightclubs in the area, although he still wasn't sure why, and silently decided that he'd do some frequenting of those places during the next few nights.

The harsh sound of his desk phone jerked him back to realty with a start.

"Violent Crimes, Carter."

"Adam, hi, it's me."

Adam smiled; only one person said that, knowing he would immediately identify her. "Hi, Catherine, how're you doing?"

"Fine, I have a quick question. Are you busy this Thursday? Casey's got the author Karin Slaughter coming. You remember you read her book *Blindsighted*, and I was wondering if you'd like to go and hear her talk. I'm going with Megan, Marla and Casey."

"That's sounds fun, and ordinarily I'd love to join you, but I'm horribly busy at the moment with the murders. Let's talk more tonight; perhaps we can take in a movie or something this Saturday instead."

"Okay, phone me later tonight. Love you."

"Love you, too."

That was good. He'd do some gay bar hopping over the next few nights. Either that or he'd try to talk Jack into doing it again.

Jack flopped his lanky body into the chair beside Adam's desk and gave him his best lopsided grin.

"You're not gonna believe this one, buddy."

"What's up?"

"We got the fiber tests back on the second young lovely we found in the cemetery and guess what?"

"I'm dying to know. What?"

"We got a blue and white fiber that matches the one we found on Jessica Stillwell. What in the hell do you figure is going on?" Jack looked at Adam.

"They know what it's from?"

"It's a terry cloth fiber like the kind you'd commonly find in towels or washcloths. How's that grab you?"

"Christ, are you telling me our perp is either washing them or drying them off after he's done his thing." Adam stared at Jack. "That's too weird."

"Sure looks like it. Scary thought, isn't it?"

"Sure as hell is. That makes it sound like a serial. I was really hoping we weren't gonna get into that again."

"Yeah, me too, we sure don't need any more bodies popping up." Jack crossed his legs. "At least they didn't find anything on the antique dealer. That really woulda got me crazy."

"He didn't fit the young tall blond category either, so I think we're gonna be able to write that one off to natural causes."

"I sure hope so. My personal theory is that the dude was trying to get himself off or getting some help with that pursuit and the effort got to be too much for him. I hope I never get that old. I'd rather be dead."

"I wouldn't worry about that, Jack; it's much more likely you're gonna wind up getting shot by a jealous husband."

"Well, if I've got to go, that's the way I want to do it, in the throes of passion."

"Good thought, but right now let's see what we can do to track down this damn fiber."

Chapter 20

Klaus was still swearing to himself in German. "That sonofabitch, I can't believe he double-crossed me. After all those friendly emails, I would've given him his thirty percent commission on the pastels. Wasn't enough, I guess. The greedy bastard. Thank God I still have the little oil paintings. I'd better get back to the room and get rid of Appleby's wife. What damnable luck!"

His upper chest was painful, but he was nearly positive that the bullet hadn't hit bone or an essential organ. He had movement enough in his left arm and shoulder to continue with what he needed to do. He would just disinfect the wound and bandage it to stop the flow of blood. With that in mind, the first stop he needed to make was at any pharmacy he could find on his way back to the motel.

Hard as he tried, he was unable to summon up much emotion over the untimely death of Hans. The man had spent as much time annoying him as he had helping him. He didn't look at the shooting as the loss of a friend as much as he did a release from bad American television and Country and Western music. He'd never even learned whether or not Hans had a wife or children or scarcely any other details about his personal life. He chose to look at the whole episode as just the loss of one more soldier in the ongoing war against the Jews. He was also thankful that he'd brought his overcoat along and had left it happily folded in the back seat. He'd need it for his visit to the CVS pharmacy he'd spied on his right and in getting back into the motel without drawing attention.

As Klaus entered the room that had become his second home, he was pleased to find that nothing had changed. Thank God the maids had heeded the 'Do Not Disturb' sign. Mildred was exactly as he'd left her, tied to one of the chairs in front of the television, which they'd left on at low volume. The only difference was the small pool of liquid that had spread over the brown shag carpet at her feet. The smell bothered him a little, but as for cleaning up, that was the motel's problem; they'd probably cleaned up worse.

"How are you doing my dear? I'm afraid I'm going to need your help for just a little bit, and then I'm going to let you go. You'd like that wouldn't you?"

Mildred's eyes still had the same pleading look they'd had from the beginning. They were saying, "Please God, just let me go," as clearly as words would have.

"Good, my dear. Just let me get my jacket and shirt off, then you can do your good deed, and I'll set you free. Okay, when I untie you and take your gag off, do you promise me you'll be a good girl and not do anything silly?"

Mildred's vigorous nodding of her head indicated she was more than willing to do whatever was required to obtain her freedom.

Klaus examined his wound in the bathroom mirror and was pleased to find it was a through and through. The exit wound looked nasty, but there was nothing to be done except disinfect it and bind it up as well as could be done under the circumstances.

He wasn't quite as happy with his appearance in the mirror. His face looked like milk that had been left in a warm room for about a month, with that pasty curdled look that would draw sighs of pity from the casual observer who would figure this poor old man was on his way out, the victim of some dread disease.

He went back into the pastel blandness of the room and untied Mildred. Her short white hair had managed to get itself rumpled despite her being confined to the chair, and the first thing she did was try to fluff it into some sort of shape. Very womanly thought Klaus. She was having a little difficulty getting her plump legs to work, and Klaus gave her the assistance she needed to cross the short distance between the bedroom and the bathroom. He noted that her hands and arms were trembling, whether from being tied up or from fear he wasn't sure. It really didn't matter as long as she was able to help him get his bandage securely in place.

Mildred's oval face was puffy, probably from crying, but it was still obvious that she'd been very attractive as a younger woman. The bright blue eyes still gave her the look of a very pretty older woman, albeit slightly overweight.

"Take this disinfectant and apply it liberally to both sides of this wound in my shoulder. Do you understand?"

Once again Mildred nodded. She was either temporarily unable to speak, or she was still too terrified to do so. She simply did as she was told.

"Now apply this bandage to the wounded areas on both sides and wrap up the whole thing. Not too tight you understand, just tight enough so that it will stay in place. Do you understand?"

"Yes."

Good, she was still capable of speech, and after a few fumbling attempts, she was finally able to get the bandage into place to Klaus's satisfaction.

"Fine, now listen to me very carefully. You stay here in the bathroom for at least one hour while I do some packing and some other things I have to do. Then you will be free to leave. Do you understand?"

"Yes."

"Good, then we won't have any problems, and I can be on my way home."

Klaus went back to his generic bedroom, threw the few articles of clothing that remained in the blond wood bureau and the remaining shirts hanging on the eight hangers they'd been allocated into his suitcase. He once again wondered about the hangers that had metal tops and could not be removed from the sturdy metal pole they encircled. Was the theft of hangers a major problem in this country? He no longer cared one way or another. He left Hans's clothes where they were, as he obviously wasn't going to need them.

He closed his suitcase for what he hoped would be the last time and took a long last look at the green and blue bedspreads that lay undisturbed and uncaring. They matched the blue and white wallpaper and blue curtains; what more did they need to do?

One last check on Mildred found her sitting primly on the throne in the bathroom, legs together with her hands smoothing the blue print dress she'd been wearing for the last few countless hours and staring straight ahead into nothingness.

"You will wait one hour before you leave. Do you understand?"

One last tentative nod indicated that she understood.

"Please say goodbye to your husband for me. I'm afraid I don't have the time to make a personal call. I shall bid you *auf Wiedersehen* then."

Mildred said nothing, just stared at him with those wide-set blue eyes as though he were an alien presence. Klaus abandoned the room, stopped briefly at the front desk, headed for the rented Lexus containing the two little paintings safely locked in the trunk, and prepared to make the beginning of the final steps that would bring him back to his beloved homeland. The first step, of course, would be the short ride to the Savannah Airport.

The tall blond paced back and forth across the small motel room. It wasn't just the loss of the Degas pastels and the money that drove her to her current state of fury; it was the humiliation of being taken by the little prick who had stolen them. A vow was made that some where, some how there'd be a way to wipe that smirky little grin off his face permanently. Dreams of castration and firing a bullet up his rectum drifted through the red haze of anger. The only problem at the moment was that there was no way to locate him. Maybe going to Savannah International might be worth a shot. It wasn't much of a hope, but it was the only thing to do for the moment. If he wasn't there, only one thing was for sure; someone was going to pay for this little debacle before this night was over.

Chapter 21

Casey was disturbed. The talk given by Karin Slaughter to her students had gone remarkably well because the students asked lots of interesting questions and Karin was a lively speaker, but the subject matter of *Blindsighted* was a harsh one and this coupled with the accounts in the Savannah papers about the discovery of a second nude young female murdered in Bonaventure Cemetery had set Casey's mind reeling. The newspapers were now reporting that neither of the victims seemed to have been sexually abused, but Casey still found herself frightened by the events. She couldn't help remembering what had happened to her two years ago and shudder for those poor young women whose lives had been so brutally cut short.

After thanking Karin and seeing her off, Casey, Megan, Marla and Catherine went out to Dingus Magee's, a local restaurant and bar, for coffee and an early evening snack. As usual, the place was filled with the university students who had decided that a couple of beers were infinitely superior to doing homework. A rather flushed, red cheeked young woman who declared herself to be their server, Maggie, took their order and departed with as much speed as she could muster in the direction of the kitchen.

"So what did you guys think? I thought she was fascinating and so good with the students."

"I'm not sure about teaching books about serial killers," Megan gave a shudder. "Our students might get ideas, and I get chills down the length of my spine." She turned to Marla. "What do you think?"

"Karin was interesting as hell, and I loved her book, but I couldn't keep myself from thinking about the next step. Where do we go from here? Will we have more and more serial killers? You're right; it's scary as hell."

"I can't help but think that the more disjointed our society gets and the more people there are that feel they've been outcast, the worse it's going to get. Not only will there be more serial killers, but there'll be more and more people who just pick up guns and start shooting at anyone in sight."

"Yeah, Catherine, unfortunately that does seem to be the road this country's taking, yet at this point it still seems to be a primarily male thing, and I find that interesting."

"I do too, Marla," Casey interjected. "How long do you think it's going to be before women start getting into this type of thing?"

Catherine shrugged her shoulders. "I don't know, but I feel that the women of today are just as capable of feeling sexual rage as men are, and they use guns as well as other deadly weapons; how long can it be before one of them turns into a serial killer? How do you all feel about that?"

"It scares the hell out of me, but as long as you, Megan, or Casey aren't the first, I guess I'll have to take my chances."

Although all four laughed at Marla's latest observation, it was equally obvious to each of them that the talk given by Karin Slaughter had touched something buried deep within them all, some little spark of fear that had lain dormant prior to listening to her.

The racket being created by a group of about a dozen young male students gathered around a large round wooden table was now making conversation difficult, if not impossible, so the four friends decided to hit the road.

They carefully worked their way through the various groups of students engaged in a variety of activities, paid their checks and headed out into a dark, gloomy nightfall, which was giving every indication of planning to rain. It wasn't going to be a pleasant rain but one of those cold, bitter rains that cut through all the way to the bone and chills from the inside out.

"Okay, that was fun, Megs. What are you and Marla up to for the rest of the evening?"

"Unfortunately Marla has to go to work; she's got the late shift at the agency the next few nights. I guess I'll just go home and play with the cat. How about you?"

"Oh I've got a hot date with a pile of essays. Aren't I the lucky one? What about you, Catherine? Are you seeing Adam?

"No, he's pretty busy at the moment with the murders of those two young women. I'll just go to my apartment and read. See you all."

As Megan and Marla walked off in the direction of their car, Casey was once again caught up in what a striking couple they made. Both so tall they looked like the vanguard of some Amazon army.

That same evening at 7 p.m. Jack drifted into the Mirror Image, feeling only slightly less conspicuous than he had when he was there the first time. He briefly wondered again if it might not have been wise to bring his fellow officer Jim Davis along with him. He just hadn't been sure if Jim could handle this without going off on a tangent. Jim was as straight as a curtain rod, and it showed.

The scenario hadn't changed. The dimly lit bar area with the wine glasses sparkling in their overhead racks held half a dozen patrons sitting in pairs talking quietly. The dark green booths looked nearly black in what passed for lighting, and he could make out another ten or twelve people sitting together at various tables throughout the hazy, smoke-filled atmosphere. There was some music emanating from somewhere in the distance, which he assumed was supposed to lend an air of romance and intimacy to the proceedings. He still wasn't really secure with being in a place where guys were after guys and women were after women, but he was determined to catch their killer, and if this is what it took, he'd do it.

Jack took a seat at the bar on one of the red leather stools which would have been gaudy in any other place but this and watched while Larry, the young blond bartender, broke off his conversation with the two men he 'd been talking to and glided his way.

Christ, this guy should be a dancer, not tending bar. Jack thought.

"Yes, sir, nice to see you again. Dewar's for you?"

"You remembered me?"

"Yes, sir. I have a great memory for faces and drinks." Larry laughed.

"That's pretty impressive."

"Okay, Dewar's coming right up."

Larry had a smile that looked like he'd cut it out of Men's World and glued it on his face. If there was such a thing as perfection in a smile, this was it.

Jack muttered, "Kudos to your orthodontist," under his breath and swiveled around on his stool to get a better look at the room. He counted eight women, or what looked like women, and ten men. Pretty slow at the moment, but maybe it would pick up as the night wore on.

"Here we go, sir, Dewar's on the rocks. Are we alone this evening, or will someone be joining us?"

Jack briefly mused. Someone may be with you, but I'm pretty damned sure no one is going to be joining me. Keeping this thought to himself, he simply said, "No, I'm alone for the evening."

Larry gave him an understanding wink and said, "Hey, you never know what life will bring you on any given night. Keep a good thought." With that he drifted off in the direction of the two men he'd been talking to when Jack came in, leaving him to sip his drink slowly and study the mirrored bar area for new arrivals.

He was nearly at the bottom of his glass when a new figure entered the bar. This one was a tall blond with close cut hair framing her delicate face. She was clad entirely in black with a tight fitting black cashmere sweater over a very short black mini skirt. A black leather jacket with silver studding completed the ensemble. She stopped in the doorway, surveyed the room, then headed in the direction of the bar choosing a stool three down from him. She worked her way carefully onto the stool and crossed her long shapely legs. Jack watched this action closely. It was his theory that men in drag had much more muscle development in their calves than real women did. He'd watched several films on men working as drag queens before he'd developed this thought and had convinced himself that his point was valid.

"Yup, look at those muscles; this has got to be a guy in drag."

The only problem was how was he going to prove it without getting himself into more trouble than he wanted to handle? Perhaps he should ask her if she'd accompany him to the men's room. He compromised by nodding in her direction and was rewarded by a nod in return with full seductive lips curved upward at the corners in a mildly salacious fashion.

"Mind if I join you?" he said.

"No, that would be nice; why don't you just slide on down a couple of seats?"

"Thanks, it gets a little lonely staring at myself in the mirror. My name's Jack Malloy. Yours?"

"Sylvia Gordon. Do you come here often?"

"Nah, just once in a while. I'm pretty busy most of the time."

"I can imagine; you're not bad looking."

"Thanks, I can certainly say the same for you."

"You're too kind. I just do the best with what I've got."

"Well, from what I can see, you've got quite a lot to work with."

"You flatter me, Mr. Malloy."

"Jack, please."

"Sure, Jack, please call me Syl, all my friends do. Did you come here just for the conversation, or do you also intend to get in some dancing?

We ought to do a slow dance together. That would be a first for this place, a man and a woman dancing together. How outrageous do you feel?"

"I think I'll wait a little while, I don't want to get anybody upset. Besides, I'm enjoying the conversation, Syl."

"Me too, it's nice to be able to talk to someone who doesn't have his hand on my thigh in the first thirty seconds. Incidentally, I'm a very open person and an honest one. I like to get things started in a way that keeps them from coming back to bite me later. I'm bisexual. Hopefully you won't find that offensive, but it's just the way I am."

"No, not at all, I've been known to go in more directions than one in my time, and the last thing I would find you is offensive."

"Good, I'm glad that's out of the way. Now, what do you do for a living, Jack?"

"I'm, ah, between jobs at the moment."

"I see; and when you're not between jobs?"

"Mostly sales."

"Anything in particular?"

"Well, I was doing kitchen appliances for a while and some insurance work. I think I'd like to try something new though, now that I'm getting older."

"Oh hell, you're not that old. What are you twenty-five?"

"Now you're the one doing the flattering. I'm a little past that I'm afraid."

"I wouldn't worry about it. I'm closing in on thirty myself, though my friends are kind enough to say I don't look it."

"You certainly don't. I wouldn't have put you past twenty-five at the most."

"God, I love a man who can lie with a straight face; you're okay in my book, Jack."

"What do you do for a living?"

"Well, I've done a little bit of modeling, and I still take a job whenever I can get one. For steady money though, I work at the local Medical Examiner's office as a forensic technician."

"Now that sounds interesting."

"Sometimes yes, sometimes no. Oh there's a cute little number coming in. Give me your masculine opinion of that one, Jack."

Jack turned in time to catch the latest group entering the bar through the padded scarlet swinging doors. Whenever he looked at those doors, he couldn't help but think he was in a French whorehouse. There were three of them, all college-aged and giggling together. This was obviously an excursion into the forbidden unknown for the three young women who probably prided themselves on having the nerve to enter this nether world that their parents had warned them about. Two of the girls were brown-haired and rather on the mousy looking end of the scale. The third was blond with hair that reached past her shoulders. She was exceptionally pretty with a slender, but well proportioned figure, and she was obviously fond of tossing her hair back in a motion that looked more practiced than natural.

"I assume you mean the blond, Syl."

"Oh yes, the other two are cute enough, but the blonde's dynamite, and she knows it."

"I'd have to agree with your assessment of the facts; she is exceptionally cute. That is if you like them that young."

"Yup, and I bet you she thinks she's really something by showing up in a gay bar. Something to tell all her little friends about. She ought to know that's a good way to get herself hurt."

"What do you mean?"

"Very few gays or lesbians like to think of themselves as a cute little sideshow to be visited at the whim of nervy little straights showing off for their friends."

"You don't think anyone would actually hurt them, do you? I mean they may be a little naïve, maybe even a little stupid, but I don't think they mean anyone any harm."

"You're missing the point, Jack. If you don't belong in this world, stay the hell out of it. I mean, I personally don't care, but I've known people who might be prone to teaching that group a little lesson in pain. "

"You're kidding, who?"

"Oh, let's just forget about it. They're just a smart-ass group of little punk teeny boppers anyway."

"True, but I still can't imagine anyone wanting to actually hurt them. You say you've known people who actually would?"

"Yeah, but that was a long time ago. Why don't we just forget about that and get back to talking about something more interesting?"

"I find this pretty interesting, Syl. Has anyone ever hurt you? I would certainly hope not."

"Some things are best left in the past, Jack. I've been hurt, and I've done some hurting, but it's nothing I want to talk about with anyone."

"Sure, I can understand that. It's just that you seem so special to me. I can't even imagine anyone wanting to hurt you."

"See, that just goes to prove the old saying 'appearances can be deceiving.' That's part of the reason I like being so tall. People tend to think a little harder when they're facing a tall person than they do when they're facing a short one."

"I never thought about it that way. How tall are you anyway, if you don't mind my asking?"

"I don't. I'm 5'10 ½" when I'm standing in my stocking feet or when I'm lying down, if you're interested in that fact. When I put on a nice pair of heels, however, I can bring myself up to eye level with most people, including men."

"When you consider how attractive your eyes are, that's got to be a real asset."

"Sometimes yes, sometimes no. There are people I've met who are intimidated by my height."

"Well, I'm not one of them. I like it."

"Yes, but you're how tall? You must be over six foot yourself?"

"I'm six one."

Sylvia smiled, drawing Jack's attention to her mouth, which was at once both attractive and sensuous. Her teeth were small and perfect and whiter than they had any right to be. Jack had to admit to himself that this tall, extremely attractive blond captivated him. She (or he) radiated a natural sexuality that couldn't be ignored, and she did it with very little effort. He almost found himself wishing that he'd been wrong about her calves and hoping that she'd turn out to be a woman and prove his latest theory wrong. Two female couples had begun to dance to Johnny Mercer's *Autumn Leaves* under a mirrored ball in the ceiling, which reflected the dim lights in the bar and made odd flickering patterns on the wooden floor and the dancers.

"Well, what do you think, Jack? If we're ever going to stir this place up by dancing, this is the time."

"Yeah, good idea. It might even spook our little trio of debs thinking they've walked into a straight bar. Let's do it."

Dancing with Sylvia was like dancing with a feather. She moved with a natural grace that was enough to make even Jack feel like a good dancer. He'd always thought of himself as having two left feet, but gliding around the floor with this lighter than air gamine was a brand new experience for him. Strangely enough, none of the other bar patrons seemed to be paying any attention to them, which he found just a little odd. Sylvia put her left arm around his neck and pulled him closer. The soft mounds now pressed against his chest certainly felt real, and he allowed one hand to rest just at the top of her round buttocks, and they felt real as well. He'd now convinced himself that this definitely was a woman. He chided himself briefly about forgetting about the real reason he was here, and how the rest of the department would react if they could see him now and then said to hell with it and allowed himself to settle into enjoying the warm feeling of the dance.

When he felt himself still moving a few beats after the song had stopped, he really began to worry about the state of his mental health. This was completely out of character with the Jack Malloy he usually was: ambitious, hard-working, determined to succeed. Police work had become his mistress, separating him from the mundane emotional stresses suffered by his contemporaries. What the hell had happened to him over the course of the last couple of hours? He should be asking more questions, not dancing with some pretty woman.

As they worked their way back onto the barstools, Jack caught the smiling glance of the bartender being cast in his direction as he methodically polished glasses. Jack was in an emotional state somewhere between feeling foolish and being in lust. He was struggling desperately to get the old Jack back in control again.

"Thank you, Syl, that was very nice."

"Yes, it was, you're an excellent dancer."

"I'm afraid I have to give all the credit to you; normally I'm all feet."

"Well, you couldn't tell it from what you did out there just now."

"Syl, would you get angry if I asked you a very personal question?"

"That depends on the question."

"I've really enjoyed this evening, but I'd really like to know if you're a guy or a gal?"

"Well, since you say you've gone both ways what possible difference could it make? Besides I have this feeling that you just might find out for yourself soon enough."

Jack felt his face begin to redden and fixed his attention on his empty glass of Dewar's.

"Does that mean I might get to see you again?"

"Yes, I'd like that, but for right now I've got some things I need to do, so I have to be going. How about we meet here again on Saturday night and pick up where we left off?"

"Great, I guess I'll see you then, but I've got to say I' m sorry to see you go so soon."

"Me too, but I'll be looking forward to Saturday."

"Yeah, me too. See you then." Jack stared after Sylvia as she strode briskly to the door. She walked like a man, but hopefully she was a woman.

"Can I refill this glass for you, sir?"

"What? Oh, no thanks, I've got to be going."

Jack paid his bar tab and headed through the French whorehouse doors back towards where he'd left his car. He had some serious thinking to do, and he wasn't going to get it done in this bar. It wasn't until he reached his house that he realized he had neither an address nor a telephone number for the captivating Sylvia, but he did have Adam's number, and it was still fairly early, definitely time to get back to what his life was really about.

Tarka was in a grumpy mood. His human companion wasn't holding up her end of the relationship, as she should have been. While your average cat should not be required to do physically taxing jobs during the day, that did not mean he didn't have plenty of time to think, and it didn't mean he was without emotional needs.

The female had arrived at the proper time but had paid virtually no attention to him. She was disconcerted to the point that she'd put his food in his water dish and thrown his favorite paper bag nesting spot into the trash bin. Tarka had stomped back and forth across the kitchen in a way that should have made Casey aware that she was being remiss in her duties. Not only had she seemed not to notice his snit and try to make it better through patting him, but she'd also stayed only a few minutes and then left again.

Tarka tried to assuage his anger by taking a nap on the bed after forcing down his soggy supper, but this wouldn't be the end of this insulting day. He had his ways of getting Casey's attention, and after a good sleep, he'd decided on the nastiest thing he could do. That would let her know that she wasn't dealing with someone who could be ignored and expect to get away with it scot-free.

Tarka was convinced that the female human's lack of attention to the important details of cat care had something to do with the ringing of the stupid thing she put in her ear. Noisy things that rang had their place of course; they could be batted around the kitchen floor as a plaything if there wasn't anything else to do, but the amount of time and energy the female was wasting in staring at the thing was way out of proportion to its value as a toy.

Megan had spent the last hour dusting the apartment. She'd even been reduced to actually taking down and washing the yellow patterned curtains in the bedroom. "God, how I hate it when you have to work nights, Marla. What the hell's the use of a committed relationship if you spend half your night at work?"

She took a few minutes to run her eyes over the titles of the paperbacks on the second shelf. Nothing there she hadn't read at least twice.

Maybe that's what I'll do. I'll go down to the library and see what they've got that's new and exciting. Maybe I can find a Sue Grafton or a Patricia Cornwell I haven't read; darn, I wish they'd write faster, Megan thought to herself, then looked at her watch, 8:45. No good going to the library as it closed at 8:00. Anyway I really don't feel like reading anyway, and there's nothing but crap on the T.V. I could always talk to the stupid cat for a while, but she never has anything interesting to talk about. Shit, I think you're losing it girl. Megan took time enough to check the refrigerator in the small kitchenette but closed the door before giving herself a chance to check its contents fully.

Putting more calories on your hips isn't the answer, tubbo. Think, think, there's got to be something to do that 's fun. I know. I'll call Catherine. She said she wasn't doing anything tonight. Maybe we can have a drink together. Where the hell did I put her number? What time is it? 9:30, perfect time to go clubbing. God, I haven't done that in a while. It'll be fun."

The call from Mildred brought Ben Appleby out of his chair like a flash.

"Mildred, where are you, honey? Are you okay? Are you by yourself?"

"Yes, yes, Ben, I'm fine. My teeth still hurt some and the finger they tore the nail off is killing me, but other than that I'm just fine. I'm at the Abercorn Holiday Inn in the lobby. The older man let me go and left to go somewhere. Can you come and get me, Ben? I need to take a shower and lie down in my own bed."

"You bet, hon, I'm on my way; just stay right there - don't move."

"Don't worry about me, Ben. I'm not going anywhere - just hurry."

"I'll be there in ten minutes."

"Oh and Ben..."

"Yes?"

"You've got some explaining to do."

The tall blond crossed her legs and glanced at the clock over the entrance to the main concourse area of Savannah International. The last flight out of the airport was boarding and due to leave in fifteen minutes. All the concessions were closed or closing. The book and gift shop had closed at 10:00 p.m., and Starbucks, Burger King, and The Country's Best Yogurt had followed minutes later. The small bar area had hung in until about 11:30, but they too had at last pulled the steel screen across their entrance. She'd positioned herself on one of the wooden benches lining the concourse area where she could view the entire area without being easily seen.

During the time she'd been sitting, there had been a couple of possibilities, but covert closer inspection had made her positive that the man who'd shot at her in the Publix lot was not one of those boarding a plane on this particular evening. The only possibility here was that he'd reached the airport before she had and had boarded quickly. A better possibility was that he hadn't returned to the airport at all but had found another method of leaving town.

Interestingly enough, she had thought for a second that she'd caught sight of the older man who had also been in the parking lot, but he'd been a long way off and had turned in the opposite direction and left before she had had a chance to identify him. By the time she'd reached the top of the down escalator for a better look, he was nowhere in sight. She'd let it go at that. He wasn't really the one she was looking for anyway. She wanted the little prick that had stolen her Degas pastels. He was the only one that counted at the moment. She made her way across the carpeted lobby down the escalator and headed through the revolving door towards short-term parking where she'd left her car. "You little bastard, you're not home free; somehow I'll find you, but for the rest of this night I'm gonna let someone else pay your bill," she muttered to herself.

Megan and Catherine were having a great time. They'd grabbed one of the dark back booths at the Mirror Image and were enjoying watching the variety of people frequenting the bar on this particular night as much as they were gleefully agreeing that this was a much better activity than staying home alone being dutiful.

At the moment, they were busily watching the tableau that was unfolding a couple of tables away from their booth. A couple had entered the Mirror Image either unaware or uncaring that it was a gay bar. They had sat facing each other unsmiling and talking in subdued tones, and it was obvious to even the most casual observer that they weren't having a particularly good evening. The man ordered something from the menu while the female was satisfied with a glass of wine. Just before the arrival of the man's food, the woman stood up with a furious look on her face and threw her glass of wine in the man's face. He showed a complete lack of emotion over this turn of events and calmly opened his napkin-wrapped utensils as the somewhat bewildered looking waiter put his plate down in front of him. The woman spun on her heels and headed through the back door of the bar in the direction of the parking lot.

"Wow, did you see that, Catherine? I thought they only did that in movies."

"You've got that right. I've never actually seen anyone throw a drink in somebody's face for real before."

"And do you believe it, the guy's sitting there calmly eating his dinner. Now that's what I call control."

"I wonder what it was all about. I've never seen anyone as angry as she was. I'd have to believe that's the end of that relationship."

Megan was amused by Catherine's obvious efforts to keep her slender form from shaking with laughter. She too was making a concentrated effort to keep herself from staring too obviously at the serenely dripping figure at the table, who seemed oblivious to everything and everyone around him. Megan and Catherine were just getting themselves back under control when the man's female companion came charging back through the rear door of the bar.

Without a word she marched back to the table they'd been sharing, picked up the man's drink and dumped it into his lap. "There, now you've got four f - -ing flat tires. F - - you." With that said, she whirled around and headed into the night for a second time.

The man looked up briefly as the woman reached his table, fork suspended in mid air. He watched her pour his drink into his lap without saying a word and then completed eating the forkful of food that was temporarily hanging in space before placing a napkin in his wet lap. After that minimal effort to dry himself, he once again returned to his meal.

"Holy shit, if I ever write a book, this has got to be in it. I've never seen anything like that and probably never will again." Megan laughed and turned away from staring at the man.

"Certainly made my night. I'm glad I came."

"Yeah, me too, unfortunately I've got to get going. Can I give you a lift anywhere?"

"No thanks, Megs. I walked here and I'd like to walk back. I need the exercise. I only live about a half mile from here. Do you know the Morris duplexes?"

"Oh yeah, I know where they are. Not that far from Forsyth Park. But I thought you lived near the mall."

"I used to, but I moved a few months ago. This apartment complex is really nice and new. It's not very far. Maybe you and Marla could come over some night, and we could all shoot the breeze. Don't forget to tell her about our little experience here tonight. She'll die laughing."

"You've got that right. Thanks for joining me; you turned a boring evening into a fun one."

"Hey, I had a good time too, Megs; let's do it again soon."

The two women left the Mirror Image and headed in opposite directions with a smile and wave.

Chapter 22

Adam was in what had to constitute one of the most exhilarating moments of his life. The seduction of the tall blond kneeling over him in the darkened bedroom was perfection. She was all satin and lace with skin that felt like it had been soaked in baby oil. The single small lamp on the bureau cast seductive shadows over everything and made her body a kaleidoscope of warm pinks and browns and pale alabasters. She removed her clothes so slowly with such cat-like grace that he was nearly wild with need by the time she finally got down to her panties.

It was at this point that the telephone next to his bed brought him back to conscious reality with its harsh insistent clamor. Sweating profusely, it took him a couple of seconds to wipe the moisture off his face and bring himself to the realization that he'd been dreaming. He was in his own bright yellow bedroom and alone He looked at his clock: 12:35 a.m.

"Yeah, this is Carter; what is it?"

"Jack here; we've had another woman attacked, but this time the perp was disturbed so she's still alive. They've taken her to Memorial."

"Sweet Jesus, is she badly hurt?"

"No, I don't think so. I've got two of the team at the scene of the crime. Why don't you and I head over to Memorial Hospital?"

"Good idea, I'll meet you there."

Adam dressed hurriedly, got in his sturdy tan Crown Victoria and headed for Waters Avenue. He'd only been in a hospital twice in his life - last year for a gunshot wound in the foot and the first time as a result of a car accident. He'd wound up in Medical Memorial on both of those occasions. As he pulled into the visitors' parking, he spotted Jack's green Escort parked three spaces down from where he put his own car.

"Good, he's already here."

He hurried towards the main entrance of the attractive glass and brick facility. Jack was leaning against the wall a few feet from the reception desk, talking to a rather pretty young nurse. Leave it to good old Jack to make good use of his waiting time. He was probably regaling her with his brave adventures as a Savannah Police detective.

"Hi, Jack, how is she?"

"Adam, I've got some shocking news. It wasn't a girl, it was Catherine."

"Catherine, oh my God. Is she hurt? What the hell was she doing out in Savannah this late?"

"I haven't yet spoken to her. Thought you'd want to do that. I just got her ID from one of the uniforms who was first on the scene. I didn't want to tell you on the phone, because I thought you'd drive like a madman if you knew it was Catherine."

As he was speaking, Jack was striding into the hospital trying to keep up with Adam who was almost running.

"Did you find out what room she's in while you were hanging around chatting up the staff?"

"Yup, she's in 411."

As the two men rode the elevator to the fourth floor, Adam felt an overwhelming fear. If anything happened to Catherine, what would he do? She'd become such an important part of his life. Only the other day they'd been talking about moving in together but couldn't make up their minds which of their places they liked better.

No one at the main desk on the fourth floor paid much attention to their arrival, so they simply checked the room number indicators posted on the pale blue walls and headed down the corridor in the direction of 411.

As the two men turned the corner into room 411, they were met head on by a senior nurse, Ruth Moore according to her name tag, who looked like she could have given Hulk Hogan a run for his money. Her salt and pepper hair was pulled back in a severe bun that was matched by equally severe gray eyes, which looked like they hadn't smiled in the last decade. Nurse Moore was built more like a barrel than she was a woman, and her unlipsticked mouth turned down at the corners in what had to be a permanent grimace. This was not a woman whose main asset seemed to be tolerance.

"Detectives, you have fifteen minutes, no more. We can't have Ms. Sherman getting all upset, can we? She's already been through enough of an ordeal."

Adam took this bit of information as more of an order than a request.

"Yes, ma'am, ah Nurse Moore, we'll make it just as brief as we can."

"Good, I'll be back in fifteen minutes."

Nurse Moore spun on her heel and headed out of the room with a precision that would have made a drill sergeant proud, lifting her massive chest to the fullest extent possible as she did so.

"Catherine, darling Catherine. How are you? What the hell were you doing out so late? Were you walking in the park? Thank God you're okay." Adam gently bent down to kiss Catherine's white face. A large bandage almost covered her fair hair, but her green eyes still sparkled up at him.

"It's okay, honey. I'm fine. Well, not totally fine, because I've got a pretty big bruise on the back of my head, but I'll live. So stop panicking."

"But what on earth were you doing out so late. I thought you'd said that you were going to go home after the talk."

"I was, but then Megan called and suggested we go out and we decided to go to the Mirror Image for a drink. You know Megan always likes that place." Catherine looked into Adam's furious face. "Yes, I know you've been doing some investigating of that place, but it's not as if we're eighteen and the murders were of young girls, not forty-year-old women like me. Anyway, the streets were pretty crowded right until I got to the apartment."

"So, did you take a short cut through the park?"

"Yes, that's exactly what I did. And that's the last thing I remember. What happened to me?"

"You were so lucky," - Jack looked down at his notebook - "an older man, a Mr. Branch, was walking his dogs and he disturbed whoever was attacking you. We'll be interviewing him later on today. At this point we don't know if the perp is connected to the murders, or you were just the victim of a random mugging. Could you have been followed from the club?"

"Maybe. I really didn't notice anyone in particular as I walked up the squares. Just before the apartment, I was vaguely aware of someone tall in my peripheral vision, but I could be wrong."

Adam held Catherine's hand and squeezed it. "Oh my love, thank goodness you're not badly hurt. I just can 't bear to think of that."

Catherine smiled at him. "I'm sorry to have worried you so much. Nothing like this has ever happened to me. Do make sure you thank the old man, won't you."

It was at this point that the formidable Nurse Moore re-entered the room hands clutching a rather nasty looking needle.

"I'm afraid it's time for a little more blood, Ms. Sherman. Gentlemen, it's time for you to go."

"Why do you need more blood? You already have about a gallon, and I'm feeling fine."

"Doctor's orders. Better safe than sorry."

"Yeah right."

"I'll be back in the morning sometime, and as soon as the doctor says you can leave, call me, and I'll pick you up. Do you have your cell phone with you?" asked Adam.

"Yes, it's in my purse. I think the police gave that back to me. Can you check in the night table?"

"Yes, it's here. I love you, sweetie." Adam bent once again and gave Catherine a soft kiss on the mouth.

Adam and Jack headed down the hospital's pale blue corridor in the direction of the polished chrome elevators, deftly avoiding a patient who obviously couldn't sleep and was strolling the halls with his IV in hand. Adam resolved that death would be infinitely superior to a prolonged illness and vowed to eat his service weapon before allowing Nurse Moore or someone like her a shot at him in a prone and helpless position.

"Thank goodness she wasn't hurt worse than she was. The man with the dogs must have scared the perp off. Do we know his address, Jack?"

"Yeah, I got a call from one of the guys," Jack looked at his notebook; "305 Taylor. Okay, tell you what, let's meet at the station later this morning, and we'll go and see Branch around 9:30."

"Fine. I'll see you then."

During their weekly Thursday morning department meeting, Captain Barton studied the anxious faces around the table and gave a summary of what had occurred in their jurisdiction over the last few weeks.

"Okay, gentlemen, let's go over what we've got so far. For one thing, we have a rather large German national who was gunned down in the parking lot of Publix three days ago. We know him as Hans, but we know his passport is a fake so we have not, as of yet, been able to determine his true identity.

"It would seem this is the same man who with another older German stole two paintings from an art restorer in Statesboro named Greg Burke about a week ago. They also perpetrated an assault on Mr. Burke and his partner Des Durden. Mr. Burke was kind enough to come in and give us a positive identification of the dead man he knew as Hans.

"Now we come to our witnesses in the parking lot shooting. Not a lot of help there, I'm afraid. As nearly as we can tell, there were four people involved, the two Germans, another man who drove away in a car that no one got a plate number on and a tall blond female.

"The best we can do on the color of the car was that it was either white, tan, brown or some combination of them all. The tall blond is interesting because of the information we've received concerning the murders that have occurred recently as well as an assault. All of those crimes have involved a tall blond of indeterminate sex.

"There may or may not be a tie-in between the parking lot shooting and the murders and assault I just mentioned. At this point we don't have enough evidence to make a judgment on whether or not they' re connected.

"Jack, Adam, any of you other guys got anything you'd like to add at this point?"

Chapter 23

Klaus's shoulder had subsided into a dull but persistent ache, and he tried to ignore it as best he could. He'd have to take a look at the wound sooner or later, but that would have to wait until he could settle somewhere. He spotted the blond before she could get a good look at him at Savannah Airport and beat a hasty retreat. A confrontation with the third victim of the afternoon's robbery was something he didn't need right at that point in time. He decided to skip his flight out of Savannah and headed the Lexus south onto Route 95 in the direction of Jacksonville, Florida. He might be able to track Schultz, but his priority was his father's paintings. He'd pull off Route 95 a few miles south of Savannah and get a room for the night. In the morning, he'd continue on to Jacksonville and book a new flight back to Germany.

Joey Morrisey checked his eyes in his bathroom mirror trying to convince himself that they weren't bloodshot enough to look like miniature Polish flags. If lunchtime yesterday had been a debacle, then what word could you use for last night's disaster? He really didn't want to think about it. It was bad enough that he had to go into that stupid bank and grovel in front of that supercilious idiot Campion, with memories of his recent frustration still vivid in his mind, but he also had to find some excuse for the old fool to explain his absence from work yesterday afternoon. His life was turning to shit right in front of his eyes. His eyes moved to the panty hose hanging over the shower curtains and the red panties he'd tossed in the corner. The panties clashed desperately with the lavender striped wallpaper and the mauve fixtures in the little room.

"I should have worn my purple set. I'm too upset to handle this right now. I'll just tell him I got sick from the shrimp I had at lunch. He'll have to believe it; what's he gonna do - fire me for one little offense? After all I've been there three years, and this is the first time I've ever done anything like this. God, I'd love to tell him and that whole frigging bank to kiss my ass." He muttered to himself.

131

Joey stumbled back into his bedroom and opened his closet, half of which consisted of the suits and jackets he wore to work on a regular basis and the other half his drag outfits. "How about if I just put on this low-cut little red number, Mr. Asshole Campion, and show up at work in full drag. Let's just see how you'd react to that, you pompous moron."

He settled instead for a gray pinstripe suit with a light blue shirt and patterned tie. As of this very moment he still couldn't afford to quit his place of employment, no matter how much he hated it. A glance around the bedroom lifted his spirits, if only slightly. Joey had dozens of pictures of him alone and with friends on every flat surface in the room as well as permanently displayed on his walls. He particularly liked the ones he'd taken on his visits to various nudist colonies over the course of the last few years. There was nothing like nudity to bring out a person's true character. Once he'd had his operation, he vowed to spend as many weekends in the nude as possible. His photos were intermingled with prints of many of the paintings he loved. He was determined that some day he'd have the originals hanging throughout the mansion he intended to own.

Joey adjusted his tie in the mirror until it looked perfect. Now he was ready to face the world and, unfortunately for him, that stone-faced old bucket of shit, Walter Campion.

David Rothschild spread the three little Degas pastels out in front of him on the bedspread in the motel room where he'd spent the night. They made quite an attractive little grouping. He felt absolutely no remorse over what he'd been required to do to get them. They had, after all, belonged to his family for generations prior to the rise of the Nazis. He hadn't actually stolen them; he'd just returned them to their rightful owner, himself. The acquisition of the $1,000,000 bank check had definitely been a real bonus, but the way he saw it, it was only fitting to be rewarded for the kind of risk he had to take in doing what he did.

He smiled as he recalled how angry he'd been when pressed into the Special Services section of the Mossad, the Israeli's Secret Service. He hadn't migrated to Israel just to wind up in the God damned army. He was too bright for that. He had other things on his mind, like making money, lots of it. How was he to know at the time just how good a computer expert they'd turn him into? It had all worked out in the end just perfectly.

He was sitting in a motel room with the equivalent of about $5,000,000, his laptop and a Mossberg directional indicator that told him exactly where the old German was. He'd had time enough to hide the tracking device before he put a round into the big Kraut and wounded the older one, but not enough time to find out what they'd done with the two little paintings they'd stolen. It would probably be the first and last time he'd come face to face with an ex-SS member and shoot to wound him, not to kill him. Now all he needed to do was follow along behind the fool in the black Lexus across the motel courtyard, and his mission would be complete or, at least, almost complete. The only other loose end was the tall blond. She would also have to be dealt with before he could enjoy the rewards of his hard work in peace. She would be even easier than dealing with the old Kraut. The tall blond was stupid enough to be actually looking for him. That would be her worst mistake, in fact, a fatal mistake; he'd make sure of that.

When Klaus woke, the first thing he became aware of immediately was the pain in his shoulder. Advil wasn't going to do it this time; he'd just have to bear it as best he could. He struggled out of bed and went into the little bathroom. He thought about a shower but only briefly. The water pounding against his wound would generate more pain than he cared to deal with right at the moment. He'd settle for cleaning it and redoing the bandage that would have to suffice for now. Everything seemed to look in order. The wound looked painful, which it was, but the disinfectant seemed to be doing its job properly, and Klaus pronounced himself fit for travel. "As though you have any other choice, old man," he told himself under his breath.

As he left the bathroom, he took a quick peek through the heavy green drapes he'd drawn over the window of the little motel room. All seemed to be in order. The Lexus with its precious paintings secured in the trunk was waiting patiently for him just where he'd left it. The sky was slate gray with a definite promise of rain hidden in the somber morning clouds. But not even the rain would deter him this morning. Jacksonville Airport lay no more than a hundred miles to the south of his rented room. With a little luck he'd be sitting in the lounge in a couple of hours waiting for his flight to be called.

He packed his few belongings and quickly put his bag and his lap top in the back of the Lexus, all the while checking the area for anything unusual. Nothing seemed out of place. A quick trip to the motel office to drop off the room key, and he could bid farewell to the lovely state of Georgia for the last time. As Klaus returned to the car and prepared to back out and head for Route 95, he once again failed to notice the little blue car that was also preparing to leave the motel, the same little blue car he'd seen many times before but had never actually taken any note of - a mistake he probably never would have made as a younger man.

Adam and Jack drove in the direction of Abercorn in silence. Adam had managed to get about three hours sleep but had been at work by 7:30. He only hoped that what he might learn from the old man who'd spooked the perp at last night's incident would tie some strings together for him and give him a sharper view of what was going on. He desperately needed to know if this latest incident was connected to the previous murders, and if it was, to get an idea of who his suspect might be.

Jack had also spent part of the night working on some leads that he'd been following for the last few weeks. He wasn't sure they might be related to last night's mugging, but he'd decided he must run his ideas past Adam just in case they were. As they drove to Mr. Branch's house, he said, "I've been looking at some old cases and I came up with something kind of interesting."

"What?"

"It seems we've been having a little run of nuisance calls over a period of the last few months. The interesting part is that they all involve young women."

"What sort of nuisance calls we talking about?"

"Nothing real nasty. Crank phone calls, messages painted on cars and walls. In four cases there was breaking and entering involved with some nasty terms scrawled on walls and clothing torn up, that sort of thing."

"What are you getting at?"

"It was all directed at young, good-looking blond women. The idea sort of floated around in the back of my mind that it might be connected in some way to the murder cases we're working on. What do you think?"

"Hey, anything's possible. Why don't you put together what you can on the incidents when you get back to the station, and we'll go over it when we're done with Ed Branch. We sure as hell can't afford to overlook any possibility at this point. I don't want another murder on our hands. Good work, Jack."

"Thanks, partner."

"It's me. You'll never guess what happened?" Casey recognized Megan's voice although there was something strange in her tone.

"What? What's happened?"

"Catherine was mugged last night and is in Memorial Hospital. Adam just called me. He was absolutely furious with me."

"Why would he be furious? What have you got to do with Catherine being mugged?"

As Megan told Casey all about going to the Mirror Image with Catherine and then what Adam had told her happened to Catherine afterwards, Casey could understand why Adam might be upset. She'd seen how he'd been getting ever more in love with Catherine even if he didn't always show it. It was typical that he'd feel protective and obviously she could have been badly hurt.

She said as much to Megan, and added, "I'm not really sure why he should be so upset with you. After all you did offer her a ride. Just because she chose to walk. She's a grown woman after all. And it wasn't that late you said. At eleven o'clock there's always loads of people around downtown."

"Yeah, I know. But I'm wondering if this was just a mugging, or if there's some connection to those other murders. After all they were blondes, too." Megan sounded worried.

"Yes, but they were young and Catherine's twenty years older."

"Yes, but she looks pretty young and especially from the back, you couldn't tell."

"True. God, what a thought. You'd better be a lot more careful than you usually are. Did you get hold of Marla?"

"Yes, she's all upset too. I think I might even look into an alarm system at this point."

"I know what you mean. You and I seem to have had our share of being the victims of crime. We don't need any more. Fortunately I have Tarka to let me know of impending doom with his meowing, but he'd let anyone in who gave him some food. But you know what, I've got an idea. How about if we do something proactive for a change? What do you think about you and Marla and me going to the Mirror Image on Saturday? Something might just click in your brain. You might even see someone you saw on the night you and Catherine were there."

"Gosh, I don't know. You're much braver than me, but maybe if there were three of us and we don't walk anywhere after, I don't see why not. Let me talk to Marla about it. I feel as though I should be doing something, and I suppose as long as we all stick together, it should be safe enough."

"That's great! Are you feeling any better?"

"Yes, I am, Case, thanks for being there."

"Anytime, best buddy, you know that."

"Time for class. I'll talk to you later, okay?"

"Yeah, give me a call tonight after you talk to Marla. I'll think about getting a sign that says "Warning Guard Cat on Duty." Do you think that would help?"

"Casey, you're hopeless, but I love you anyway. Talk to you later."

Chapter 24

As Adam and Jack pulled into the far end of Taylor Drive, a light rain began to fall. They hurried to the bright blue front door and knocked. A tall white-haired man answered, dressed in jeans and a yellow Polo shirt. Adam and Jack showed their identification. "Mr. Branch? Ed Branch?"

"Yes, that's me; come in, gentlemen. I presume you've come about the assault I witnessed last night. Bad business."

Adam and Jack followed him into a neat living room filled with antique furniture. Adam's eyes widened. Even though he only knew a little about antiques, he could see the fine patina on the highboy in the corner and that the cherry desk was an exquisite little piece. A further glance around the room revealed some oil paintings and two beautiful porcelain figures on the mantelpiece above the fireplace in the center of the room. Mr. Branch had money, no doubt about it.

"Can I get you some coffee, detectives?"

"No thanks, Mr. Branch." Jack pulled out his notebook. "Now tell us what happened last night. How come you were out walking so late?"

"I always take my Corgis out last thing before I go to bed. You can hear them now; I've shut them in the kitchen. As I live alone, I confess I keep rather odd hours, so I usually watch the late movie which ends around 11 o'clock. Last night the movie ended at 11:15, and I got the dogs and had been walking maybe five minutes or so."

"Do you just go the length of Taylor, sir?"

"It varies. Sometimes I walk around the block; sometimes I go to Forsyth Park. Anyway yesterday I had just entered the park. There are some trees just there, and it was rather dark because one of the streetlights was out.

As I got to the spot, the dogs started barking like crazy. At first I couldn't see anything, but then the moon came out from behind some clouds and shone directly on this figure who was on the ground. I didn't know what to think, so I instinctively ran forward. I think I shouted something like 'Are you all right?'

137

"It was only then that I noticed this tall, thin second person had his arm raised, and I saw the glint of light on what I presumed was a knife. I admit I was scared, but I just let go of the leads and the dogs took off. They're feisty little creatures. They went hurtling off, and the man just took off like a bat out of hell. He sure could run. He had these very long legs, and in a flash he was gone, and I couldn't see where he went. Misty ran after him for a bit, but then I think her lead got tangled, because when she came back, she was half strangling herself with it. Tango was snuffling around the young woman on the ground, so I stayed there to check if she was okay. She had a cell phone in her purse, so I phoned 911 right there, and your guys came pretty quickly and took her off to Memorial. I never even asked her name. I was pretty shaken at that point. You just don't expect violent crime around here. It's not a totally crime free area, but I've always felt very safe here. Not any more, I guess."

"Well, Mr. Branch, thanks a lot. The woman's name is Catherine Sherman and she's a counselor at Carter University. We've already visited her in the hospital, and she wanted us to give her your name so she could thank you yourself. I reckon you saved her life. If the perp was carrying a weapon, he probably was out to hurt her," said Adam. "One more thing, you keep saying he; are you sure the perp was a man?"

"It's funny you should say that, because after I got back home, I sat a while and had a brandy to calm my nerves. I kept thinking about the person, and I could have sworn it was a male until Misty chased him, but then, you know, he ran more like a woman. Women run differently from men; I'm sure you've noticed that at some time or another. They tend to hold their arms closer to their bodies. That's what this person did, so maybe it was a woman. But I can't be sure. If it was a woman, she was pretty tall, at least 5'10" or even 6' and thin. She was wearing black pants and a jacket and some sort of baseball cap, so I didn't see the color of hair, but she was white. I should have mentioned that, I'm sorry."

"No matter, Mr. Branch, you've been very helpful. We'll pass your description around, and if we do catch him or her, perhaps you'd be willing to come and make a formal identification."

"Of course, but I don't know if I could identify her. I didn't really get a good look, but I'll do anything to help. Are you sure you wouldn't like a coffee now?"

"No thanks, we have to be off."

As Adam and Jack left Mr. Branch, they both turned to each other. "Nice guy and pretty observant, but we still don't know if this person is male or female, or is the killer," said Jack.

"Yeah, this sure is frustrating, but I have a gut feeling this was our insulin killer, and if Misty and Tango hadn't been around, Catherine might now be dead. God, what a thought." Adam shuddered.

At that moment, Adam's cell phone rang. "Hi, my love. He does? That's great news. I'll drop Jack off at the station and be right over. Will you stay at my place for a few days? Good." He replaced the phone. "That was Catherine. The doctor says she can go home, but must rest for a few days. I'll swing by her place, after I've dropped you off and get her some clothes. Then I'll come back to work later today. Okay?"

"Sure, that sounds fine."

Later that afternoon, Adam caught up with Jack in the station. "Hi partner, what have you got?"

"Some kind of interesting stuff. The victims of the various nuisance crimes I pulled up are all young and all blond. What does that tell you?"

"Tells me we've got somebody with a thing against young blonds. Any of the scenes have fingerprints or anything tangible to help us out?"

"Nope, the perp is pretty careful, must be wearing gloves. We don't have a single print that can't be accounted for. The forensic boys do have a few fibers from the four break-ins, but that won't be of much use to us until we can find something to match them to."

"Great, let's haul in every tall blond in Savannah and start going through their wardrobes." Adam joked.

"With our luck the perp would live out of town; next thought?"

"Has anyone involved with any of these little escapades gotten a look at this wacko?"

"Not according to the reports of the guys who got assigned to the cases I've reviewed. No one seems to have seen a thing."

"That figures. Why do I feel like I'm riding a merry-go-round?" Adam shook his head. "I just keep grabbing for the brass ring and coming up with nothing but air."

"How about doing some interviews with the victims? Do you think that might be worth a shot?" Jack asked. "The perp did take some things from the spots he hit. It might help us to know exactly what."

"Let's do it. What have we got to lose? What's he taking?"

"Mostly underwear, stuff like that."

"That's interesting especially since we've never found the clothes of the two murder victims. Maybe there is a connection here somewhere. Start making some calls, buddy; let's see what we can find out."

Marla was cooking Megan her favorite shrimp Alfredo. As she busied herself preparing the meal, she thought about Megan's suggestion to re-do the walls. Maybe a darker paint or wallpaper might help. It was so light in the little kitchen that it almost made her eyes glaze over. Perhaps something in a mauve or a light blue might relieve the whiteness of the area and give her something to focus on other than the dinner she had heating on the stove. Megan was sprawled in one of the chairs in the adjoining dining area enjoying the view through the sliding glass doors that led to their tiny patio area. Small as the patio was, Megan had managed to cram in at least a dozen plants of various types next to a statue of a girl on a dolphin which happily spewed a stream of water into the circular pool at its base.

They were both excited about the girls' night out at Patricia's house, but a little worried that Catherine wouldn't feel well enough to come. Megan had told her who was coming and it sounded fun. None of the other women attending were gay, but neither she nor Megan saw any problems developing from that. They had each other and that was quite enough.

"How you doing in there, Marla? It smells great. Can I help with anything? I'm getting hungry."

"Just keep your jeans on. It's almost ready. You can fill my wine glass if you'd like. "

"Got ya. Coming right up."

Marla carried the hot dishes over to the glass-topped dining table they shared on those rather rare occasions when they were both home for supper at the same time and set one dish down in front of the now fully alert Megan. "Anything else you need before I sit down?"

"Nope, I'm good to go. I already put the cheese on the table and some bread and butter if you want some."

"No bread for me, thanks."

"It looks delicious, Marla. Thanks for all the effort."

"I wish I could do this every night. I kind of enjoy it. By the way, have you seen Pussy?"

"No, she hasn't shown up for her supper yet, but if I know Pussy, she'll be stomping in shortly to chew on a few more cords or something else of mine."

"Yeah, she is bad like that. Now tell me the deal for tomorrow night again. We're going to the Mirror Image with Casey to see if you can spot anyone who might have been there the evening that Catherine got assaulted?"

"Yup, that's the idea. I don't think there's a snowball's chance in hell that anything helpful will occur, but you know how excited Casey gets when there's even the remotest possibility of an adventure."

"She is brave. I think it's all those mysteries she reads." Marla forked up another mouthful of her Alfredo. "This is good even if I say it myself."

"Yeah, it's delicious. Thanks for fixing it. You know Casey, everything seems to be a game to her, and she's always up for any excitement. Nothing's going to slow her down."

"Well, good for her. I just think she should be a little more careful, especially after what happened to Catherine."

"Please, don't even talk about it. What's happened to all those young women is bad enough. Thank goodness Catherine wasn't badly hurt."

"Actually, Megs, I never really cared that much for Catherine. Still, I wouldn't wish anything nasty to happen to her."

Megan choked on her linguini. "Wow, you surprise me. I didn't know that. What is it about Catherine that you don't like?"

"I think she's a little bit too prissy and self-opinionated. I guess she just reminds me too much of my grand-mother."

"Now, this sounds interesting, Marla. Tell me more."

"No, forget about it. Let's just enjoy our dinner. We'll talk about it some other time."

"God, you always say that. I'd love to hear every little detail of your life."

"No, you wouldn't. Most of it's boring as day old shit."

Megan was caught off guard by the sudden smile she caught on Marla's lips; the subject they'd been discussing seemed rather serious to her and certainly not a cause for levity.

"What are you smiling about? Did I say something funny?"

"No, talking of Catherine, I thought of her fair hair, and I just had a flashback to that fancy dress party we went to a couple of weeks ago and you posing in that Bo Peep outfit. I loved you in your blond wig with pigtails and freckles. Did we ever get our pictures back from that?"

"Nope, I keep forgetting to pick them up from CVS. I'll try to remember them tomorrow. I was pretty adorable, wasn't I? Maybe we could go out at Christmas to one of the bars on River Street where they'll have a costume party."

"Yeah, what a good idea. I don't usually like costume parties, but if you wear that outfit, I'll feel as if my date for the evening is about eleven years old, and if I go dressed again as Vampira, I'll spend the entire evening thinking that everyone who sees us suspects I am actually drinking your blood."

"That was a fun night. A repeat would be great. Marla, that was a terrific meal, my love. I think I'll take a little stroll around the neighborhood to work it off and see if I can't spot Pussy. Want to come along?"

"Nope, I'm exhausted from slaving over a hot stove, and I've got to prepare a report for tomorrow's meeting. I'll be in the study. Hurry back."

"I will; see you in a little while."

Megan put on her jacket and walked towards the front door while Marla contentedly rubbed her stomach and headed for the computer. All in all, it had been a very nice evening so far.

As Klaus passed the Florida state line, he was beginning to feel better. Sure, his shoulder still ached, but he was only a few miles from Jacksonville Airport. Even though this journey hadn't accomplished everything he'd hoped it would, he was returning with the two precious little paintings, and it wasn't his fault that the deal on the Degas pastels had gone wrong. The Lexus hummed along smoothly, and he judiciously observed the posted speed limit. This was no time to make a stupid mistake. Klaus was even enjoying the silence inside the car - no more Country and Western music to intrude into his thoughts. He wasn't even remotely worried about what the police might be doing about Hans. They'd both been supplied with aliases and false papers, and it would be a long time, if ever, before the police figured out who Hans really was. He even ran his own real name over in his mind. "Wilhelm Wolfe, that's who you are old man." He'd almost forgotten that during the seeming eternity he'd been calling himself Klaus.

The exit to the airport loomed ahead; only one more mile and he'd be making the last leg of this nightmare expedition into this foreign and inhospitable land. Klaus headed towards long term parking as he neared the airport. There was no need to bother returning the Lexus to the rental agency. They'd eventually find it in long term parking, and even though they'd be upset by that, exactly what could they do about it? He'd be long gone and untraceable back in his beloved Munich. He put the Lexus in park and popped the trunk. After removing his bag and his laptop from the back seat and putting them on the roof, he walked back to the trunk and prepared to remove the two little treasures that had been the whole point of his trip.

As he gazed down at the little package, he almost wished he could view the paintings one more time before he boarded the plane, but that would be dangerous as well as stupid. He'd simply put the package in the overhead along with his laptop and dream about removing the brown paper and bubble wrap to show them to Hilda before selling them and enjoying the proceeds. One final fond gaze and he'd make his way to the ticket counter inside the airport and be on his way.

Before he could lift the small package out of the trunk, Klaus became aware of something terribly wrong. He could no longer breathe. Something was cutting into his neck with a vicious pressure. He raised both hands in an effort to pull the savage pain away from the area of his jugular, but it was of no use. The hands that held the wire slicing into his throat were too strong for him to dislodge. He could neither remove the choking wire nor make a sound, and he knew he was going to die in the long term parking lot of Jacksonville Airport without being able to do a single thing about it. He could feel his vision begin to fade as his lungs made their final efforts to breathe life-sustaining air into themselves. His fingers were getting sticky, and he didn't need to look at them to know that there were little rivulets of blood washing over his hands and wrists. Even the pain began to fade as blackness wrapped its enveloping cape over his last few moments on earth. As he died, his last thoughts were of a black uniform with death heads on the collars.

David Rothschild held the wire he'd placed around the old German's throat until he was completely sure the old man was dead. He removed the paintings and then dumped the body unceremoniously into the trunk of the Lexus. A second quick glance around the area told him there was still no one around who might have viewed the last moments of Klaus Kruger or whatever his name really was. A faint smile crossed his face; just one more little string to tie up, and he'd be able to retire and enjoy his new wealth. A cleverly placed message on the Internet should do the trick in wrapping up the final stage of this little adventure. Life could be so very good if you just knew how to play the game correctly. He left the suitcase and the laptop sitting on the roof of the Lexus. He didn't need them, and he'd made damn sure the old Kraut didn't either.

The tall blond had spent the last several hours working the computer with one single thought in mind - to find some sort of message that would provide a lead to the theft of the Degas. It was the only avenue left open that offered any hope of recovery of either the pastels or the money. It was closing in on midnight when the coded message hit the

Internet with the long-awaited clue as to where they could be found. Whoever was sending the message was an idiot; an eleven-year-old child could have seen through it. "Have completed mission in Savannah. Little Albert wants instructions to bring presents home. Immediate reply requested." It was coming out of a Ramada Inn in Jacksonville, Florida. What a moron! She'd leave tomorrow and finish this business.

Chapter 25

Joey Morrisey sat on his favorite bench in Johnson Square and tried to concentrate on the tuna grinder he'd gotten from the Subway a block down from where he worked. The looming heroic statue of Nathaniel Greene that dominated the center of the little square held little interest for him at this point, as he'd already seen it a thousand times. There were, of course, the ubiquitous pigeons waddling back and forth as they always did, hoping desperately that someone would drop something edible. Screw you, you nasty little bastards. I'd sooner throw this thing in the garbage before I'd give you a single crumb, he thought.

The pigeons, for the most part, ignored Joey's tirade and continued their little circling patterns around and under the bench he was sitting on. Joey made one clumsy attempt to stomp on one of them but missed his mark badly and had to make do with cursing at them. The pigeons moved out of the way of his feet and closer to another human who was willing to share his food.

Nothing seemed to be going quite right for Joey at the moment. Here it was Saturday, a time he should be off from work, enjoying himself, but, oh no, here he was halfway through another stupid day at the bank because of a special audit they were conducting on one of the bigger estates he had valued. Just another injustice that someone was going to have to pay for, and tonight might be a very good night for that purpose. They could control his days, but there wasn't a single thing they could do about what he did with his nights. He dejectedly threw the remainder of his grinder into a trash bin as he slowly walked back in the direction of the bank. Payback is a bitch. Someone was going to find that out before the night was over.

Although it was Saturday, Adam, too, was hard at work and making a concerted effort without a great deal of success to get the piles of paper on his desk into some kind of order. He had a lot on his mind and shuffling all this paper wasn't helping anything. Catherine was getting better, and everyday her head hurt less, she was getting more fidgety. This morning she'd told him quite sharply that she needed to get back to her own place.

At first she'd been happy to be fussed over by him, but very soon he'd realized that she was one independent woman who hated lying on the sofa doing nothing but watching daytime television. Finally, he'd agreed that he'd take her home after work today and had left her talking on the phone to Casey.

He'd got over his anger at her foolishness in going to the Mirror Image, but still held some resentment towards Megan. If she wanted to take risks, that was one thing, but she shouldn't have involved his beloved.

He and Jack had at least made some progress on the nuisance cases. Most of the articles missing from the apartments of the young women who had been victimized were panties, bras and nightwear. The clothing that the intruder left behind in three of the break-ins had been slashed or cut up. This perp was obviously someone who had a serious hatred of young blond women. Adam even pressed a forensics team into service in the hopes that they might find something helpful. They hadn't found any useful prints, but they came up with something that might prove helpful if they could get their hands on a suspect. Some blond hairs had been found at one of the scenes that did not belong to the owner. They were, in fact, not even human hair, but rather a synthetic fabric which would only be found in a blond wig, leaving Adam and Jack to ponder the fact that their suspect might very possibly not be a blond at all but rather someone wearing a blond wig.

Upon learning the information, Adam's mind immediately went back to the tall blond Jack had met at the Mirror Image, and his upcoming date to meet her or him again tonight. Jack was looking forward to their next assignation with a combination of fear and hopefulness. He'd told Adam that he had been quite taken with the tall, sexy blond, but he had now decided in his own mind where this thing was going, nowhere. He'd already broken the cardinal rule of police work - never get involved with a possible suspect - which included most of the tall blonds in Savannah at this point. While Adam felt happy that Jack had found someone he liked at the Mirror Image, he too knew how dangerous it was for his partner to get into anything with anybody even remotely suspicious at this point.

"Adam, Adam, Earth to Adam. You in there somewhere, partner?"

Adam had been so lost in thought that he hadn't been aware of Jack coming up beside his desk, much less speaking to him. "What? Oh yeah. What's up?"

"That photograph we've been running on the local TV of the last murder victim has brought in over a hundred calls. I doubt any of them are going to be terribly useful, but we've got to track 'em all down, just in case. I've got a couple of uniforms to help me out. I'll let you know if we get anything. Oh, by the way, we've already had four confessions to the crime, but none of them seems to know how he killed her, so I don't think we'll be going anywhere with that. I'll talk to you later."

"Okay, thanks."

Adam fought the urge to dump his entire in-tray in his wastebasket and went back to contemplating what he might do about perking up Catherine's spirits when he took her home later that evening. He decided a large bunch of flowers couldn't harm.

Casey breakfasted at Clary's as she loved to do on Saturdays and then decided to do a little antiquing. After browsing through Cassandra's on Broughton Street, she decided to head back up Abercorn Street once again in the direction of Ben Appleby's. As she pulled into Collier Street, she noticed Greg's blue Chevy van parked behind Ben's van.

Oh good, Greg and Des are here; I haven't seen them in a while. She thought as she climbed the steps to Ben's antique shop and pushed the two buttons, one on either side of the door, which would signal Ben that customers had arrived, whether he was on the first floor or the second. In a few moments, Ben opened the door, his face breaking into a good-natured smile when he saw who was there.

"Casey, good to see you. No Megan with you? Come on in. Greg and Des are here too, so we can have a nice little get-together."

"Ben, how have you been? I haven't seen you in a while."

"Well, the best I can say is that it's been up and down. Come on in, and I'll tell you all about it."

Casey joined Greg and Des in the crowded first floor parlor that Ben used to display his antiques and gasped at appropriate intervals as Ben, Greg, and Des related their tales of adventure they'd experienced with the theft of the two little paintings by the Germans and the subsequent death of the one named Hans.

"That's amazing, all of this over two paintings. Wait till I tell Megan; she'll never believe it. Do you know what happened to Mr. Kruger? And is Mildred OK now?"

"Oh yes, she's finally getting past the trauma of what happened. She's still very upset by the whole episode, but I'm sure she'll get over it in time. We don't know what happened to Kruger, but it was Greg who identified Hans. Also, the two little paintings were a lot more than they seemed to be. Greg and Des had discovered that one of them had Camille Pisarro's signature on it, and the other was by Paul Cezanne. No wonder they were so anxious to get their hands on them. They must have known what they really were from the beginning and were more than happy to do whatever it took to get them. I'm just glad none of us got too badly hurt in the process."

"How about you, Greg? Are you okay now?"

"Oh, yeah, I'm doing fine with the exception of the fact that Des seems to find it necessary to tell me at least twelve times a day about how she saved my life."

"Well, I did. If I hadn't shown up when I did, they might have killed you. It was me and my two-by-four that saved the day."

"Des rides to the rescue again. Just like you did last year. Where would these men be without you, right?"

"That's what I keep telling Greg, but he just won't buy into it."

"Let me get a bottle of wine from upstairs," said Ben, "and we'll have a little toast to just that very thought. I'm the first to admit that being alive is better than having paintings, no matter how valuable they are. I can't help wondering where the little darlings wound up though. I wonder if they've found a home back in Germany?"

Casey was pleased that her friends had come through their hair-raising experience relatively unharmed. There was a tiny area in the back of her mind that sort of wished she could have been a little closer to all the action that had taken place. Not that she wanted a repeat of her horrific time with Earl and Jimbo or even with Stewart, but a little adventure might be fun. Maybe tonight at the Mirror Image might prove exciting.

Chapter 26

The sun was flirting with a grouping of little white clouds playing hide-and-seek as the tall blond wheeled the green Ford Taurus off Interstate 95 onto the exit ramp that represented the last couple of miles into Jacksonville Airport. Timing was critical in this most important of projects. It was 3:00 p.m., and this job had to be completed in enough time to ensure her arrival back in Savannah before 8:00. It would be close, but it could be done, had to be done. It was slightly less than a two-hour drive from Savannah to Jacksonville, so 6:00 p.m. would need to be the completion hour. No problem.

The shadows were already beginning to lengthen appreciably, and darkness would begin its descent very shortly as it always did in November in the Southeast. The Ramada Inn loomed ahead on the tall blonde's right and caused the driver to shift positions behind the steering wheel in anticipation. Nerves were a big part of this little game. While the blonde's right hand controlled the steering wheel, the left smoothed the fabric of the satin red sheath over long silken thighs. If this project were to be successful, looks would play a major role. Sexuality was not only a fun part of living, it was also a potent weapon to be used as required. She hoped that the desk clerk would be male. It was easy to convince them that a blond was always dumb and always in need of help. A female clerk would make life a little more difficult, but the plan for gaining access to the room of the thief who'd stolen the Degas pastels and fired the shot that barely missed would work. People, especially people who worked in motels, always went out of their way to help a tall, very attractive blond who was seemingly lost and confused. In just a few more minutes, what rightfully belonged in the possession of their recent owner would be recovered. And if it resulted in one more death, that was just the way it had to be.

David Rothschild had also had an extremely interesting day. He'd spent nearly three hours hiding out in the bathroom of room 107 of the

Jacksonville Airport Ramada Inn with the shower going before he heard the muted click of the outside door that let him know his visitor had finally arrived. He didn't know if the motel would see any difference in their water bill, but he was determined to be ready when his expected visitor showed up. He was a little cramped up from sitting in the same position for all that time, but as he slipped behind the door, he was ready, as was the little Beretta he held in his right hand with its faithful silencer attached. When this last loose end was tied up, he could be out and gone with his newly found wealth securely under his arm. He hadn't made any pretense about hiding the paintings or the briefcase with the pastels and check inside. Everything had to appear as normal as possible for this to work.

His visitor glided across the room without making a sound, and he watched from behind the bathroom door as she paused just outside the opaque white shower curtain for an instant with a rather nasty looking .38 special held at shoulder height.

"Hi, I was wondering when you were going to show up."

The blond spun around, and David deftly removed the pistol from her hand as she turned to face him. God, she wasn't just tall and pretty; she was flat-out gorgeous. His face must have held the same look of surprise as hers now did.

"You stole my pastels, you prick."

"Now, now, let's not get testy. It was only business. Unfortunate that you had to get in the way of all this, but that's the way it goes sometimes. I trust you didn't exactly come by them honestly, now did you?"

"That's none of your business, asshole. If you intend to kill me, let's just get it over with."

"Oh, I really don't see the need to be all that hasty. Why don't we just step into the bedroom and talk about it? Okay, stop just there by the foot of the bed. I'm going to make a quick check to make sure you're not hiding anything under your clothes. Don't take it personally."

"Screw you."

"Such language, my, my, my."

As David ran his free hand over the tall but soft form in front of him, he checked all the areas including the most intimate ones where she might have something hidden and found nothing other than a bra and panties under the dark clothing.

"Okay my dear, take your clothes off very slowly. You don't have to turn around; you can keep your back to me if you want to."

The tall blond slowly unzipped the red dress and let it fall to her feet. "Why am I bothering to do all this if you're going to kill me anyway?"

"Yes, that's true, but that can go quickly and without pain, or I can shoot you in the stomach first and watch you writhe around for an hour or two before I finish you off. It's your choice."

"I see, and how exactly do you intend to cover up this little thing about them finding a dead woman in your room?"

"No problem. I'm going to use your very own little .38 to put a bullet into your pretty little head and then put the gun into your hand. By the time they figure out it wasn't a suicide, I'll be long gone, and I know how to cover my tracks, my dear."

"What about the old German? He won't give up that easily."

"Ah yes. Unfortunately for him, he's now residing in the trunk of his rented Lexus. I've got an idea it's going to be a while before they find him."

"Tied up all the strings, have we Mr. ____?"

"Rothschild, David Rothschild. Nice to meet you, Miss, if only for the briefest of times. Now get on with it, and we can get this thing finished."

"Okay, Mr. Rothschild, if you're going to insist on killing me, you might as well get a good look at what you're wasting."

As the tall blond turned slowly toward him, David watched the movement of her slender fingers as they began to unclasp her front-opening bra. Both the bra and panties were black, edged with lace. The bikini panties barely covered her pubic area, and he could spot little tendrils of dark curly hair poking their way out of the sides of her tiny panties. As she unclasped her bra to reveal her upthrusting breasts, David was lost for a second in the remarkable perfection of her body. God, she was superb! - so much so that he hardly noticed that she had taken a step forward in his direction. He was so taken by the moment that his right hand holding the Beretta dropped a few inches in the direction of the carpet. The flash of her right arm and hand was so quick that he barely had time to realize that a movement had taken place before he felt the pain in his right wrist. The Beretta hit the carpet with a plop as he lost all sensation in his right hand. He scarcely had time to ponder the unexpectedness of this event before her hand rose with astonishing speed and chopped him expertly on the side of his neck rendering him semi-conscious and on his way to the floor.

"Jesus Christ, she'd had a needle concealed in her bra."

His first mistake had been a bad one, he thought, as the drug-induced blackness began closing in. The blond quickly retrieved her dress and calmly put it back on. She picked up the briefcase and the little package, being careful to take a washcloth from the bathroom and wipe any possible prints off anything she might have touched and left the scene quietly, wondering how the motel maids were going to handle this one. She carefully put the 'Do Not Disturb' sign on the door of the room and wiped down the doorknob - another job well done. Now all that was required was to get into her car and head back to Savannah, first to drop the package off in her rented motel room safe, change her clothes and then get home. She wondered how she'd be described to the police by the desk clerk. A tall blond with sunglasses and a hanky over her mouth because she had a cold, and oh yes, she was wearing a gorgeous red dress. Not too much to go on.

Jack was doing his very best to make himself presentable.

"God damn it," he muttered. He'd gotten a little too close with the razor again and had been rewarded with a second tiny drop of blood running down his chin. It was the fault of the stupid frosted mirror. He couldn't see properly in it and it needed changing. He didn't like the pale green of the rest of the bathroom either. That was the trouble with buying an older home which still had those 1970's touches - avocado and harvest gold. He'd redecorated the bedroom and living room as soon as he'd moved in. The shag carpeting was impossible to live with, but having restored the beautiful hardwood floors, Jack had decided he couldn't cope with the expense of altering the bathroom for a while. So the avocado fixtures and cream and green flowery wallpaper glared at him every morning, which never helped his moods.

"Hi, remember me, Jack Malloy? Sure is good to see you again, Sylvia. I've been thinking about you." God, did that sound lame or what? Even Jack had to avoid his own eyes in the mirror on that one. "Hi, Sylvia, good to see you again. What's new?"

God, what a slick talker I am. I sound like I've been housed in a monastery for the last ten years. Oh well, I'm just going to have to come up with something when I get there that won't make me sound retarded. Why was he even worrying? It wasn't as if he wanted to seduce this woman. He had his job to think of and it was important to him. What was it with this Sylvia woman? He couldn't understand, but she seemed to fascinate him, much like the snake must have fascinated Eve. Oh well, no use worrying about it right now.

What am I going to do if she wants to come back here? Shit! No, no, that's a complication I don't need. Why am I even thinking along those lines? Why does she intrigue me so much? Could she have something to do with the murders? If that's the case, I'd be better off getting Adam to go with me. My God! I think I'm going crazy. Time to go, perhaps she won't even be there anyway, and then all this fuss will have been for nothing.

Jack had, of course, completely convinced himself that the lovely Sylvia had to be a woman. There was no way that his mind could accept that she might be a man in drag. Despite the many females he'd dated, his ego concerning women was quite fragile.

His best suit was hanging on the closet door, along with a blue shirt and a white shirt, fresh from the dry cleaners. He'd even picked out a new tie and had his shoes polished. The suit looked pretty good, a nice mixture of dark blue interwoven with strands of gray, not bad. He decided to wear the blue shirt and put that on, followed by freshly laundered shorts and socks. This was the most effort Jack had put into dressing for a date in quite some time. It was all beginning to make him a little dizzy, and he couldn't push down the feeling that he might be making a total fool of himself.

Across town Megan was also preparing for the big night out at the Mirror Image. She'd started dressing at 8:00 when Marla got home, and she was still at it. Megan had chosen a dark blue dress in a clingy crepe, which hugged the curve of her hips without accentuating the fact that her belly was rounder than it needed to be. Marla, of course, was a vision in green, with a form-fitting mid-thigh length sheath that showed off her superb legs and splendid breasts to their best advantage.

"God, you look good in that. We should get dressed up more often."

"You're not so bad yourself, Miss Muller; pretty good looking couple, I'd say."

"No, I really mean it. I get so used to myself dragging around in my baggy old stuff that I astound myself when I actually get dressed up."

"Yeah, I get a little tired of the business stuff I have to put on every day too. I'd almost forgotten what I looked like with legs, not too bad, I might add."

"Marla, you look sensational, and you know it; don't pull that false modesty stuff on me. I know you too well for that."

"Don't push me, Muller, or I'll pull your little blond wig out of the closet and make you wear it. Do you think I look too tall in these heels?"

"Hey, tall is good. We both can attest to that. I think we make a stunning couple; what do you think?"

"Yeah, we're great. Are you almost ready? I want to get there a little early so we can pick the booth we want and get something to eat."

"I'm about as ready as I'm ever going to get, but I don't know about eating. I don't want to bust out of anything important like my dress."

"Don't worry, Megs. The fabric looks pretty sturdy to me. Now get your cute little butt in gear, and let's get out of here. It's almost 9:30."

Casey arrived at the Mirror Image to find Megan and Marla holding down a booth near the back of the nightclub where the light was the dimmest - it paid not to be seated in the better lit places within the bar. The walls were covered with a dark red patterned wallpaper, and there were countless photos signed by well-known local personalities covering nearly all the available surfaces.

"Hi, you two, how you doing?"

"We're good. We just finished slopping down a plate of ribs and fries each so we're both full but happy. "

"Aha - I knew there had to be a good reason why you got here before I did. I had macaroni and cheese, my good old standby and great for counteracting any drinking I might do. So, Megan, have you spotted anything or anyone exciting yet?"

"Not so far. It's been pretty dead in here, but it's early and the night's still young," said Megan.

"We've got the perfect spot. We can see everyone that comes in, but they can't see us until their eyes become accustomed to the murkiness. What could be better?" Marla added.

The rest of the customers in the club at this point consisted of two women and three men at the bar, a mixed couple, male and female, in the booth next to the window and three other couples seated at various points around the room. Golden Boy was working the bar and two bored-looking waitresses were taking care of the floor customers.

"What do you think of the blond at the bar? Look at the length of those legs," asked Megan.

Marla turned to look at the blond and shook her head. "She may be pretty, but I bet she's one of those snotty art students who believes she's just the hottest thing that ever lived."

"Gosh, Marla, aren't you over-reacting just a hair. She's probably a very nice person if you get to know her," said Casey.

"I doubt that. Look at the way she's drinking a martini. She impresses me as a superior little bitch who probably has a rich daddy and thinks she can get away with murder."

"Remind me not to get on your bad side," Casey said, looking a little startled at the vehemence in Marla's voice.

"Oh, you don't have anything to worry about. You're great." Marla gave Casey a smile.

"Thank God for that."

"Well, let's get off that subject. How about the couple up front? They're starting to look a little puzzled. Do you think we should go over there and tell them they're not alone? That there is one other hetero person in the place, so they can relax."

"No, let 'em worry about it for a while."

"So, Megan, you don't see anyone who looks even vaguely familiar?"

"Not a soul. Whoops, I spoke too soon. That's Jack Malloy who just walked in the door. He and Adam have been so pissed at me. Maybe I ought to hide." Megan slid lower on her seat. "I wonder why he's here?"

Casey turned round. "Is he alone?"

"Yes, he's alone, but it doesn't look as if he's seen us; he's headed for the bar."

"Oh, shit."

"What's the matter, Marla?"

"My beeper just went off. I've got to get to a phone; there's one down by the ladies room, right?"

"Yes, there is. Please don't tell me you're going to have to leave us right in the middle of the evening. You spent all day at work. Can't you ever have any time off?"

"Let me go make a quick check to find out what's going on. I'll be right back."

As Marla quickly rose and headed down the hall in the direction of the rest room, Casey sensed an immediate dampening of Megan's mood.

"Don't worry; it's probably nothing."

"I hope not, but there are times when I find myself really hating her job. Her stupid clients always seem to have some desperate need for her just when we're starting to have fun."

Jack took a red stool at the bar, shading his eyes with his hands and trying to adjust his vision to the dim lights. He saw no sign of Sylvia in the place and busied himself for a few moments studying the stunning young blond a few stools down from where he was sitting. She was in a form-fitting blue dress with a slit that went almost to her hip, and the front of her dress was cut low enough to more than adequately display her ample bosoms. She was quite a package; unfortunately she looked barely twenty-one despite her martini glass.

"Good evening, sir; nice to see you here again. Are you having Dewar's on the rocks?"

"Sure, that would be great."

"You haven't happened to see the young lady I was talking with the last time I was in here have you?"

"No, I thought I did for a second, but then I looked around, and she wasn't anywhere in sight. Probably my imagination. I'm sure she'll be in later."

"Hopefully. Not much of a crowd here yet."

"No. We really don't start to fill up until about midnight, and from that point on we're really jammed. Let me know when you're ready for a refill."

"Thanks, I will."

It was at this point that Jack spotted Megan and Casey in one of the booths near the back of the room, left his stool and walked over.

"Megan, Casey, what are you doing here? I would have thought your last visit here, Megan, would have been quite enough excitement to last you a while." Jack's sarcastic tone caused Megan's own anger to rise.

"Don't be angry at me, Jack. Just because Catherine wanted to walk even after I'd offered her a ride doesn't make me responsible for what happened to her. I have every right to go to a club if I want to." As Jack started to say something, Megan held up her hand to stop him. "No, I haven't finished. I have to tell you that I was a little bit pissed when Adam called me and yelled at me. I'm horribly upset about what happened to Catherine, but let's face it a mugging can happen to anyone in a big city. So just get off my case."

"Now hold it there, Megan. I don't know what Adam said to you, but the reason he may have been upset is because Catherine knew we were staking out this place because we think it might have some connection to the other murders. He just couldn't understand why she and you would come to this particular club at this time."

"Sorry. I didn't mean to snap at you, but I have to repeat I'm not Catherine's keeper, and I knew nothing about a stakeout."

Casey interrupted. "Stakeout, that sounds exciting. Can you tell us more?"

"Nothing much to tell. We've been going to many of these clubs around the city."

"So, is that what you're doing here tonight?" Casey stared intently at Jack.

"No, tonight all I'm doing is expecting to meet a contact, a woman of course."

"Yeah, yeah, of course." Megan couldn't keep the sarcasm out of her voice, but smiled at Jack as she said it.

"Are you and Casey just out on the town again?"

"Well, sort of. My partner, Marla, was here for a while. I was hoping to introduce you to her, but you just missed her. She got a call and she had to sort out some problems with one of her tour groups."

"That's a pity, but at least you have your old friend, Casey."

"Yes, that's a plus. Do you want to join us, Jack?"

"Well, maybe just for a couple of minutes."

"Do you have any leads on the murders, yet?"

"We've got a couple of things we're working with, Casey. It seems we may be looking for a tall person with a blond wig in case you happen to run into one."

"Well, Megan here is 5'11" in heels and she owns a blond wig she wore at a party a couple of weeks ago. Anything you want to tell us, Megs?"

"Nope, I'm not saying a word until my lawyer's present. Incidentally, if you happen to need a shorter, dark-haired suspect, I've got one right here. Excuse me you two for just a second, I'm gonna run down the hall and see what Marla's up to on the phone."

Megan, as promised, returned shortly with the disappointing news that Marla had indeed been called away on an emergency.

"It figures; she's off again. I'll be damned if I'm gonna let it ruin my evening. See that blond over there? I'm gonna ask her to dance."

Jack turned his head and was surprised to find that the woman Megan was referring to was Sylvia.

Jack hesitated. He wasn't sure if he should admit that he knew her. "Her name's Sylvia Gordon. I met her here last weekend."

"You've got good taste, Jack; she's a knockout. I don't want to step on your toes."

"No problem, go do your dancing thing then invite her back to the table."

Jack had to admit the two made an attractive couple on the dance floor even though he found himself fighting off pangs of jealousy. He reminded himself he had no ties on Sylvia. But he felt uncomfortable seeing her with Megan. Could he handle someone who was bi-sexual? That would certainly be a first for him. Perhaps he should stay away from the gorgeous Sylvia. After the music stopped, Megan and Sylvia spent a few moments talking and then walked back toward the booth where Jack and Casey were sitting.

"Jack, how good to see you."

"Same here, Syl. I was beginning to think you weren't going to show up."

"Just got here. Who's your friend?"

"This is Casey Forbes; Casey, this is Sylvia."

Both women traded hellos. Jack couldn't help but notice that Casey, while being pleasant, was more reserved than usual, and Megan sat listening to the conversation with a smile that looked like it had been painted on her face. After they had all been chatting for about fifteen minutes, Jack turned to Sylvia. "I think it's my turn. How about a dance, Syl?"

"Let's do it. I certainly enjoyed it last time."

Once Jack and Sylvia had reached the dancing area, Casey turned to Megan with a quizzical look.

"Is something the matter? You hardly said a word."

"What a bitch. I hope Jack doesn't get serious about her."

"Megan, what are you talking about? We've only just met her."

"Never mind, maybe it's me who's the bitch. She just said something that really pissed me off. Let's just get the hell out of here before they get back."

"Do you wanna tell me what she said?"

"No, not now. We'll talk about it later." After Casey and Megan left, Jack returned to the bar in the company of Sylvia and got another Dewar's. An hour later, he too said goodnight to Sylvia and headed for the door. Casey and Megan had decided to go back to Megan's apartment for a nightcap, completely unaware that what would happen next would severely alter the courses of all their lives.

Chapter 27

Joey Morrisey was having more fun than he'd had in a while. He was finally getting to release some of the tension that had been building inside him over the course of the last couple of weeks. He ran his buck knife through a cute little black number that would have looked better on him than it did on its owner. His vivid imagination allowed him to visualize a body inside it as he sliced it from hem to bodice. The two bitches that lived here deserved whatever they got parading around in their women's bodies and so contemptuous of people like himself. It was true that only one was a blond, but that made both of them acceptable targets. He'd seen the blond on several occasions at the Mirror Image, but couldn't decide if she was gay or not. Not that that really made any difference to him. He would have preferred what's-her-name from the office, but being the slutty bitch that she was, she'd been home with her boyfriend. These two should be out for the whole evening with any kind of luck at all, but he'd left the back door open just in case he had to make a quick getaway. He almost hoped someone would see him sneaking out and chuckled quietly to himself over the description the police would get.

"Oh yes, officer, it was a tall blond in a short black dress. I'm sure of that."

He crept back in the bedroom, using his small penlight. He'd already scrawled "Whore" on the wall in lipstick and urinated on the bedspread for a second time. It was time to collect his prizes for the evening, some panties and a couple of bras, and head back home where he could parade around in his new treasures in peace. It was at this point that he heard the muffled but distinct sound of a key being inserted in the front door. "Shit, they're home earlier than I thought."

Gathering himself together, Joey made a rapid but soundless beeline for the back door ready to slink off into the night after a job well done. He no sooner got the door fully open before he found himself face-to-face with a pretty brunette who was standing just outside the back door.

Before he had time to think she'd sprayed his face with the tiny canister she was holding.

"Oh my God, my God!" As his eyes streamed, and he could hardly catch his breath, she launched herself at him with a vicious kick to the groin. Joey fell to the floor, his knife spinning from his hand, positive that he'd never recover from this acute pain. He didn't know whether he should clutch his groin or try desperately to wipe his streaming eyes. The pain in both areas made him want to scream.

"Stay completely still and don't give me any problems. I'll spray you again if I have to."

"Casey, are you okay?" came from behind him. It was another woman.

"Yeah, I'm okay."

"I've called 911. Let's bring her in the bedroom and watch her."

Joey glimpsed the buck knife being picked up and found himself nearly paralyzed with fear. He'd never expected it to end like this.

Casey had been doing the best she could to cheer Megan up on the ride back to her apartment. It had put a damper on the evening when Marla had been called away to deal with some of her tourists who were having a problem on River Street, but Casey managed to put a smile on Megan's face several times before they pulled into the driveway of her apartment building and headed for their promised nightcap. Casey was the first one to spot the tiny ray of light bobbing up and down in the bedroom.

"Megan, what the hell is that light in there? Do you think Marla's home already?"

"I doubt it. If Marla were in there, she'd have all the lights on. I don't have any idea what on earth that's all about."

"Megan, give me a couple of minutes, then open the front door. I'm going to circle around to the back."

"No way, Case. We're going to call the police and let them handle it. We don't have any idea who might be in there, and if they're stealing something, it's all replaceable."

"No need to be a victim, Megs. I've got my little friend with me. Whoever is in there could be long gone by the time the cops arrive." With that, Casey scurried away in the direction of Megan's back door, reaching into her purse as she left.

"You're crazy. What the hell are you doing?" But Megan was talking to herself. She dialed 911 on her cell phone and then entered the apartment to catch the strange sight of a tall blond lying in a fetal position clutching her groin, her face streaming with tears.

"Casey, are you all right?"

"Yeah, I'm fine; grab her knife and then call the police so we can have our friend here picked up."

"I did already; just hold onto her."

"Oh, she's going to do just fine - aren't you, sweetheart? Have a seat on the bed and this will all be over in just a few minutes. Who are you anyway, and what the hell were you doing in here?"

Joey disconsolately sat on the bed without speaking. It was bad enough he was going to have to talk to the cops. He had the deep-seated feeling that all this wasn't going to go over very well at the bank.

Chapter 28

Sunday was supposed to be Jack's day off, but he'd gotten a call from an excited Adam that he felt he couldn't possibly ignore, even though it was only 6:30 in the morning.

"Jack, they've got him."

"Got who? What are you talking about?"

"They've got him - the guy that's been doing the break-ins and writing graffiti - you know, the nuisance calls you've been working on."

"Oh, yeah? How'd they catch him?"

"They caught him last night in Megan's apartment."

"Oh my God. Is she okay? Boy, that woman attracts trouble!"

"Yeah she's fine. Casey was with her. But guess what?"

"What? Cut out the guessing games and tell me what's going on."

"It was a guy in drag, blond wig and all."

"You've got to be kidding. Did you put forensics on a fiber check?"

"I've got a call in. They should be showing up any minute."

"Did you get the name of the joker?"

"Yeah, his name is Joseph Morrisey, but he calls himself Joey. He works for one of the local banks. God, they're gonna love this."

"Where is he at the moment?"

"They've got him in the tank downstairs. I thought I'd wait until you got here, and we could ask our boy a few questions - like, what have you got against women, Joey? And, have you killed any in the recent past?"

"I'm on my way, buddy. I'll be there in just a few minutes. I don't believe it, Megan's apartment. I was just speaking to her last night. That woman always seems to be in the thick of things. How great that we finally got a break. How'd they catch this guy?"

"He was doing the apartment, even had three pairs of panties and a couple of bras packed away as souvenirs, when Megan and Casey got home. Megan went in the front door while Casey went in the back and caught Mr. Morrisey right in the middle. Joey says Casey Forbes sprayed him with mace, but there was no sign of it when the uniforms showed up. She said all she did was kick him with one of the new judo moves she's been practicing."

"You know where I met Megan and Casey last night? The Mirror Image."

"The Mirror Image? What the hell were you doing there?"

"I still think our killer is involved in the gay world somehow, and I was hanging around hoping to pick something up. Seems they were, too. They had this crazy notion they might recognize someone from the night Catherine was attacked. Could be I was right if this transvestite turns out to be the one connected to the needle murders. Let me get off the phone so I can get down there, and we can start grilling our boy. See you in a few minutes."

Adam was having difficulty controlling his excitement as he sat in Interview Room 2A at the Savannah Police Department waiting for the arrival of Joey Morrisey. His feelings at this point were ambivalent. His hopes were clamoring for this to be his murder suspect, but in the common sense part of his brain, logic was trying to tell him that nuisance crimes and murder were not normally compatible within someone who was a killer. Still, it was the best thing he had to go on to date.

A tall, pale figure appeared in the doorway with Jack's hand firmly attached to his elbow.

"Christ, he's just a kid."

The young man in question was about six-foot tall with neatly trimmed brown hair and soft brown eyes. He looked like he'd been crying. His face was as smooth as a baby's behind, and he was probably quite attractive when he wasn't as pale as a ghost as he was now. He was shaking and probably terrified - some murder suspect.

"Have a seat, Mr. Morrisey. I assume you've been read your rights; is that correct?"

"Yes, sir."

"My name is Carter and the man next to you is Detective Malloy. Do you want a lawyer present before we talk?"

"No, sir."

"Okay, then, Mr. Morrissey. Just sit down and tell us what this is all about."

"Could I have some water, please?"

"Sure. Jack, could you get a uniform to bring Mr. Morrisey some water please? Is there anything else you want, Joey, coffee, cigarette?"

"No, just some water."

"Okay. Now, we're going to record the interview, do you understand?"

"Yes, sir."

"Fine. Let's start by you telling us what you were doing in the apartment where the police arrested you."

"I wasn't doing anything. I just went in to take a look around."

"Right, and while you were there, you decided to help yourself to some underwear. Why's that, Joey?"

"Okay, so I'm a cross-dresser. What's the big deal? I didn't hurt anybody."

"The big deal, Joey, is that we have you for breaking and entering, destruction of private property, and theft, to name a few. Shall I go on?"

Joey remained silent; his eyes fixed on the scarred metal table in front of him, and slowly swung his head back and forth.

"Do you know what forensics is, Joey? Forensics is where we match things like fingerprints or fibers to place a suspect at the scene of a crime. Do you know that within an hour or so my partner Jack here will have a warrant to search your place and take samples of whatever he wants to, plus search for items that might place you at the scene of other crimes we're investigating?"

Joey remained silent as two little tears worked their way down his cheeks, hung suspended on his jaw for a fraction of a second, then quietly plopped onto the table.

"Adam, why don't you leave me alone for a couple of minutes with this little shit? I'll get some answers out of him."

"Ease up, Jack. I'm sure Joey will want to be straight with us; isn't that right?"

"Okay, I'll admit to breaking into a couple of places and taking some lingerie, but I still didn't hurt anybody."

"Is that so? We've had a couple of murders of young blonds recently here in Savannah. You wouldn't know anything about that, would you, Joey?"

This question brought Joey's head up with a startled jerk. Now he looked like an animal caught in the headlights of a fast-moving car.

"Murder! Shit, I don't know anything about any murders."

"Remember what I said about the forensics, Joey. You sure you don't want to make it easy on yourself?"

"I swear I don't know anything at all about those murders. I swear it. Now I think I want a lawyer."

"Adam, please let me have some time alone with this turd."

"It's okay, Jack. If Joey doesn't want to talk to us, we'll just wait for his lawyer to show up. You're going to tell us what we want to know sooner or later, aren't you, Joey?"

"Jesus Christ! Yes, I did do the break-ins, and I did steal some underwear, and I even wrote some graffiti, but murder - never. No way, detective. Please. I'm innocent of hurting anyone. You've got to believe me, please."

"Jack, can I see you outside for a second."

The two detectives watched the shaking, frightened form of Joey Morrisey through the two-way glass and turned to face each other.

"He isn't the one, Jack."

"I'm afraid you're right. Damn! I really had my hopes up there for a minute."

"Well, get him booked on what we've got. He'll probably make bail on this, so make sure somebody's assigned to stick to him like glue. I don't want him making a single move we don't know about."

"Okay, but shit, it's right back to square one, isn't it?"

"Afraid so, partner, for right now. I'm going over to see Catherine and maybe catch a football game."

"Right."

Several days had passed. Marla had listened to Megan's tale of adventure with incredulity. A break-in had occurred right in their own apartment, and Megan had taken a part in apprehending the criminal. Marla couldn't believe it.

"God, I wish I could have seen the look on his face when he went out the back door and ran into Casey and that famous mace of hers. He must have shit in his pants."

"It was priceless. Of course, at that point we didn't even realize it was a he. He looked so good I thought he was a woman right up until the cops took his wig off. If we weren't together, I might have been interested. The only thing I don't understand is why he took three pairs of your panties and none of mine."

"Elementary, my dear Watson; I've got prettier underwear than you."

"Yeah, but he preferred my dresses. The bastard cut up three of my best ones, and you didn't lose a thing."

"Oh, yes I did. How about the bedspread I bought only last month? He pissed all over it. You didn't think I was going to keep it after that, did you? Plus, who'll wind up repainting the walls? Me, that's who! "

"Okay, I give in; all in all I guess we got away pretty lucky. What if he'd been the person who was committing those murders, and one of us had been home alone?"

"I don't even want to think about that."

What's your schedule these days, Marla? You are going to be able to come with me this week-end, aren't you?

"Sure."

"Don't forget we've got to pick up some stuff before Sunday night for Patricia's girls' night out."

"I'll let you take care of that, Megs, if you don't mind. I've got several incredibly busy days ahead of me."

"Okay, but only because I feel sorry about your bedspread. I should have gotten home a little earlier."

"So should I; I'm sorry about the Spanish tourists thing. I should have been with you. I would probably have beaten the shit out of the creep."

"Forget it, Marla. He wasn't really worth an assault charge. I'll give you first crack at the next one that breaks in here."

"You're all heart, Megs. Let's go get something to eat; crime makes me ravenous."

Chapter 29

There is a question that comes up every once in a while at parties or social gatherings or, even more rarely, on TV drama shows. "If you could know the exact time of your death, would you want to?" Elizabeth Snow didn't want to but knew she was facing it.

It was cold and she was naked. She should have been freezing to death, but she was sweating. Thin lines of spittle worked their way from the bottom of her gag and pooled on her chin. She was trying very hard to scream, but she couldn't. She was trying very hard to move her hands and feet as well, but she couldn't do that either. Her arms were pulled high over her head, making her shoulders a taut, knotted bundle of pain. Her legs were spread, and each of her feet was tied to something she couldn't see.

Unfortunately for her, she could see where she was being held, and it terrified her. It was old, musty and smelled like something had gone bad and been left to rot, of urine and a thousand other nightmarish things. It might have once been someone's bedroom, maybe even a pretty bedroom, but now it looked like nothing more than a death chamber. The remnants of what had once been patterned wallpaper lay in torn ragged brown patches on the walls and on the floor. The two windows she could see were boarded over from the outside, and if there had ever been curtains hanging there, they were long gone now. The floor was covered in dirt and debris and probably rats not only lived in this hellhole, but they undoubtedly thrived in it.

Elizabeth's wide-spread, horror-filled blue eyes were not occupied with the depressing nature of the room she was now held captive in, but more by the solitary figure squatting against the far wall. The only feature she could make out clearly was the blond hair beneath the hood; the rest of whoever had brought her to this agonized situation was hidden in the gloom that pervaded the atmosphere of the small room.

She only vaguely remembered what had happened to her. She'd been at the Mirror Image for a couple of drinks and a little dancing. She'd started to feel light-headed and a bit sick to her stomach, so she'd left to return to her car and go home. Putting the key in the car door to unlock it was the last conscious thought she'd had. And now this.

Her lone dark-hooded captor wasn't moving a muscle, not saying a word, simply sitting there on its haunches, back against the wall, playing music that drifted softly across the intervening space and forced its way into Elizabeth's unresponsive ears. It was a piano, playing songs in a rhythm that was unfamiliar to her nineteen-year-old mind. Things like this just weren't supposed to happen to a person like her on a Friday night, when she'd been having such a good time. She'd always believed that things like dying happened to people who were old and on a Monday or a Tuesday at 4:00 in the morning when there wasn't anything else to do. She twisted her body in a vain attempt to release herself from her bonds, but accomplished nothing other than to make the pain emanating from her shoulders worse.

The figure against the wall rose and moved in her direction. It was carrying something in its right hand that looked like a large needle. It stopped a few inches from Elizabeth's face, and she found herself staring into two dark brown pools of liquid hate through the mask the figure wore. She had never faced eyes like that before in her young life. The mouth said nothing, but the eyes spoke volumes. There was almost tangible hatred glowing like unearthly coals from those two eyes watching her as calmly as a cat about to destroy a bird. How could any human being be doing to her what this one was? She or he was tall enough to reach up to where Elizabeth's hands were tied and release them, allowing them to fall down behind her back. The relief Elizabeth enjoyed was short-lived; one strong arm pushed her to the ground with ease, where she lay trying to collect herself and whimpering quietly. The arms were yanked out from behind her back and pulled over her head again, but this time in a prone position. The tall silent figure retied her feet, so that her legs were spread, leaving her naked on her back and completely exposed to whatever cruelty this strange being chose to inflict. It wasn't very long before she began to know the full extent of what her fate was going to be as she felt the insertion of a needle into her armpit. It was fortunate for Elizabeth, who had always been a rather timid soul that she passed out before the last stage of the ritual began. She never would have understood why she was being washed and dried from head to foot, and her last cogent thought was of what the rats would do to her.

The ladies' night out had been a great success so far. The six women involved had chosen Semolina's Italian restaurant for their Saturday evening meal and then headed to Patricia's house to get the party going in full swing, all the while swapping tales of the week past and catching up on each other's gossip. Since five of the group worked at Carter University, they were familiar with what each other did and amused one another with horror stories of students' behaviors that bridged the gamut from the surreal to the ridiculous. Only Marla worked outside the college, and she was amusingly relating the story of how she'd been kept up until three in the morning on the previous evening by a bunch of British tourists who were visiting Savannah and had managed to make themselves sick by overeating seafood. The only one that wasn't laughing was Megan, unhappy about having had to spend another Friday night alone.

When they arrived at Patricia's, the entire group was ready for fun and games, which included a drink or two. Patricia's house was a lovely modern one story with three bedrooms, a large patio with a Jacuzzi tub and numerous planters filled with pansies. The living room, where the group was now sitting, was traditionally furnished in blues and creams, with two comfortable sofas and four large floor cushions on the highly polished hardwood floor. Numerous ornaments from Patricia's travels overseas acted as conversation pieces and two hand-sewn quilts hung on the walls. Patricia's husband, Harold, was in the National Guard and away for the weekend, so the only voices that would be heard would be those of the higher pitched feminine variety.

"Let's play Therapy," Sharon suggested.

"Goodness, I'd have thought you counselors would have had enough of that kind of thing at work," answered Casey.

"Yeah, well, this is kinda different. We just want to know all about your inhibitions and sex life, Case." Laughed Catherine.

"Okay, I'll play. Let me just get myself a hefty slug of rum and coke. I feel a need to get a little tipsy if you're going to discover the real, utterly debauched me."

As the game got under way, Casey looked around at all of her close friends. They all seemed relaxed and happy except for Megan and Marla who kept darting each other glances whenever the questions became personal. Casey suddenly felt Catherine's eyes on hers and realized that she had been staring rather obviously at Megan. She gave Catherine a quick grin and was rewarded by her raising her eyebrows interrogatively.

"Hey, Megan, you going to sleep there? It's your turn." Patricia's voice broke into her daydreaming.

"Oh sorry, let me see. Eight. Where does that put me? Oh rats, on a group therapy. That's all I need, having you all dissect my character! Who's reading the questions? Marla?"

"Okay, Megan, 'In a committed relationship how important is total honesty? A) essential, B) important but some white lies are acceptable, C) not really important.'"

"Oh, good question. I'm sure my marriage has lasted twenty-five years just because Harold and I have absolutely no secrets from each other," exclaimed Patricia.

"Maybe you're right. I knew Hank was a lying bastard which is why I divorced him," said Catherine.

"Okay, Megs, it's your question, so what do you say?" smiled Casey.

Megan looked hard at Marla. "Did you deliberately pick that question? No, I guess you couldn't do that. But isn't it appropriate! I'll say 'C' because my past is nobody's business but my own, and I certainly won't be pressured into telling all just for the sake of a game." Megan got up abruptly and stormed out into the yard.

"Wow, what was all that about?" Sharon asked, staring at Marla. "You two had a fight or something?"

"Not really, but I think I'd better go and see what's upsetting her. Sorry about that." Marla went out of the house and the other women looked at each other.

"Guess the game's over. Think I'll turn in with a book," muttered Casey. "Did you put us in our usual rooms, Trisha?"

"Yeah."

"Okay, good idea. Night all." Catherine followed in Casey's direction.

In the garden Megan sat on a bench facing the fountain. As Marla sat down beside her, she turned and said, "Guess I shouldn't have gone off the deep end. Did I upset everyone?"

"No, not really, but I guess no one's seen you lose your cool like that before. What's going on, Megs? We've been snipping at each other for weeks now. If you have some dark secret in your past that you don't want to tell me, fair enough. Or is it that you're angry about my job? You know if you want me to bare my soul about my dreadful childhood, I'll tell you. The reason I've never told you before is because I've made a huge effort to put the past behind me. I just don't like talking about it, but maybe it's time if our relationship is to continue."

"Yeah, you're right. I know I've been a bitch lately. I'm not sure what's been getting into me." Megan put her arm around Marla. "Tell me your tale of woe, hon, and I'll tell you mine. Maybe that'll work."

"The reason my name's Marla is because my grandmother was German. She left Germany at the end of the war. I think she married a serviceman, but he was never on the scene and there were no photos of him. I guess he left soon after my mother was born in 1950. My mother was terrified of Nana. She made the mistake of getting pregnant in high school with me and was never allowed to forget that she was a slut who didn't even have a high school diploma.

"My childhood was a living hell. There's no other way to put it. Nana was a compulsive cleaner. I can hear her now 'Cleanliness is next to Godliness,' she'd tell me about ten times a day. She'd make me wash my hands over and over again. And way into my teens, she'd come into the bathroom when I was in the shower or tub and take a washcloth and wash my face and neck really roughly. She'd mutter things about washing my private parts and never letting any dirty boys touch me there. When I was little, I had no idea what she was talking about.

"My mother, the stupid coward that she was, would just pretend that all the raised voices she heard in the bathroom weren't happening. I suppose she didn't see much harm in what Nana did, but God, I felt so dirty. I couldn't wait to leave home, and the minute I graduated from high school, I was out of there. I did try dating men, but the only relationship I had with a guy at university was a total loss, and he told me I was a frigid weirdo. Is that enough of my history, or do you want more details?"

"Oh Marla, I'm sorry to have made you bring all that up. It really is horrific how events in our childhoods affect us so much and for so long. I've only ever told some of my past to Casey and even with her, I never told her exactly what happened. If you don't mind, I think all that vodka I drank has made me feel really sleepy. Let's leave my grisly past for another time. I will say one thing: if you thought your childhood was bad, mine was equally so, but at least my parents are dead, so I never have to face them again." Megan walked slowly back into Patricia's house. It was sad that both she and Marla had bad memories. But was all of Marla's story true, or was it just something she'd made up to get some sympathy?

Adam sat with his feet propped up on his desk, absorbed in an interesting report that was the result of police work from several jurisdictions. It seemed that there was some connection between the man identified as Hans killed in the Publix parking lot and a corpse found in a trunk in Jacksonville, Florida. Both had apparently been using aliases, and a joint effort was being made to determine their true identities. To make matters more difficult, it appeared both were involved in the theft of two paintings and the assault on Greg Burke in Statesboro, Georgia.

Adam flipped the file onto his desk in the one clear space that remained there and popped a piece of Nicorette gum in his mouth. This stuff was all very interesting, but it didn't have anything to do with him or his cases. The discordant sound of the telephone broke into his thoughts. A call was coming in on an interdepartmental line, never a good omen.

"Hello, Carter here."

"Adam, this is O'Rourke, down at the desk; you've got another one."

"Oh shit - where?"

"An abandoned building, 1145 Barnard Street. Some kids found a body there this morning, a young blond nude female with no apparent wounds. There are two uniforms on the scene; you want me to send for the rest of the violent crimes crew?"

"Yes, please."

"Got it. How about Jack?"

"I'll call him, thanks, Mike."

"No problem. Good luck."

This was going to be another terrific day, no doubt about it. Adam had already spilled half a cup of coffee on the suit he'd just had dry-cleaned and concluded that life was shit; the only difference was the degree of depth of it you were stuck in. After making his call to Jack, Adam took enough time to make just one more.

"Mike, Adam again."

"Yeah?"

"Put out an all points on Joey Morrisey. I want him in here and as soon as possible."

"Gotcha. I'm on it."

Chapter 30

As Adam watched the scene-of-the-crime technicians working swiftly over and around the body of the latest young victim, he couldn't help but think to himself what a lousy place this was to die in. The similarity to the murder of Jessica Stillwell frightened him. It was pretty obvious why the perp liked these abandoned buildings, but the fact that the animals always seemed to get to the corpse first made him feel more than a little queasy. Even the gum he was chewing did little to mask the odor of death. He was grateful for the fact that the early November weather was cooler. If this were August, the decomposition would have been infinitely worse.

"What's the deal on the time of death?"

"According to the state of rigor I'd say late Friday night or early Saturday morning."

"Anything useful on bruising?"

"She's got ligatures on her wrists and ankles, but other than that, nothing obvious. She was on her back when she died, but the rope marks tell me she may have been vertical for a while before the perp tied her down and finished her off on the floor."

"Did you find any needle marks?"

"Looks like there may be one in her armpit like the others, but I'll need to get her back to work to make sure."

"Shit, I was afraid it was a needle again. How long before you can tell me what got pumped into her?"

"Not very long, now that we know what to look for."

"Has forensics got anything?"

"Yeah, they've got a couple of fibers, no prints yet, unfortunately. There's an interesting faint outline near the wall over there that suggests the perp had something with him that he put down on the floor, it's about 6" x 10". We've also got some footprints this time; this guy's got small feet - can't be more than an 8-1/2 sneaker. I would have thought he'd have bigger feet, don't know why."

"Could it be a woman's footprint, Mike?"

"Yeah, now that you mention it, it could be. We're getting some casts to take back to the lab; maybe that will tell us something. Where's Jack?"

"He's interviewing the three little kids who found her. Christ, they'll be having nightmares for months."

"Join the crowd. This thing is giving us all nightmares."

Adam immediately thought of Catherine. Although he loved her dearly, her independence really troubled him. And now there was another victim. He shivered. He was positive that whoever had hit Catherine was the same perp. He might not have any positive proof, but his years in police work told him he was right. Thank God Catherine was all right.

"How much longer, Jack, before we've got this thing cleaned up?"

"A few more minutes. The forensics guys are about done, and the ME's about ready to move the body. You want me to start checking the neighborhood to see if anybody saw anything?"

"Good idea. We might as well get started. You do that, and I'll go back to the station to start filling out the paperwork. I get the distinct feeling I just may have a call from Captain Barton waiting for me. "

"Maybe even the Chief, Adam. The brass isn't gonna like this much."

"Don't I know it? Check in with me if you get anything."

"You got it, partner. I'll talk to you later."

"Okay, Jack, I'll see you later. Good luck."

Adam considered calling in a profiler from the FBI as he slogged his way through the water-soaked, garbage-filled lot on the way back to his car. At the very least it might help to take some of the pressure off.

"Christ, the newspapers are gonna have a field day with this."

Adam was more accurate than his worst fears would have allowed. The front page banner on Savannah's major paper proclaimed the grizzly news to the world on the following morning: "THIRD YOUNG WOMAN FOUND MURDERED - Police have not yet released cause of death." That and an unsubstantiated report that CNN might be sending a reporter to Savannah was all that Adam needed to make his year.

Casey was on the telephone to Catherine. "Catherine, I still can't get Megan out of my head. You remember I told you about her little outburst at the club, and you saw her reaction during the game we were playing at Patricia's house on Sunday. I can't seem to get it off my mind. If you were me, what would you do? "

"Casey, you've known Megan quite a while now. What exactly are you worried about?"

"I don't know. It's just this weird feeling I have that won't go away. I know you said on Saturday that I needn't worry, that fights between couples weren't necessarily a bad thing, but I'm still bothered. Do you remember my telling you that Marla had picked up a little cat they called Pussy?"

"I don't recall; you might have."

"Well, it seems that Pussy turned up dead, and Megan didn't seem that upset by it. Now, I know that it was Marla's pet, but wouldn't you have thought she'd be just a little upset? I'd be devastated if Tarka died. I even offered to bury it for her, but she turned me down. She said she'd already disposed of it."

"Casey, some people are animal lovers and some aren't. Although there have been links made between adult sociopaths and their cruelty to animals in their childhood, I don't see Megan like that at all. Maybe she just didn't particularly like the cat. After all, from what she's said, Marla is away a lot, and so the cat care fell on her. Perhaps she just felt she was being taken advantage of.

"I know you're right. I wish I could shake this stupid feeling I have about both her and Marla. For God's sake, Megan's my dearest friend; what the hell am I thinking?"

"Casey, I'm sure you'll feel a lot better when the murders have been solved. I think we all will. This too will pass my dear, but for tonight, would you like me to come over and we can watch a stupid movie and eat popcorn?"

"That's sweet of you, but I'll be fine. I think I'll just cuddle up with Tarka and have an early night."

Adam was precisely correct. All hell had, in fact, broken loose. Information had been leaked to the press that all three girls had died as a result of being injected with drugs, but so far they had been lucky enough to keep secret the fact that insulin had been used. How much longer it would remain a secret was anybody's guess. The chief was catching hell from the mayor; the captain was catching hell from the chief, and Adam was catching hell from everybody. Worse than that, it was coming up on another Friday. What if this nut struck again? Bringing Joey Morrisey in again hadn't been any help either. The fibers they'd found didn't match anything they'd been able to find in his apartment, and he wore a size 10-1/2 shoe. Adam was reluctantly forced to release him. He decided to check the web site and learn more from the autopsy. Nothing. He called Jack.

"Hi, Jack, it's Adam; got anything new for me on the Elizabeth Snow murder?"

"Sorry, pal, you were lucky we were able to ID her for you as fast as we did. We're working with fibers we found at the scene, however, and it looks like they'll probably match those we found at the other two scenes."

"I just keep hoping something will crop up that we missed. We were able to find a couple of people she was with at the Mirror Image, but that's a dead end too. Nobody saw a thing. There were two or three tall blonds in the place, but what the hell am I supposed to do with that - arrest every tall blond woman in Savannah?"

"If you find the one you're after, can I have the leftovers? I've always had this thing for tall blonds."

"Jack, you're a prince. Keep in touch. Maybe something will crop up."

"I hope so for our sake; this is getting very nasty."

"You're not telling me anything I don't already know, pal. See ya."

Adam walked into Greg Burke's restoration studio to find Greg and Des busy at what they both were fondest of doing. Greg had his feet up on his wastebasket smoking a cigarette and Des was unwrapping a Hershy's kiss and talking about what she wanted for lunch.

"Hi, guys, I thought I'd drop by and see how you two were doing after the exciting events of the last couple of weeks. Greg, you look like you've healed up pretty well."

"Yeah, I'm doing fine."

"How about you, Des? Hit anybody in the head with a two-by-four lately?"

"Nah, but I have considered hittin' Greg on the head with a hammer if he don't get his butt into gear so we can get somethin' to eat."

"If nothing else, Des, you're predictable. I hear from the guys in robbery that they've got the thing with the paintings pretty well straightened out. Seems like they're worth a pile of money."

"I'll say," Greg sighed. "It's just a shame that Ben had to lose them like that."

"I heard they were his. At first we all thought they belonged to you."

"We tried to keep Ben out of it until we were sure Mildred was home safe and sound. After that we were able to tell the real story. Any word on the old German guy that got away or the one that got shot?"

"We think we're getting closer to an identification, but I can't tell you anything quite yet."

"How are those murder cases you're working on? Are you making any progress?"

Adam looked at Greg. "Unfortunately not a hell of a lot, I'm afraid. About all we've got going for us is that we think a tall blond may be involved, but we're not even positive of that. I might even suspect you, Des, but you're way too short. You don't own a blond wig and shoes with eight inch heels, do you?"

"No, but I think Greg does." Des busied herself by opening another chocolate while Greg idly flipped through the latest group of photos he'd just had developed.

"Ah well, it was just a thought. You know loads of people though, Des. Do you know any murderous tall blonds?"

"Well, most of the people at the Waffle House aren't very tall. The only big women I know are Marla and Megan."

"Shit, Des, they're friends of ours. They wouldn't be involved in murder. Next thing you'll be saying Casey in a blond wig."

"Well, Adam said tall blonds. Megan's naturally blond and I know she's got a wig because she came to that party we all went to in one."

"Sorry, Des, I can't believe either of them would do anything illegal much less murder. Try finding another candidate."

"How about that clown at the bank. Joey what's his name? He's always callin' us about information about art, and he sure as hell qualifies as a tall blond. Anyway, are you looking for a male or a female, Adam?"

"We're not sure at this point. But who's this guy you're talking about, Des?"

"This strange guy at First Savannah Bank. He does valuations on art for estates the bank has control of. I think he's weird enough to be involved in anythin'. He's a bit creepy, like Stewart Douglas was."

Adam remembered the business with the Douglas Funeral Home and immediately said, "No one could be as weird as Stewart, surely."

"True, but I just plain don't like him."

Adam turned to Des again, "What's this Joey's last name? We had a run in with a Joey."

"Joey Morrisey."

Adam chuckled and began to tell Greg and Des the sorry story of Joey.

When he'd finished, Des shook her head laughing. "Good old Casey, she's just like me."

"So those are the only tall blonds you know? Doesn't seem like a lot," asked Adam.

"We did have a new blond customer last month with a painting she wanted appraised. She was a real looker. Do you remember what her name was, Des?"

"Nope, all I can think of was that she said she worked in Savannah and had a day off to get up here with her paintin'."

"Was it worth anything?" Adam asked.

"Oh yeah, it was a really fine piece."

"She say where she got it?"

"Nope, and I didn't ask. If I'd known about the tall blond thing, I'd have asked her about her murderous tendencies." Greg laughed. "But maybe your tall blond doesn't come from Savannah. What about all the blonds in Statesboro? "

"Wait, I'm sure she said she worked for the City of Savannah. Does that help?"

"Sure, that narrows it down to a few thousand."

"Greg, if you'd spent half as much time concentratin' on what she was sayin' as opposed to what her butt looked like, maybe we'd have been able to help Adam solve his murders."

"And if you spent half as much of your time restoring paintings as you do thinking about eating and sleeping, I'd be a rich man, so what's your point?"

"Ah, I can see things are totally back to normal. If either of you do happen to remember her name just give me a call. You just never know."

"Sure will. Thanks for stopping by."

"Good to see you two. I'll catch you at the Waffle House one of these days."

The tall blond looked around the motel room she'd learned to loathe for what she hoped would be one of the very last times that it would be necessary. Her flight to Paris was booked for 11:00 Saturday morning, the last day of her rental on the room. She'd made arrangements to get rid of the artwork in her possession for about half of its actual worth at auction, but that still amounted to over $5,000,000. With that in hand, plus the $1,000,000 bank note she already had, she could be in

Switzerland by Monday morning opening an account that would support her in luxury for the rest of her life. All that remained was the wrapping up of a few little details, and her life in the Southern United States would be completed. She was now ready to become a woman of the world. It had taken a while, but it had been worth everything she'd had to do and more. It was the last time she'd be forced to wear that stupid blond wig and the last time she'd have to play nursemaid to a bunch of idiot unthankful tourists.

She took the package that she'd taken from David Rothschild out of the safe. She hadn't had the time to examine it till now so she couldn't resist a last peek before she let the paintings go. The second she looked closely at them, she knew something was drastically wrong. They were smudged. That was not possible; they hadn't seen daylight since she'd stolen them. What could have possibly happened while they were hidden away in the room safe? She picked them up with an emotion that was a combination of bewilderment and horror. She turned the Pissaro slowly in her hands and felt her heart constrict. These pieces weren't oils, and they weren't even very good copies of oils. They were clever copies to be sure but not the originals she'd thought she had.

"Oh my God, the pastels."

Marla opened the briefcase with trembling hands and unwrapped the three pastels. They were also nothing more than old prints with little similarity to what she'd once had in her possession. She'd been taken again.

Even though she already knew what she'd find when she looked at the $1,000,000 bank draft, there was no way to avoid checking it. In her mind she knew what it was going to tell her; "Void - For Demonstration Purposes Only."

That nasty little son of a bitch had been ready for her and he'd conned her one last time. Why hadn't she examined the contents of the package and the briefcase thoroughly in his hotel room? Because she'd been too sure of herself that was why.

"You stupid cow, you let it all get away from you."

Who knew where he was now. It was too late to try to find him again at this point. Marla dejectedly put the wig, the paintings and the briefcase under her arm and headed for the door. She'd toss the lot in a trash bin on her way out.

Now what was she going to do? Go back to her dreadful job? And what about Megan? That relationship was definitely on the skids.

179

Chapter 31

Casey had had a rough week. She'd spent every lunch hour trying to talk to Megan about what she felt inside, but Megan had been busy and appeared to be avoiding her. Casey knew that she was having troubles with Marla, but was there something more? When Jack had mentioned the blond wig, she had noticed that Megan had gone very still and quiet. What was going on?

Maybe she was the one that needed the counseling. The one thing she was sure of was that sooner or later she was going to have to face Megan with her feelings. Holding everything inside was getting harder and harder to do. Either they'd both have a great laugh over it, or Megan would wind up hating her, but no matter what happened, Casey knew she had to clear the air with Megan if they were ever going to be able to maintain their closeness. By Friday morning she made her decision. She knew Marla was away for the weekend, and it was now or never. She'd drive over to Megan's apartment tonight with a bottle of wine, and they'd let it all hang out. With her decision made, Casey spent the rest of her afternoon in nervous anticipation of what the evening might bring.

Jack pushed the remains of his chicken in honey sauce around the little black dish he'd heated it up in. It was one of those delicious Healthy Choice things he'd been trying to force himself to eat for the last few nights. He'd been working out in the police gym, much to the amusement of the ever laid back Adam and was determined to lose a couple of pounds and get rid of the small paunch he'd put on recently. However, he hadn't yet lost the five pounds he wanted to in the week he'd been on his new regime, and the idea of doing all this healthy stuff long term filled him with gloom. He tossed the remainder of the chicken in the trash and dug out from a cabinet drawer a couple of Twinkies that he always kept on hand for occasions like this.

Maybe I should get a pet.

He checked the TV guide one more time, but nothing new had been added.

He decided to drive around downtown to check out some of the clubs, but as he drove near Megan's apartment, it occurred to him to stop in and see her. He was positive she knew something, but she obviously wasn't telling. Maybe an informal visit and a cup of coffee might give him the answers he wanted. If she wasn't in, he could always take one more shot at finding Sylvia. After all, it was only 9:00. The night was young.

As Casey wound her way through the narrow streets of Savannah, wine bottle safely tucked in the passenger seat, she began to wonder if this was all a big mistake. She knew that Megan was aware that something was going on between them and was probably as eager as she was to get it out in the open. She herself was apprehensive but felt the long-term close friendship between them was worth saving under any circumstances. Casey pulled her yellow VW Beetle into the parking lot next to Megan's blue Cavalier and worked her way around to the front door of the apartment with her heart in her mouth.

"Screw up your courage, girl. This is your very best friend you're visiting. Everything will be okay if you just keep in mind how much you've been through together and how important she is to you. There's nothing she could have done that would make you love her any less," she muttered.

Casey knocked at the front door and waited for Megan to open it. Several minutes went by and nothing happened. This struck her as a little odd. She knew Megan was expecting her. Where could she be? Casey gave it a couple more minutes, then tentatively turned the handle. The door was unlocked and that too seemed a little strange with all the apprehension generated by the latest killing in Savannah. What could Megan be thinking? She pushed the door open and cautiously stepped into the small foyer.

"Megan, Megan, it's me Casey. Where are you?"

There was no reply as Casey gingerly worked her way into the dimly lit living room. There she was sprawled on the couch, apparently asleep.

"Megan, it's Casey. Are you asleep?" Still no sign of recognition. Casey began to feel an eerie sensation of fear work its way up her spine, and she held her bag containing the mace closer to her body. What in the hell was going on here?

Casey moved to the side of the couch as quietly as she could and put one hand against her friend's throat. There was a good solid pulse there, so why was she sleeping so soundly? She gave Megan's shoulders a little push in an attempt to wake her.

"Megan, wake up."

"Hi, Casey, so nice that you could join us."

Casey spun around, startled by the disembodied voice coming from the shadows at the far end of the room.

"Who? Er, it's Sylvia, isn't it? What are you doing here? What's wrong with Megan? I can't seem to wake her up."

"Not a thing, Casey. I just gave her a little something to help her sleep; she'll be fine in an hour or so."

It wasn't until Sylvia stepped further into the darkened living room that Casey noticed the automatic pistol she was holding in her right hand.

"Sylvia! What are you doing?"

"I'm just tying up some loose ends. It's a shame you had to butt in."

"What are you talking about?"

"You'll find out soon enough, but for right now, why don't you put your purse on the floor for me? We don't want to have any little accidents with anything you might have in there."

"This is crazy. What the hell are you playing at? And what have you done to Megan?

"I'm not playing at anything. It's just a shame you aren't a blond. I guess this nice wig will have to do."

"God in heaven! You're the one who's been committing the murders! Why, Sylvia, why?"

"It's a long story, Casey, and I hate to bore you with mundane details. I'm sorry that you have to be my last victim, but that's just the luck of the draw."

"What the hell are you talking about? Are you crazy?"

"Very possibly, but it's time for me to move to another part of the world and start over, but I really can't do that until I give the Savannah Police a suspect for their murders, can I?"

"There's no way you can get away with this. They're going to know it was you."

"Oh, I don't think so. By the time they get here, they're going to find Megan standing over your insulin-injected body with her fingerprints all over everything. I, of course, will be amazed when I hear of another corpse and the woman in the blond wig who did it. By the time they finish booking and processing Megan for your murder, I'll be long gone. The mickey I gave her will leave her groggy enough so that she won't even be sure whether she killed you or not. Pretty neat, huh?"

"Why us? What have we ever done to you?"

"Oh, you academics. Always looking for neat answers. Don't you know that none of this is personal? Put it down to my childhood, if it makes you feel better.

"Sylvia, if we can prove this all relates back to a brutal childhood, then a good defense attorney can probably get you off with a few years in a psychiatric hospital. You could get through this and you could enjoy a whole new life."

"Oh Casey, you are so naive; you have no idea what my life was like. Maybe you should have been around to help solve my problems when I was a kid. You might have done some good then, but now I'm afraid it's a little too late for all that."

Casey gulped. What on earth could she do to keep Sylvia's attention? "Tell me about your childhood, Sylvia. Maybe I can still help?"

"What? You want me to tell you? Okay, then, as they say in the children's books, 'Are you sitting comfortably? Then I'll begin.' I was nine, the apple of my father's eye despite the fact that I was a girl. After a series of miscarriages, my pretty blond mother, Jenny, was told that she couldn't have any more children and she and the colonel, my father, would just have to accept that my sister Jean, who was two, and I wouldn't be joined by a longed-for son. My father had probably realized this fact ages before but continued to go along with my mother's desire to have a son since this was the only way he could get her to go to bed with him."

Casey looked at Sylvia and quickly turned her head away. This was not the same woman she'd met at the Mirror Image. She didn't look like her and certainly didn't sound like her. She was happily telling her life story like it was a monologue in a drama. The whole situation seemed so rehearsed as if Sylvia had told the facts numerous times before. Yet all the while she was brandishing a gun at her. It was so weird. Casey found herself fascinated more than frightened. But all the time her mind was scurrying. How could she escape? Could she somehow knock the gun out of Sylvia's hand? She sat back in the chair. Let her ramble on. She'd think of something.

"My father was never a faithful man; according to one of my aunts, he'd eyed the bridesmaids at his wedding and seduced the au pair when my mother started to look ungainly around the seventh month of her first pregnancy. That child, a son who they christened Thomas after my grandfather, was stillborn. The shock and horror of losing a child after a problem free pregnancy changed my mother in ways that affected all of us. From being an easy going, bright, talkative woman, she became a silent, fearful, nervous person. I can remember her teasing my father out of his black moods when I was very young, but as I grew older, she seemed to cower beneath his rages. And like the big cat that he resembled, the more she appeared frightened of him, the more he terrorized her. It was as if he fed off her fear and her cringing ways."

Casey smiled encouragingly at Sylvia, thinking Sylvia certainly loved the sound of her own voice. She was clearly completely mad. But how should she react so that Sylvia didn't turn on her, didn't kill her?

Sylvia continued, seeming not to notice that Casey's eyes were darting all over the room. "It's funny, but I wasn't ever afraid of him. As I grew up, the rows between my parents grew more virulent and frequent. A part of me sympathized with my mother, but the other part just wanted to shake her and say, 'Just stand up to him. If you show him you're frightened of him, it only makes him more aggravated.'" Sylvia's voice hardened. She looked angrily at Casey. "My mother was such a stupid bitch and then she went and died." Her voice changed again, and Casey saw that she was deliberately reining in her anger. Her tone was silky as she continued. "But enough of me. Let's just get on with our game, Casey."

"But Sylvia, you haven't explained the killings to me. You said you would." Casey smiled tentatively at Sylvia; if she could just keep her talking and prevent her from losing total control, Megan might wake up, or she could think of some way to get the gun away from her.

"I don't have enough time to go into everything now. We've got to get on with our own game." Sylvia smiled in a gloating fashion, and Casey shuddered in horror. "See this lovely needle I have? By the time this is over, you'll have some idea of how bad pain can really be. Now, just do as I say and go into the bedroom and take your clothes off. If you make me put a bullet in your head, you're going to make me have to change my whole story. It'll still work, but it would be messier."

As Sylvia motioned in the direction of the bedroom with the deadly-looking weapon she held, Casey was astounded by the change that had come over her face. She was still a beautiful woman, but her expression had turned to stone. Instead of normal lively brown eyes, her eyes had become flat hard pools of hatred without humanity or mercy. The woman who stood in front of her now was lost to all reason, incapable of pity or any other human emotion, except for cold murderous rage. Casey had no alternative but to go into the bedroom and begin to remove her clothes. Sylvia was considerably taller than she was and probably a lot stronger. She frantically thought of her can of mace nearby, but so far away, in the living room.

Sylvia watched her strip without comment, waiting until she was completely naked, before telling her to lie down on the bedspread. Holding the revolver in her left hand, she bent to handcuff Casey's left hand to the headboard of the queen-sized oak bed.

Casey started to shake. Immediately her mind flashed back to her terrible ordeal at the hands of the McLeans. Sylvia couldn't rape her, but the violation and fear she was feeling was almost as bad as before. But as she looked into Sylvia's eyes, anger swept over Casey. There was no way she'd ever allow herself to be a victim again. She would fight for her life with what she had left, her brains and her words.

"Sylvia, there's still plenty of time to change this."

"If you don't shut the hell up, I'm going to have to gag you. Here, let me play some music for you. It's by Scott Joplin. Have you ever heard of Scott Joplin, Casey? He was my mother's favorite. She used to play it in our sitting room every time Daddy played his little games with me. The louder I'd cry out for her, the louder she'd play it. Now it's my theme music. Isn't it pretty?

"After I inject you, I'm going to give you a bath like Mommy used to do for me, but I'll be gentle and I'll dry you off with this fluffy towel which I'll leave in Megan's bathroom. Won't that feel nice? Oh, I'm sorry; you won't be able to feel anything at that point, will you? So I guess you'll just have to take my word for it." Sylvia gloated and Casey tensed.

As Sylvia struggled to cuff her right hand and still keep her covered with her gun, Casey launched herself forward. All her years of judo training had made her legs very strong and as she connected with Sylvia's stomach, she screamed, "Megan! Help! Help!"

Jack Malloy pulled into the parking lot of Megan's apartment complex, one hand on the steering wheel and the other nervously brushing his hair into place. He put the car in park, then almost switched it back into reverse before killing the engine. He still wasn't sure whether coming here was a good idea or a bad one. He stepped out of the Crown Vic, automatically patting his weapon, then headed for the front door of Megan's apartment.

Jack knew Megan had to be home, as he'd seen her car in the parking lot, but he stopped before ringing the bell. Every year of experience he'd had on the police force told him something wasn't quite right. The front door was ajar. Only a couple of inches, but it was enough to set off Jack's alarm systems. No one, especially a woman alone, left her door even slightly open in Savannah at night anymore. He also thought he'd seen Casey's car in the parking lot, but there were no lights on in the apartment, no voices, only the very dim sound of a radio coming from somewhere in the interior of the apartment. He was about to open his mouth and shout out "Hi, is anyone home in there?" when he heard the sound of a voice that sounded distinctly like Casey's coming from an area off to his right that was probably a bedroom. He couldn't make out all the words clearly, but the tone was terrified. He slowly edged his way into the dark interior of the house to be greeted by the sight of Megan lying awkwardly on the couch, obviously out like a light. After a quick check of her pulse, he inched his way in the direction of the music. He slowly removed his .38 from his shoulder holster and paused beside the door where the voice he'd heard seemed to come from.

"Megan! Help! Help!"

It was Casey, and she was in trouble. Jack ran to the source of the cry and threw open the bedroom door, to be greeted by the astonishing sight of a tall blond with a gun in her hand rolling around on the bed with Casey. She whirled as the door flew against the wall, her face distorted by rage. "What?"

"Sylvia?" was all Jack got out before she trained the gun on him with the quickness of a cat. This was beyond belief. Jack had no time to sight his weapon or even take decent aim; he simply reacted. His bullet took her about two inches below her navel and sent her reeling into the wall and then sideways into the closet, clutching her stomach. Three long strides took him across the room where he kicked the weapon away from her reach. As the woman he knew as Sylvia lay moaning quietly on the floor of the closet, he turned his attention to the naked form of Casey.

"Casey, what in the name of God is going on here?"

"You just caught your murderer, Jack; now would you please unlock me and give me something to put on?"

Jack backed away from the figure of the wounded woman in the closet and used his master key to unlock the handcuff. He handed Casey his jacket, which she gratefully used to cover most of her nude body, and Jack sat slowly down beside her in a complete state of confusion.

"Let me call 911, and then you can fill me in on what in hell this is all about." He looked again at Sylvia whose pain-filled eyes glared at Casey.

"You should have said you were sorry. Why didn't you say you were sorry?"

Epilogue

Adam Carter turned to Jack Malloy, handing him a thick file. "Well, I reckon that wraps it up. Your Sylvia Gordon certainly had a horror story to tell about her father raping her one Halloween when she was nine and continuing to do so until she grew tall enough to fight back. She never did say if he molested her younger sister, but the way she spoke about her, I have a feeling he didn't and that might have been why she picked on blondes to murder."

"But didn't the psychologist say her mother was also a blonde?"

"Yes, so the mother might have been the cause of the blonde fixation. Her mother's dying last year was probably the catalyst that pushed her over the edge and on her murdering spree. Sylvia kept saying that she'd never get a chance now to make her mother admit her complicity in the rapes. She obviously knew it was going on because she played music loud to stop her hearing Sylvia's cries, and then bathed her afterwards."

"God what a terrible woman she must have been." Jack shuddered. "I can never get over how many sickos there are in the world."

"Ain't that the truth!"

Megan settled back in Casey's comfortable armchair and took another sip of her glass of Chardonnay. She smiled at Casey.

"Well, it's just you and me again, kiddo. I guess I don't have good luck picking partners."

"Do you want to talk about Marla? We don't have to if you don't want to. I still can't believe that we both survived Sylvia. Listening to her talk about her childhood and learning the rest of her story from Adam, I almost felt sorry for her. Well, I did feel sorry for the child she'd been, but it's hard to believe that a woman like that can become a serial killer. I mean she seemed a bit self-centered at the club, and I confess she irritated me, but Adam was saying that she might have gone on killing for years if they hadn't caught her."

187

"What a terrifying thought. At least she's in custody now and will be going down for the rest of her life. God, when I woke up and found you and Jack in the apartment and Sylvia bleeding everywhere, I couldn't believe it. I still don't totally understand Marla's reaction when she came home. I almost thought she was somehow involved, but I guess not. "

"What did she say?"

"She said she was relieved that I was okay, but she acted so weird, kind of disappointed. I just can't fathom her out. She's been nagging me for ages about my past. I know she thinks I'm the odd one not wanting to talk about my dad and everything that happened to me as a kid, but to some extent I feel I'm past that. My folks are dead. Paul's dead, and I just have to get on with my life as best I can. All this thrashing over the past does nothing for me. When you had the whole McLean thing, we talked, but I'm not one to want to bare my soul all the time."

"Do you think it's more that you didn't want to bare your soul to Marla? Perhaps you didn't really trust her not to misuse the knowledge in some way. I always feel you and I are close, and you're really there for me. You feel the same way, don't you?"

"Oh, I do. You're definitely my best buddy." Megan leaned towards Casey and gave her a hug.

"That's all that matters. I don't care if you tell me all the grisly details about your dad. It's enough that I know he made you miserable. We don't need to keep on about it."

"Yeah, you do understand. Anyway you know that I've been feeling really terrible recently. I've had all these wicked mood swings. Things just came to a head that night, and Marla and I had an almighty row and agreed to split. She's also far too money-minded for me. Let's face it. What do I give a damn about clothes or designer stuff? I don't."

"You'll find someone else, not to worry. In the meantime we can just hang out together, but guess what? I have no intention of ever going to the Mirror Image again."

"I'll second that."

Tarka, who had been busy eating Megan's gift of some nice flounder, chose this moment to come in and settle himself on Megan's lap. "My God, Case, this cat smells wonderful. What have you done to him?"

"I took him to the cat grooming place. His fur was so knotted up and he just smelt bad, so I spent my hard earned cash in making him beautiful. Doesn't he look great? We could show him and win first prize."

Tarka looked balefully at Casey. "Don't even think about it, human. What I had to put up with at that grooming place was utterly beneath my dignity. If you think I'm going to be a show cat, I'll run away."

"You know, Megs, I do have one more question to ask you. You're always so nice to Tarka and I really thought you were sort of a cat person, but you seemed to really dislike Pussy, and you weren't at all upset when she died. Why was that?"

"I'm not really sure. I was really pissed that Marla got her and then just dumped all the care on to me. The final straw came when the damn animal chewed my brand new bag. It'd cost me a fortune, and when I came home to find teeth marks all over it, I just lost it. Next thing I knew Pussy was missing, and I felt so guilty because I'd thrown her outside and locked the cat flap so she couldn't come in. I never told Marla I did that."

"So when she turned up run over, you were kinda relieved?"

Yeah, exactly. I know I sounded hard and unfeeling when you asked me about her, but I was. I love Tarka, but really don't want a cat of my own. I just can't be bothered."

"Fair enough. Now how about pouring me some more wine and let's decide which video we'll watch."

Marla was not only dejected over the recent loss of the fortune in art works that had been in her possession, she was also bored. She had been planning a future of freedom and ease where she could travel at will and live wherever she pleased. Now she was once again trapped in the same old job in the same old location. In addition to losing the money, she'd also blown her relationship with Megan. She'd been very fond of Megan although she wasn't quite sure if love was part of the deal in her own mind. She knew she'd get past that loss at some point; there were a million good looking women out there who would be delighted with her attentions. It just all seemed so completely unfair.

She decided to do something she rarely did, watch a little TV. Maybe hearing about someone else's problems might make her own seem a little more palatable. Aside from that, there wasn't a single thing she really felt like doing at the moment.

The Fox Network group was its usual happy self, jabbering away about this and that and the other thing while seemingly remaining totally unaffected by the death and tragedy throughout the world they were reporting on. She was almost at the point of turning them off and reading a magazine when a familiar name caught her attention.

"David Rothschild, an Israeli citizen is currently being held in a Newark jail after having been picked up on the New Jersey Turnpike while driving a rental car which was reported stolen by Dollar Rental late yesterday. It seems that Mr. Rothschild did not return the vehicle on the required date, so the rental agency reported it stolen, which is their standard policy in such situations.

Imagine the surprised faces on the agency personnel when they opened the trunk and found three pastels by the French artist Edgar Degas and two paintings, one done by Camille Pissaro and the other by Paul Cezanne. In addition to the art work, they also found a draft on a German bank for $1,000,000.

"No explanation has been forthcoming on how or why Mr. Rothschild happened to have these items in his possession. The Degas pastels were stolen from the Berlin Museum during World War II. The origin of the two paintings is unknown at this time. Mr. Rothschild is currently being held without bond on charges of Grand Theft Auto. Authorities say they intend to investigate the matter thoroughly and further charges may follow.

"Now for a truly miraculous story about a cat that managed to find its way home after being lost by its owner on a trip from Missouri to Texas."

Marla missed the next few minutes of news because she was laughing too hard to hear it. The little bastard had got what he deserved after all. It was almost enough to make her believe that there was some justice in life after all. She began to feel a bit better than she had in several days and was about to turn off the TV and get some lunch when one last news story caused her to pause.

"We have another story today concerning stolen art. A report has come out of the Netherlands that the National Museum was robbed Tuesday night by an unknown burglar or burglars. Three Rembrandts were cut out of their frames and removed. It is not yet known how the thieves got into or out of the Museum. A nationwide alert has been issued for the apprehension of the thieves and the return of the portraits."

Marla stared at the screen for a few more seconds as the news program went into commercial, then hit the power button on her remote to turn off the set. She picked up her organizer and scanned ahead for what she had going for the next couple of weeks. There was little doubt in her mind that a tour group to Amsterdam might be just what the doctor ordered to cure her case of depression. Life was definitely starting to look up again.

OTHER BOOKS AVAILABLE FROM
TWENTY FIRST CENTURY PUBLISHERS

CASEY'S REVENGE

Is this the best of all possible worlds? Well, almost, or so Casey Forbes thinks. She is a college professor with a successful career and good friends; boyfriend trouble in the past, perhaps, but who hasn't? And her prospects are excellent.

But no woman can expect to descend into the real life nightmare, that envelopes Casey ... out of nowhere.

Mary Charles's heroine is forced to confront the darkest side of human nature and the most bestial of acts committed by man. Yet it is the strength of will, the trauma inflicted on Casey's personality and the resourcefulness of the female psyche that Mary Charles explores in this novel. What does it take to survive overwhelming adversity and does Casey have it?

Many dream of revenge but wonder if they have within themselves the capacity to carry it out. Can Casey? And is the price going to be too high?

Read this thriller and one thing is certain: don't ever let this happen to you.

Casey's Revenge by Mary Charles
ISBN 1-90443-06-5

THE RELUCTANT CORPSE

"Stewart Douglas could not, under any circumstances, be considered your average human being. He'd always been a fan of agony as long, of course, as it wasn't his own." Well, Stewart is the local mortician, and maybe he has a less than healthy interest in the job. Every community has its secrets, and Savannah, Georgia, is no exception. The questions are: exactly what are those secrets, and who do they belong to?

Mary Charles introduces us to a community of characters, and although we do see the mortician at work, everything is comfortably tranquil, or so it seems. But strange things are afoot. Who can you trust? It may be best to let things rest, but events have their own momentum.

There is a foray into the antique art market, which gives the plot a subtle twist, and as the sinister undertone begins to take on real menace, you will be unable to put down this exciting suspense novel.

"Set within the confines of Savannah and Southeast Georgia, The Reluctant Corpse confronts the reader with frightening images lurking just behind closed doors and stately homes. Well written and enjoyable." William C. Harris Jr. (Savannah best-selling author of Delirium of the Brave and No Enemy But Time).

The Reluctant Corpse by Mary Charles
ISBN 1-904433-16-2

RAMONA

How did a little girl come to be abandoned in the orange scented square of the Andalusian City of Seville? Find out, when the course of her life is resumed at age seventeen.

Ramona catches the mood of Europe in transition, as Ramona, brought up in a quiet village in southern Spain, moves into the cosmopolitan world. Her strange background holds a mystery, revealed as the novel develops, but then events take on a different hue as a new perspective emerges. But that is not all, and reality seems to bend further, but does it?

From a novel within a novel, we move on to ... well, let's not say. Read it, and the author challenges you to predict each step of the unfolding plot, and just when it defies belief, read on - you will believe.

Ramona by Johnny John Heinz
ISBN: 1-904433-01-4

MEANS TO AN END

Enter the world of money laundering, financial manipulation and greed, where a shadowy Middle Eastern organisation takes on a major corporation in the US. As the action shifts through exotic locations, who wins out in the end? Certainly, the author's first hand experience of international finance lends a chilling credibility to the plot.

As well as being a compelling work of fiction this book offers, in a style accessible to the layman, a financial insider's insight into the financial and moral crisis, which broke in the early millennium, in the top echelons of corporate America.

Means to an End by Johnny John Heinz
ISBN: 1-84375-008-2

THE SIGNATURE OF A VOICE

The Signature of a Voice is a cat-and-mouse-game between a violent trio, led by a psychopathic killer, and a police officer on suspension. Move and countermove in this chess game is planned and enacted. The reader, in the position of god, knows who is guilty and who plans what, but just as in chess, the opponents' plans thwart one another. The outcomes twist and turn to the final curtain fall.

There is a sense of suspense but also anger as the system seems to be working against those who are fighting on the side of right, while the perpetrators of vicious crimes seem able to operate freely and choose to do what they wish. They choose the route of ultra-violence to stay ahead of the law in an otherwise tranquil community: they plan and execute, in all senses of the word. Is it possible to triumph over this ruthlessness?

The Signature of a Voice by Johnny John Heinz
ISBN: 1-904433-00-6

TARNISHED COPPER

Tarnished Copper takes us into the arcane world of commodity trading. Against this murky background, no deal is what it seems, no agreement what it appears to be. The characters cheat and deceive each other, all in the name of grabbing their own advantage. Hiro Yamagazi, from his base in Tokyo, is the biggest trader of them all. But does he run his own destiny, or is he just jumping when Phil Harris pulls the strings? Can Jamie Edwards keep his addictions under control? And what will be the outcome of the duel between the hedge fund manager Jason Serck, and brash, devious, high-spending Mack McKee? And then one of them goes too far: life and death enters the traders' world........

Geoff Sambrook is ideally placed to take the reader into this world. He's been at the heart of the world's copper trading for over twenty years, and has seen the games - and the traders - come and go. With his ability to draw characters, and his knack of making the reader understand this strange world, he's created an explosive best-selling financial thriller. Read it and learn how this part of the City really works.

Tarnished Copper by Geoffrey Sambrook
ISBN 1-904433-02-2

OVER A BARREL

From the moment you land at Heathrow on page one the plot grips you. Ed Burke, an American oil tycoon, jets through the world's financial centres and the Middle East to set up deals, but where does this lead him? Are his premonitions on the safety of his daughter Louise in Saudi Arabia well founded? Who are his hidden opponents? Is his corporate lawyer Nicole with him or against him?

As the plot unfolds his company is put into play in the tangle of events surrounding the 1990 invasion of Kuwait. Even his private life is drawn into the morass.

In this novel Peter depicts the grim machinations of political and commercial life, but the human spirit shines through. This is a thriller that will hold you to the last page.

Over a Barrel by Peter Driver
ISBN 1-904433-03-0

THE BLOWS OF FATE

It is a crisp clear day in Sofia and three young friends are starting out in life, buoyant with their hopes, aspirations, loves. But this is not to be, as post war Eastern Europe comes under the grip of its brutal communist regime. Driven from their homes and deprived of their basic rights, the three friends determine to escape ... but one of them cannot seize that moment. It may seem that life cannot become worse for the families who are ostracised and trapped in their own country, but the path of hopelessness descends to the concentration camps and unimaginable brutality.

For those who escape there is the struggle to survive, tempered by the kindness they encounter along their way. We see how talent and determination can win through. Yet, though they may have escaped those terrible years in Bulgaria, they can never escape their personal loss of family, homeland, friends and love that may have been.

While life is very difficult for the three friends, they do not forget each other. After forty years of separation, they meet. For each one fate has prepared a surprise....

Can beauty, art and love eclipse the manmade horrors of this world? You will think they can, as Antoinette Clair brings out the beautiful things in life, so that the poignancy of her novel reaches into the toughest of us, and moves to tears.

This is a tale of beauty, music and a grand love, but it is also expressive of the sad recurring tale of Europe's recent history.

The Blows of Fate by Antoinette Clair
ISBN 1-904433-04-9

THE GORE EXPERIMENT

William Gore is not a mad scientist: he is a dedicated medical researcher working on G.L.X.-14, an AIDS serum. He is on the brink of a major breakthrough and seeks to force the pace, spurred on by his knowledge of the suffering to be spared, if he is right, and the millions of lives of AIDS victims to be saved. But as things begin to go askew, how far dare he go? What level of risk is warranted? What, and who, is he prepared to sacrifice? The answers become worse than you can imagine as William Gore treads a path to horror.

The Gore Experiment may be fiction, but it addresses real issues in the world of experimental vaccines, disease-busting drugs and genetic engineering. Is science unknowingly exposing us to risk through overconfidence in ever narrowing fields of expertise, ignorant of ramifications? Or is the red tape of bureaucracy signing the death warrants of the terminally sick? Well, William Gore at least is confident. He is convinced of what he must do. Should he do it?

This is not a book for the faint-hearted. H. Jay Scheuermann adds a new high-tech dimension to the traditions of vampires, Jekylls and Hydes as William Gore paves his own road to hell. But there is a twist....

The Gore Experiment by H. Jay Scheuermann
ISBN 1-904433-05-7

SABRA'S SOUL

From the heart of the California rock music scene comes this story of much more than just love and betrayal.

Does Sabra know who she is? She thinks she is a loving mother and a trusting wife, but her husband Logan, a powerful figure in rock music, seems consumed by commitments to his latest band, 23 Mystique. Sabra begins to feel that something is missing, to feel a yearning for something more. Is she too trusting and too slow to spot Logan's lapses in behaviour?

When Sabra meets the pop idol of her sub-teen daughters, things begin to change. She can't believe the attraction growing in her for this youthful figure, her junior by several years.

Lisa Reed paints a picture of virtue and vice in this tale of love, lust, betrayal and drug-induced psychosis, set amidst the glitter of the rock scene. It is not fate that leads these people on but their own actions. Can they help it and where does it lead?

Who better than Lisa Reed, with her access to the centre of rock, to weave this tense plot as it descends from the social whirl into the deadly serious. If you are a successful rock star, this is a book for you, and if not ... well, read on and dream.

Health warning: this book contains salacious sex scenes demanded by its setting.

Sabra's Soul by Lisa Reed
ISBN 1-90443307-3

FACE BLIND

From the pen of Raymond Benson, author of the acclaimed original James Bond continuation novels (Zero Minus Ten, The Facts of Death, High Time to Kill, DoubleShot, Never Dream of Dying, and The Man With the Red Tattoo) and the novel Evil Hours, comes a new and edgy noir thriller.

Imagine a world where you don't recognize the human face. That's Hannah's condition - prosopagnosia, or "face blindness" - when the brain center that recognizes faces is inoperable. The onset of the condition occurred when she was attacked and nearly raped by an unknown assailant in the inner lobby of her New York City apartment building. And now she thinks he's back, and not just in her dreams.

When she also attracts the attention of a psychopathic predator and becomes the unwitting target of a Mafia drug ring, the scene is set for a thrill ride of mistaken identity, cat-and-mouse pursuit, and murder.

Face Blind is a twisting, turning tale of suspense in which every character has a dark side. The novel will keep the reader surprised and intrigued until the final violent catharsis.

Face Blind by Raymond Benson
ISBN 1-904433-10-3

CUPID AND THE SILENT GODDESS

The painting Allegory with Venus and Cupid has long fascinated visitors to London's National Gallery, as well as the millions more who have seen it reproduced in books. It is one of the most beautiful paintings of the nude ever made.

In 1544, Duke Cosimo de' Medici of Florence commissioned the artist Bronzino to create the painting to be sent as a diplomatic gift to King François I of France.

As well as the academic mystery of what the strange figures in the painting represent, there is the human mystery: who were the models in the Florence of 1544 who posed for the gods and strange figures?

Alan Fisk's Cupid and the Silent Goddess imagines how the creation of this painting might have touched the lives of everyone who was involved with it: Bronzino's apprentice Giuseppe, the mute and mysterious Angelina who is forced to model for Venus, the brutal sculptor Baccio Bandinelli and his son, and the good-hearted nun Sister Benedicta and her friend the old English priest Father Fleccia, both secret practitioners of alchemy.

As the painting takes shape, it causes episodes of fear and cruelty, but the ending lies perhaps in the gift of Venus.

'A witty and entertaining romp set in the seedy world of Italian Renaissance artists.' Award-winning historical novelist Elizabeth Chadwick. (*The Falcons of Montabard, The Winter Mantle*).

'Alan Fisk, in his book Cupid and the Silent Goddess, captures the atmosphere of sixteenth-century Florence and the world of the artists excellently. This is a fascinating imaginative reconstruction of the events during the painting of Allegory with Venus and Cupid.' Marina Oliver, author of many historical novels and of Writing Historical Fiction.

Cupid and the Silent Goddess by Alan Fisk
ISBN 1-904433-08-4

TALES FROM THE LONG BAR

Nostalgia may not be what it used be, but do you ever get the feeling that the future's not worth holding your breath for either?

Do you remember the double-edged sword that was 'having a proper job' and struggling within the coils of the multiheaded monster that was 'the organisation'?

Are you fed up with forever having to hit the ground running, working dafter not smarter - and always being in a rush trying to dress down on Fridays?

Do you miss not having a career, a pension plan or even the occasional long lunch with colleagues and friends?

For anyone who knows what's what (but can't do much about it), Tales from the Long Bar should prove entertaining. If it doesn't, it will at least reassure you that you are not alone.

Londoner Saif Rahman spent half his life working in the City before going on to pursue opportunities elsewhere. A linguist by training, Saif is a historian by inclination.

Tales from the Long Bar by Saif Rahman
ISBN 1-904433-10-X

COUSINS OF COLOR

Luzon, Philippines, 1899. Immersed in the chaos and brutality of America's first overseas war of conquest and occupation, Private David Fagen has a decision to make - forsake his country or surrender his soul. The result: A young black man in search of respect and inclusion turns his back on Old Glory - and is hailed a hero of the Filipino fight for independence.

Negro blood is just as good as a white man's when spilled in defense of the American Way, or so Fagen believed. But this time his country seeks not justice but empire. Pandemonium rules Fagen's world, Anarchy the High Sheriff, and he knows every time he pulls the trigger, he helps enslave the people he came to liberate.

Not just an account of an extraordinary black solider caught in the grip of fate and circumstance, Cousin*s of Color* tells the story of Fagen's love for the beautiful and mysterious guerilla fighter, Clarita Socorro, and his sympathy for her people's struggle for freedom. *Cousins* also chronicles Colonel Fredrick Funston's monomaniacal pursuit of victory at any cost and his daredevil mission to capture Emilio Aguinaldo, the leader of the Philippine revolution. Other characters include the dangerously unstable, Captain Baston, particularly cruel in his treatment of prisoners, and Sergeant Warren Rivers, the father Fagen never had.

Himself a Vietnam combat veteran, author William Schroder hurtles us through the harsh realities of this tropical jungle war and provides powerful insight into the dreams and aspirations of human souls corrupted and debased by that violent clash of cultures and national wills. Based on actual events, David Fagen's pursuit of truth and moral purpose in the Philippine Campaign brings focus to America's continuing obsession with conquest and racism and provides insight into many of today's prevailing sentiments.

Cousins of Color by William Schroder
Hardcover - ISBN 1-904433-13-8
Paperback - ISBN 1-904433-11-1

EVIL HOURS

"My mother was murdered when I was six years old." Shannon has become used to giving this explanation when getting to know new arrivals in the small West Texas town of Limite. She has never hidden the truth about her mother, but she is haunted by the unresolved circumstances surrounding her mother's murder and the deaths of a series of other women around the same time. It is when she sets about uncovering the truth, with the help of an investigator, that the true depravity of Limite's underbelly begins to emerge.

The very ordinariness of the small town lends a chill to *Evil Hours*, as revelations from a murky past begin to form a pattern; but much worse they begin to cast their shadow over the present.

As Shannon delves behind the curtain of silence raised by the prominent citizens of Limite, she finds herself caught up in a sequence of events that mirror those of the previous generation…and the past and the present merge into a chilling web of evil.

In *Evil Hours* Raymond Benson revisits his roots and brings to life the intrigue of a small West Texas Town. Benson is the author of the original James Bond continuation novels: *The Man With the Red Tattoo*; *Never Dream of Dying*; *DoubleShot*; *High Time to Kill*; *The Facts of Death*; and *Zero Minus Ten*. He has recently released a thriller set in New York, *Face Blind*.

Evil Hours by Raymond Benson
ISBN 1-904433-12-X

PAINT ME AS I AM

What unique attribute dwells within the creative individual? Is it a flaw in the unconscious psyche that gives rise to talent, influencing artists to fashion the product of their imagination into tangible form, just as the grain of sand gives rise to the precious pearl? Or is it more?

To the world around him, Jerrod Young appears to be a typical, mature art student. He certainly has talent as a painter, but hidden within the darkest corners of his mind are unsavory secrets, and a different man that nobody knows.

H. Jay Scheuermann, author of The Gore Experiment, gives us another great psychological thriller, delivering a chilling look inside the psyche of a man whose deepest thoughts begin to assume control over his actions. The needs of the darkness within him seem to grow with each atrocity, his ever-increasing confidence fueling an inexorable force for evil.

Hell is not a place, but a state of mind, a state of being: it exists within each of us. We like to believe we can control it, but the cruel alternative is that our choices have already been made for us. Jerrod has accepted his truth, and is resolved to serve his inner demon.

Special Agent Jackie Jonas has been given her first assignment, a case that may mark the beginning and the end of her FBI career, as it leads her into a web of violence and deception, with each new clue ensnaring the lives of the ones she loves....

This gripping story brings to life the awful truth that the Jerrod Young's of this world do, in fact, exist. It could be one of your co-workers, the person behind you in the supermarket checkout line, or even the person next door. Can you tell? Are you willing to stake your life on it?

Paint Me As I Am by H. Jay Scheuermann
ISBN 1-904433-14-6

EMBER'S FLAME

"He could focus on her intelligent conversations and the way her aqua blue eyes lit up when they were amused and turned almost gray when they were sad. It was easier to admire the strength she carried in her soul and the light she carried in her walk. Now, seeing her in five inch heels and hot pants…"

Ember Ty is majoring in journalism. Graced with stunning looks, she finances her studies by dancing in a strip club. She has a hot boyfriend in a rock band, a future writing about the music world, and yes, she's working hard to achieve it.

But it all starts to go wrong. There is a predator on the loose, and Ember is sucked into a nightmare that none of us would care to dream, let alone live.

Vulnerable and threatened, Ember is drawn into a love triangle that might never have been, with the man she is to marry and the man she knows she can never have.

Ember's Flame by Lisa Reed
ISBN 1-904433-15-4

THE AFFAIRS OF STATE

A philandering president. Rumors about The First Lady. Public lies about private lives. Talk about impeachment. Unstable world events that could lead to war. Sound familiar?

It should. It was all possible in 1940.

Immediately after Franklin Roosevelt won an unprecedented third term and World War 2 was heating up, a brand new radio network aired information about the First Family that was true but had never been made public.

Michael Audray, the network's high-profile host of the most listened-to radio program in the country, asked *the* question that set off a chain of events that changed modern history before and after Pearl Harbor.

The Affairs of State is about power politics, broadcasting, private lives and the public's right to know. It's fiction, but it meshes with the historical record and asks questions that challenge us to face the moral ambiguity that emerges.

The Affairs of State by Tim Steele
ISBN 1-904433-17-0

SINCERE MALE SEEKS LOVE AND SOMEONE TO WASH HIS UNDERPANTS

Colin Fisher is long-divorced with two grown-up children and an ageing mother in care. He is not getting any younger. Perhaps it is time to get married again. There are hordes of mature, nubile, attractive, solvent (hopefully) women out there, and marriage would provide regular sex and companionship, and someone to take care of the tedious domestic details that can make a man late for his golf and tennis matches. All Colin needs to do is smarten up a bit, get out more and select the lucky woman from amongst the numerous postulants. What could be easier?

International best-sellers by Christopher Wood include:

A Dove Against Death; Fire Mountain; Taiwan; Make it Happen to Me; Kago; 'Terrible Hard', Says Alice; James Bond, the Spy Who Loved Me; The Further Adventures of Barry Lyndon; James Bond and Moonraker; Dead Centre; John Adam, Samurai.

Christopher Wood has written the screenplays for over a dozen movies, including The Spy Who Loved Me and Moonraker, two of the most successful James Bond films ever made. *"Laugh-out-loud-funny…deeply touching…I really enjoyed this book. Mark Mills, author of Amagansett."*

Sincere male seeks love and someone to wash his underpants
by Christopher Wood
ISBN 1-904433-18-9

ARCHIPELAGO

If you haven't yet, you soon will hear about the Archipelago Company. They run the utopia that is the independent economy orbiting London and the whole raft of money-making schemes that goes with it. Let London sink under the weight of congestion charges, an uncontrolled building boom, high prices and limited employment. The Archipelago doesn't need to help it along. It can just help itself to bits of the action that come floating by. Simple!'

So for the man on the M25, and business, this utopia can only be a win-win, or so it would seem. Perhaps we should take a closer look at the conflicting interests of the members of the team running the Archipelago Company. In this best of all possible worlds of tomorrow that is here today, we see a financial institution that has come down in the world, a university that wants to be a business, an IT company, not too ambitious, that just wants to run the country.

There are rich pickings for the bottom feeders: a language school with delusions of grandeur, a mysterious firm of Swiss lawyers and individuals participating in this grand scheme who are seeking to connect with their inner demons.

Virtue has to be its own reward, since no-one will give it the time of day.
Archipelago by Saif Rahman
ISBN 1-904433-22-7